*My dearest Catherine, I miss you my darling, as I always do, but today is especially hard because the ocean has been singing to me, and the song is that of our life together. . . .*

And so the story begins, about a woman who no longer believed in love, and a man who thought he could never love again—until they found each other.

# MESSAGE IN A BOTTLE

"Deeply moving, beautifully written, and extremely romantic."
—*Booklist*

"Brew the tea or pour a glass of wine—whatever is your pleasure. And settle in for Nicholas Sparks's latest book . . . you're in for another treat."
—*Oakland Press*

"Sparks is on a roll."
—*Atlanta Journal-Constitution*

"Nicholas Sparks has written this summer's *The Bridges of Madison County*."
—*Wall Street Journal*

"Beautifully romantic."
—*Kliatt*

"A book that will stay with you always."
—*Salisbury Post*

*Please turn the page for more reviews. . .*

# MESSAGE IN A BOTTLE
# RIDES A WAVE OF PRAISE!

Also by Nicholas Sparks

*The Notebook*
*A Walk to Remember*

# NICHOLAS SPARKS

# MESSAGE IN A BOTTLE

**WARNER BOOKS**

NEW YORK    BOSTON

Warner Books

Time Warner Book Group
1271 Avenue of the Americas, New York, NY 10020
Visit our Web site at www.twbookmark.com.

Printed in the United States of America

First Trade Printing: December 1999
10   9

**The Library of Congress has cataloged the hardcover edition as follows:**

Sparks, Nicholas.
    Message in a bottle / Nicholas Sparks.
        p.    cm.
      ISBN 0-446-52356-9
      I. Title.
    PS3569.P363M47    1998
    813'.54—dc21
ISBN 0-446-67607-1 (pbk.)                                    97-39158
                                                                   CIP

For Miles and Ryan

# ACKNOWLEDGMENTS

This book would not have come about without the help of many people. I'd especially like to thank Catherine, my wife, who supports me with just the right mixture of patience and love.

I'd also like to thank my agent, Theresa Park, of Sanford Greenburger Associates, and my editor, Jamie Raab, at Warner Books. This book could not have been written without them. They are my teachers, my colleagues, and my friends.

Finally, there are those people who deserve my heartfelt gratitude as well. Larry Kirshbaum, Maureen Egen, Dan Mandel, John Aherne, Scott Schwimer, Howie Sanders, Richard Green, and Denise DiNovi—you all know your role in this project, and I thank you for everything.

# PROLOGUE

*The bottle was dropped overboard on a warm summer evening, a few hours before the rain began to fall. Like all bottles, it was fragile and would break if dropped a few feet from the ground. But when sealed properly and sent to sea, as this one was, it became one of the most seaworthy objects known to man. It could float safely through hurricanes or tropical storms, it could bob atop the most dangerous of riptides. It was, in a way, the ideal home for the message it carried inside, a message that had been sent to fulfill a promise.*

*Like that of all bottles left to the whim of the oceans, its course was unpredictable. Winds and currents play large roles in any bottle's direction; storms and debris may shift its course as well. Occasionally a fishing net will snag a bottle and carry it a dozen miles in the opposite direction in which it was headed. The result is that two bottles dropped simultaneously into the ocean might end up a* continent apart, or even on opposite sides of the globe. There is no way to predict where a bottle might travel, and that is part of its mystery.

This mystery has intrigued people for as long as there have been bottles, and a few people have tried to learn more about it. In 1929 a crew of German scientists set out to track the journey of one particular bottle. It was set to sea in the South Indian Ocean with a note inside asking the finder to record the location where it washed up and to throw it back into the sea. By 1935 it had rounded the world and traveled approximately sixteen thousand miles, the longest distance officially recorded.

Messages in bottles have been chronicled for centuries and include some of the most famous names in history. Ben Franklin, for instance, used message-carrying bottles to compile a basic knowledge of East Coast currents in the mid-1700s—information that is still in use to this day. Even now the U.S. Navy uses bottles to compile information on tides and currents, and they are frequently used to track the direction of oil spills.

The most celebrated message ever sent concerned a young sailor in 1784, Chunosuke Matsuyama, who was stranded on a coral reef, devoid of food and water after his boat was shipwrecked. Before his death, he carved the account of what had happened on a piece of wood, then sealed the message in a bottle. In 1935, 150 years after it had been set afloat, it washed up in the small seaside village in Japan where Matsuyama had been born.

The bottle that had been dropped on a warm summer evening, however, did not contain a message about a shipwreck, nor was it being used to chart the seas. But it did contain a message that would change two people forever, two people who would otherwise never have met, and for this reason it could be called a fated message. For six days it slowly floated in a northeasterly direction, driven by winds from a high-pressure system hovering above the Gulf of Mexico. On the seventh day the winds died, and the bottle steered itself directly eastward, eventually finding its way to the Gulf Stream, where it then picked up speed, traveling north at almost seventy miles per day.

*Two and a half weeks after its launch, the bottle still followed the Gulf Stream. On the seventeenth day, however, another storm—this time over the mid-Atlantic—brought easterly winds strong enough to drive the bottle from the current, and the bottle began to drift toward New England. Without the Gulf Stream forcing it along, the bottle slowed again and it zigzagged in various directions near the Massachusetts shore for five days until it was snagged in a fishing net by John Hanes. Hanes found the bottle surrounded by a thousand flopping perch and tossed it aside while he examined his catch. As luck would have it, the bottle didn't break, but it was promptly forgotten and remained near the bow of the boat for the rest of the afternoon and early evening as the boat made its journey back to Cape Cod Bay. At eight-thirty that night—and once the boat was safely inside the confines of the bay—Hanes stumbled across the bottle again while smoking a cigarette. Because the sun was dropping lower in the sky, he picked it up but saw nothing unusual inside, and he tossed it overboard without a second glance, thereby insuring that the bottle would wash up along one of the many small communities that lined the bay.*

*It didn't happen right away, however. The bottle drifted back and forth for a few days—as if deciding where to go before choosing its course—and it finally washed up along the shore on a beach near Chatham.*

*And it was there, after 26 days and 738 miles, that it ended its journey.*

# CHAPTER  1

*A* cold December wind was blowing, and Theresa Osborne crossed her arms as she stared out over the water. Earlier, when she'd arrived, there had been a few people walking along the shore, but they'd taken note of the clouds and were long since gone. Now she found herself alone on the beach, and she took in her surroundings. The ocean, reflecting the color of the sky, looked like liquid iron, and waves rolled up steadily on the shore. Heavy clouds were descending slowly, and the fog was beginning to thicken, making the horizon invisible. In another place, in another time, she would have felt the majesty of the beauty around her, but as she stood on the beach, she realized that she didn't feel anything at all. In a way, she felt as if she weren't really here, as if the whole thing was nothing but a dream.

She'd driven here this morning, though she scarcely remembered the trip at all. When she'd made the decision to come, she'd planned to stay overnight. She'd made the arrangements and had even looked forward to a quiet night away from Boston, but watching the ocean swirl and churn made her realize that she didn't want to stay. She would drive home as soon as she was finished, no matter how late it was.

When she was finally ready, Theresa slowly started to walk toward the water. Beneath her arm she carried a bag that she had carefully packed that morning, making sure that she hadn't forgotten anything. She hadn't told anyone what she carried with her, nor had she told them what she'd intended to do today. Instead she'd said that she was going Christmas shopping. It was the perfect excuse, and though she was sure that they would have understood had she told them the truth, this trip was something she didn't want to share with anyone. It had started with her alone, and that was the same way she wanted it to end.

Theresa sighed and checked her watch. Soon it would be high tide, and it was then that she would finally be ready. After finding a spot on a small dune that looked comfortable, she sat in the sand and opened her bag. Searching through it, she found the envelope she wanted. Taking a deep breath, she slowly lifted the seal.

In it were three letters, carefully folded, letters that she'd read more times than she could count. Holding them in front of her, she sat on the sand and stared at them.

In the bag were other items as well, though she wasn't ready to look at those yet. Instead she continued to focus on the letters. He'd used a fountain pen when he'd written them, and there were smudges in various places where the pen had leaked. The stationery, with its picture of a sailing ship in the upper right hand corner, was beginning to discolor in places, fading slowly with the passage of time. She knew there would come a day when the words would be impossible to read, but hopefully, after today, she wouldn't feel the need to look at them so often.

When she finished, she slipped them back into the envelope as carefully as she'd removed them. Then, after putting the envelope back into the bag, she looked at the beach again. From where she was sitting, she could see the place where it had all started.

She'd been jogging at daybreak, she remembered, and she could picture that summer morning clearly. It was the beginning of a beautiful day. As she took in the world around her, she listened to the high-pitched squawking of terns and the gentle lapping of the waves as they rolled up on the sand. Even though she was on vacation, she had risen early enough to run so that she didn't have to watch where she was going. In a few hours the beach would be packed with tourists lying on their towels in the hot New England sun, soaking up the rays. Cape Cod was always crowded at that time of year, but most vacationers tended to sleep a little later, and she enjoyed the sensation of jogging on the hard, smooth sand left from the outgoing tide. Unlike the sidewalks back home, the sand seemed to give just enough, and she knew her knees wouldn't ache as they sometimes did after running on cemented pathways.

She had always liked to jog, a habit she had picked up from running cross-country and track in high school. Though she wasn't competitive anymore and seldom timed her runs, running was now one of the few times she could be alone with her thoughts. She considered it to be a kind of meditation, which was why she liked to do it alone. She never could understand why people liked to run in groups.

As much as she loved her son, she was glad Kevin wasn't with her. Every mother needs a break sometimes, and she was looking forward to taking it easy while she was here. No evening soccer games or swim meets, no MTV blaring in the background, no homework to help with, no waking up in the middle of the night to comfort him when he got leg cramps. She had taken him to the airport three days ago to catch a plane to visit his father—her ex—in California, and it was only after reminding him that Kevin realized he hadn't hugged or kissed her good-bye yet. "Sorry, Mom," he said as he wrapped his arms around her and kissed her. "Love you. Don't miss me too much, okay?" Then, turning around, he handed the ticket to the flight attendant and almost skipped onto the plane without looking back.

She didn't blame him for almost forgetting. At twelve he was in that awkward phase when he thought that hugging and kissing his mom in public wasn't *cool.* Besides, his mind was on other things. He had been looking forward to this trip since last Christmas. He and his father were going to the Grand Canyon, then would spend a week rafting down the Colorado River, and finally go on to Disneyland. It was every kid's fantasy trip, and she was happy for him. Although he would be gone for six weeks, she knew it was good for Kevin to spend time with his father.

She and David had been on relatively good terms since they'd divorced three years ago. Although he wasn't the greatest husband, he was a good father to Kevin. He never missed sending a birthday or Christmas gift, called weekly, and traveled across the country a few times a year just to spend weekends with his son. Then, of course, there were the court-mandated visits as well— six weeks in the summer, every other Christmas, and Easter break when school let out for a week. Annette, David's new wife, had her hands full with the baby, but Kevin liked her a lot, and he had never returned home feeling angry or neglected. In fact, he usually raved about his visits and how much fun he had. There were times when she felt a twinge of jealousy at that, but she did her best to hide it from Kevin.

Now, on the beach, she ran at a moderate clip. Deanna would be waiting for her to finish her run before she started break-fast—Brian would already be gone, she knew—and Theresa looked forward to visiting with her. They were an older cou-ple—both of them were nearing sixty now—but Deanna was the best friend she had.

The managing editor at the newspaper where Theresa worked, Deanna had been coming to the Cape with her hus-band, Brian, for years. They always stayed in the same place, the Fisher House, and when she found out that Kevin was leaving to visit his father in California for a good portion of the summer, she insisted that Theresa come along. "Brian golfs every day he's here, and I'd like the company," she'd said, "and besides, what else are you going to do? You've got to get out of that apartment sometime." Theresa knew she was right, and after a few days of thinking it over, she finally agreed. "I'm so glad," Deanna had said with a victorious look on her face. "You're going to love it there."

Theresa had to admit it was a nice place to stay. The Fisher House was a beautifully restored captain's house that sat on the edge of a rocky cliff overlooking Cape Cod Bay, and when she saw it in the distance, she slowed to a jog. Unlike the younger runners who sped up toward the end of their runs, she preferred to slow down and take it easy. At thirty-six, she didn't recover as fast as she once had.

As her breathing eased, she thought about how she would spend the rest of her day. She had brought five books with her for the vacation, books she had been wanting to read for the last year but had never gotten around to. There just didn't seem to be enough time anymore—not with Kevin and his never-ending energy, keeping up with the housework, and definitely not with all the work constantly piled on her desk. As a syndicated columnist for the *Boston Times*, she was under constant deadline pressure to put out three columns a week. Most of her co-workers thought she had it made—just type up three hundred words and be done for the day—but it wasn't like that at all. To constantly come up with something original regarding parenting wasn't easy anymore—especially if she wanted to syndicate further. Already her column, "Modern Parenting," went out in sixty newspapers across the country, though most ran only one or two of her columns in a given week. And because the syndication offers had started only eighteen months ago and she was a newcomer to most papers, she couldn't afford even a few "off" days. Column space in most newspapers was extremely limited, and hundreds of columnists were vying for those few spots.

Theresa slowed to a walk and finally stopped as a Caspian tern circled overhead. The humidity was up and she used her forearm to wipe the perspiration from her face. She took a deep breath, held it for a moment, then exhaled before looking out over the water. Because it was early, the ocean was still murky gray, but that would change once the sun rose a little higher. It looked enticing. After a moment she took off her shoes and socks, then walked to the water's edge to let the tiny waves lap over her feet. The water was refreshing, and she spent a few minutes wading back and forth. She was suddenly glad she had taken the time to write extra columns over the last few months so that she would be able to forget work this week. She couldn't remember the last time she didn't have a computer nearby, or a meeting to attend, or a deadline to meet, and it felt liberating to be away from her desk for a while. It almost felt as if she were in control of her own destiny again, as if she were just starting out in the world.

True, there were dozens of things she knew she should be doing at home. The bathroom should have been wallpapered and updated by now, the nail holes in her walls needed to be spackled, and the rest of the apartment could use some touch-up painting as well. A couple of months ago she had bought the wallpaper and some paint, towel rods and door handles, and a new vanity mirror, as well as all the tools she needed to take care of it, but she hadn't even opened the boxes yet. It was always something to do next weekend, though the weekends were often just as busy as her workdays. The items she bought still sat in the bags she'd brought them home in, behind the vacuum, and every time she opened the closet door, they seemed to mock her good intentions. Maybe, she thought to herself, when she returned home . . .

She turned her head and saw a man standing a little way down the beach. He was older than she, maybe fifty or so, and his face was deeply tanned, as if he lived here year-round. He didn't appear to be moving—he simply stood in the water and let it wash over his legs—and she noticed his eyes were closed, as if he were enjoying the beauty of the world without having to watch it. He was wearing faded jeans, rolled up to his knees, and a comfortable shirt he hadn't bothered to tuck in. As she watched him, she suddenly wished she were a different kind of person. What would it be like to walk the beaches without another care in the world? How would it be to come to a quiet spot every day, away from the hustle and bustle of Boston, just to appreciate what life had to offer?

She stepped out a little farther into the water and mimicked the man, hoping to feel whatever it was that he was feeling. But when she closed her eyes, the only thing she could think about was Kevin. Lord knew she wanted to spend more time with him, and she definitely wanted to be more patient with him when they were together. She wanted to be able to sit and talk with Kevin, or play Monopoly with him, or simply watch TV with him without feeling the urge to get up from the couch to do something more important. There were times when she felt like a fraud when insisting to Kevin that he came first and that family was the most important thing he'd have.

But the problem was that there was always something to do. Dishes to be washed, bathrooms to be cleaned, the cat box to be emptied; cars needed tune-ups, laundry needed to be done, and bills had to be paid. Even though Kevin helped a lot with his chores, he was almost as busy as she was with school and friends and all his other activities. As it was, magazines went straight to the garbage unread, letters went unwritten, and sometimes, in moments like these, she worried that her life was slipping past her.

But how to change all that? "Take life one day at a time," her mother always said, but her mother didn't have to work outside the home or raise a strong and confident yet caring son without benefit of a father. She didn't understand the pressures that Theresa faced on a daily basis. Neither did her younger sister, Janet, who had followed in the footsteps of their mother. She and her husband had been happily married for almost eleven years, with three wonderful girls to show for it. Edward wasn't a brilliant man, but he was honest, worked hard, and provided for his family well enough that Janet didn't have to work. There were times when Theresa thought she might like a life like that, even if it meant giving up her career.

But that wasn't possible. Not since David and she divorced. Three years now, four if you counted the year they were separated. She didn't hate David for what he had done, but her respect for him had been shattered. Adultery, whether a one-night stand or a long affair, wasn't something she could live with. Nor did it make her feel better that he never married the woman he'd been carrying on with for two years. The breach of trust was irreparable.

David moved back to his home state of California a year after they separated and met Annette a few months later. His new wife was very religious, and little by little she got David interested in the church. David, a lifelong agnostic, had always seemed to be hungry for something more meaningful in his life. Now he attended church regularly and actually served as a marriage counselor along with the pastor. What could he possibly say to someone doing the same things he'd done, she often wondered, and how could he help others if he hadn't been able to control himself? She didn't know, didn't care, really. She was simply glad that he still took an interest in his son.

Naturally, once she and David had split up, a lot of her

friendships ended as well. Now that she was no longer part of a couple, she seemed to be out of place at friends' Christmas parties or backyard barbecues. A few friends remained, though, and she heard from them on her answering machine, suggesting that they set up a lunch date or come over for dinner. Occasionally she would go, but usually she made excuses not to. To her, none of those friendships seemed the way they used to, but then of course they weren't. Things changed, people changed, and the world went rolling along right outside the window.

Since the divorce there had been only a handful of dates. It wasn't that she was unattractive. She was, or so she was often told. Her hair was dark brown, cut just above her shoulders, and straight as spider silk. Her eyes, the feature she was most often complimented on, were brown with flecks of hazel that caught the light when she was outside. Since she ran daily, she was fit and didn't look as old as she was. She didn't feel old, either, but when she looked in the mirror lately, she seemed to see her age catching up with her. A new wrinkle around the corner of her eye, a gray hair that seemed to have grown overnight, a vaguely weary look from being constantly on the run.

Her friends thought she was crazy. "You look better now than you did years ago," they insisted, and she still noticed a few men eyeing her across the aisle in the supermarket. But she wasn't, nor ever would be, twenty-two again. Not that she would want to be, even if she could, unless, she sometimes thought to herself, she could take her more mature brain back with her. If she didn't, she'd probably get caught up with another David—a handsome man who craved the good things in life with the underlying assumption that he didn't have to play by the rules. But dammit, rules were important, especially the ones regarding marriage. They were the ones a person was never supposed to break. Her father and mother didn't break them, her sister and brother-in-law didn't, nor did Deanna and Brian. Why did he have to? And why, she wondered as she stood in the surf, did her thoughts always come back to this, even after all this time?

She supposed that it had something to do with the fact that when the divorce papers finally arrived, she felt as if a little part of her had died. That initial anger she felt had turned to sadness, and now it had become something else, almost a dullness of sorts. Even though she was constantly in motion, it seemed as if nothing special ever happened to her anymore. Each day seemed exactly like the last, and she had trouble differentiating among them. One time, about a year ago, she sat at her desk for fifteen minutes trying to remember the last spontaneous thing she'd done. She couldn't think of anything.

The first few months had been hard on her. By then the anger had subsided and she didn't feel the urge to lash out at David and make him pay for what he had done. All she could do was feel sorry for herself. Even having Kevin around all the time did nothing to change the fact that she felt absolutely alone in the world. There was a short time when she couldn't sleep for more than a few hours a night, and now and then when she was at work, she would leave her desk and go sit in her car to cry for a while.

Now, with three years gone by, she honestly didn't know if she would ever love someone again the way she had loved David. When David showed up at her sorority party at the beginning of her junior year, one look was all it took for her to know she wanted to be with him. Her young love had seemed so over-whelming, so powerful, then. She would stay awake thinking about him as she lay in her bed, and when she walked across campus, she smiled so often that other people would smile back whenever they saw her.

But love like that doesn't last, at least that's what she found out. Over the years, a different kind of marriage emerged. She and David grew up, and apart. It became hard to remember the things that had first drawn them to each other. Looking back, Theresa felt that David became a different person altogether, although she couldn't pinpoint the moment when it all began to change. But anything can happen when the flame of a relationship goes out, and for him, it did. A chance meeting at a video store, a conversation that led to lunch and eventually to hotels throughout the greater Boston area.

The unfair thing about the whole situation was that she still missed him sometimes, or rather the good parts about him. Being married to David was comfortable, like a bed she'd slept in for years. She had been used to having another person around, just to talk to or listen. She had gotten used to waking up to the smell of brewing coffee in the morning, and she missed having another adult presence in the apartment. She missed a lot of things, but most of all she missed the intimacy that came from holding and whispering to another behind closed doors.

Kevin wasn't old enough to understand this yet, and though she loved him deeply, it wasn't the same kind of love that she wanted right now. Her feeling for Kevin was a mother's love, probably the deepest, most holy love there is. Even now she liked to go into his room after he was asleep and sit on his bed just to look at him. Kevin always looked so peaceful, so beautiful, with his head on the pillow and the covers piled up around him. In the daytime he seemed to be constantly on the go, but at night his still, sleeping figure always brought back the feelings she'd had when he was still a baby. Yet even those wonderful feelings didn't change the fact that once she left his room, she would go downstairs and have a glass of wine with only Harvey the cat to keep her company.

She still dreamed about falling in love with someone, of having someone take her in his arms and make her feel she was the only one who mattered. But it was hard, if not impossible, to meet someone decent these days. Most of the men she knew in their thirties were already married, and the ones that were divorced seemed to be looking for someone younger whom they could somehow mold into exactly what they wanted. That left older men, and even though she thought she could fall in love with someone older, she had her son to worry about. She wanted a man who would treat Kevin the way he should be treated, not simply as the unwanted by-product of someone he desired. But the reality was that older men usually had older children; few welcomed the trials of raising an adolescent male in the 1990s. "I've already done my job," a date had once informed her curtly. That had been the end of that relationship.

She admitted that she also missed the physical intimacy that came from loving and trusting and holding someone else. She hadn't been with a man since she and David divorced. There had been opportunities, of course—finding someone to sleep with was never difficult for an attractive woman—but that simply wasn't her style. She hadn't been raised that way and didn't intend to change now. Sex was too important, too special, to be shared with just anyone. In fact, she had slept with only two men in her life—David, of course, and Chris, the first real boyfriend she'd ever had. She didn't want to add to the list simply for the sake of a few minutes of pleasure.

So now, vacationing at Cape Cod, alone in the world and without a man anywhere in the foreseeable future, she wanted to do some things this week just for herself. Read some books, put her feet up, and have a glass of wine without the TV flickering in the background. Write some letters to friends she hadn't heard from in a while. Sleep late, eat too much, and jog in the mornings, before everyone got there to spoil it. She wanted to experience freedom again, if only for a short time.

She also wanted to shop this week. Not at JCPenney or Sears or places that advertised Nike shoes and Chicago Bulls T-shirts, but at little trinket stores that Kevin found boring. She wanted to try on some new dresses and buy a couple that flattered her figure, just to make her feel she was still alive and vibrant. Maybe she would even get her hair done. She hadn't had a new style in years, and she was tired of looking the same every day. And if a nice guy happened to ask her out this week, maybe she'd go, just to have an excuse to wear the new things she bought.

With a somewhat renewed sense of optimism, she looked to see if the man with the rolled-up jeans was still there, but he had gone as quietly as he had come. And she was ready to go as well. Her legs had stiffened in the cool water, and sitting down to put on her shoes was a little more difficult than she expected. Since she didn't have a towel, she hesitated for a moment before putting on her socks, then decided she didn't have to. She was on vacation at the beach. No need for shoes or socks.

She carried them with her as she started toward the house. She walked close to the water's edge and saw a large rock half-buried in the sand, a few inches from a spot where the early morning tide had reached its highest point. Strange, she thought to herself, it seemed out of place here.

As she approached, she noticed something different about the way it looked. It was smooth and long, for one thing, and as she drew nearer she realized it wasn't a rock at all. It was a bottle, probably discarded by a careless tourist or one of the local teens who liked to come here at night. She looked over her shoulder and saw a garbage can chained to the lifeguard tower and decided to do her good deed for the day. When she reached it, however, she was surprised to see that it was corked. She picked it up, holding it into better light, and saw a note inside wrapped with yarn, standing on its end.

For a second she felt her heart quicken as another memory came back to her. When she was eight years old and vacationing in Florida with her parents, she and another girl had once sent a letter via the sea, but she'd never received a reply. The letter was simple, a child's letter, but when she returned home, she remembered racing to the mailbox for weeks afterward, hoping that someone had found it and sent a letter to her from where the bottle washed up. When nothing ever came, disappointment set in, the memory fading gradually until it became nothing at all. But now it all came back to her. Who had been with her that day? A girl about her age . . . Tracy? . . . no . . . Stacey? . . . yes, Stacey! Stacey was her name! She had blond hair . . . she was staying with her grandparents for the summer . . . and . . . and . . . and the memory stopped there, with nothing else coming no matter how hard she tried.

She began to pull at the cork, almost expecting it to be the same bottle she had sent, although she knew that couldn't be. It was probably from another child, though, and if it requested a reply, she was going to send it. Maybe along with a small gift from the Cape and a postcard as well.

The cork was wedged in tightly, and her fingers slipped as she tried to open it. She couldn't get a very good grip. She dug her short fingernails into the exposed cork and twisted the bottle slowly. Nothing. She switched hands and tried again. Tightening her grip, she put the bottle between her legs for more leverage, and just as she was about to give up, the cork moved a little. Suddenly renewed, she changed back to her original hands . . . squeezed . . . twisting the bottle slowly . . . more cork . . . and suddenly it loosened and the remaining portion slipped out easily.

She tipped the bottle upside-down and was surprised when the note dropped to the sand by her feet almost immediately. When she leaned over to pick it up, she noticed it was tightly bound, which was why it slid out so easily.

She untied the yarn carefully, and the first thing that struck her as she unrolled the message was the paper. This was no child's stationery. It was expensive paper, thick and sturdy, with a silhouette of a sailing ship embossed in the upper right hand corner. And the paper itself was crinkled, aged looking, almost as if it had been in the water for a hundred years.

She caught herself holding her breath. Maybe it was old. It could be—there were stories about bottles washing up after a hundred years at sea, so that could be the case now. Maybe she had a real artifact here. But as she scrutinized the writing itself, she saw that she was mistaken. There was a date on the upper left corner of the paper.

July 22, 1997.

A little more than three weeks ago.

*Three weeks? That's all?*

She looked a little further. The message was long—it covered the front and back sides of the paper—and it didn't seem to request any reply of sorts. A quick glance showed no address or phone number anywhere, but she supposed it could have been written into the letter itself.

She felt a twinge of curiosity as she held the message in front of her, and it was then, in the rising sunlight of a hot New England day, that she first read the letter that would change her life forever.

*July 22, 1997*

*My Dearest Catherine,*

*I miss you, my darling, as I always do, but today is especially hard because the ocean has been singing to me, and the song is that of our life together. I can almost feel you beside me as I write this letter, and I can smell the scent of wildflowers that always reminds me of you. But at this moment, these things give me no pleasure. Your visits have been coming less often, and I feel sometimes as if the greatest part of who I am is slowly slipping away.*

*I am trying, though. At night when I am alone, I call for you, and whenever my ache seems to be the greatest, you still seem to find a way to return to me. Last night, in my dreams, I saw you on the pier near Wrightsville Beach. The wind was blowing through your hair, and your eyes held the fading sunlight. I am struck as I see you leaning against the rail. You are beautiful, I think as I see you, a vision that I can never find in anyone else. I slowly begin to walk toward you,* and when you finally turn to me, I notice that others have been watching you as well. "Do you know her?" they ask me in jealous whispers, and as you smile at me, I simply answer with the truth. "Better than my own heart."

I stop when I reach you and take you in my arms. I long for this moment more than any other. It is what I live for, and when you return my embrace, I give myself over to this moment, at peace once again.

I raise my hand and gently touch your cheek and you tilt your head and close your eyes. My hands are hard and your skin is soft, and I wonder for a moment if you'll pull back, but of course you don't. You never have, and it is at times like this that I know what my purpose is in life.

I am here to love you, to hold you in my arms, to protect you. I am here to learn from you and to receive your love in return. I am here because there is no other place to be.

But then, as always, the mist starts to form as we stand close to one another. It is a distant fog that rises from the horizon, and I find that I grow fearful as it approaches. It slowly creeps in, enveloping the world around us, fencing us in as if to prevent escape. Like a rolling cloud, it blankets everything, closing, until there is nothing left but the two of us.

I feel my throat begin to close and my eyes well up with tears because I know it is time for you to go. The look you give me at that moment haunts me. I feel your sadness and my own loneliness, and the ache in my heart that had been silent for only a short time grows stronger as you release me. And then you spread your arms and step back into the fog because it is your place and not mine. I long to go with you, but your only response is to shake your head because we both know that is impossible.

   And I watch with breaking heart as you slowly fade away. I find myself straining to remember everything about this moment, everything about you. But soon, always too soon, your image vanishes and the fog rolls back to its faraway place and I am alone on the pier and I do not care what others think as I bow my head and cry and cry and cry.

   *Garrett*

CHAPTER 2

*H*ave you been crying?" Deanna asked as Theresa stepped onto the back deck, carrying both the bottle and the message. In her confusion, she had forgotten to throw the bottle away.

Theresa felt embarrassed and wiped her eyes as Deanna put down the newspaper and rose from her seat. Though she was overweight—and had been since Theresa had known her—she moved quickly around the table, her face registering concern.

"Are you okay? What happened out there? Are you hurt?" She bumped into one of the chairs as she reached out and took Theresa's hand.

Theresa shook her head. "No, nothing like that. I just found this letter and . . . I don't know, after I read it I couldn't help it."

"A letter? What letter? Are you sure you're okay?" Deanna's free hand gestured compulsively as she asked the questions.

"I'm fine, really. The letter was in a bottle. I found it washed up on the beach. When I opened it and read it . . ." She trailed off, and Deanna's face lightened just a bit.

"Oh . . . that's good. For a second I thought something awful happened. Like someone had attacked you or something."

Theresa brushed away a strand of hair that had blown onto her face and smiled at her concern. "No, the letter just really hit me. It's silly, I know. I shouldn't have been so emotional. And I'm sorry for giving you a scare."

"Oh, pooh," Deanna said, shrugging. "Nothing to be sorry about. I'm just glad you're okay." She paused for a moment. "You said the letter made you cry? Why? What did it say?"

Theresa wiped her eyes, handed the letter to Deanna, and walked over to the wrought-iron table where Deanna had been sitting. Still feeling a bit ridiculous about crying, she did her best to compose herself.

Deanna read the letter slowly, and when she finished, she looked up at Theresa. Her eyes too were watering. It wasn't just her, after all.

"It's . . . it's beautiful," Deanna finally said. "It's one of the most touching things I've ever read."

"That's what I thought."

"And you found it washed up on the beach? When you were running?"

Theresa nodded.

"I don't know how it could have washed up there. The bay is sheltered from the rest of the ocean, and I've never heard of Wrightsville Beach."

"I don't know, either, but it looked like it had washed up last night. I almost walked by it at first before I noticed what it was."

Deanna ran her finger over the writing and paused for a moment. "I wonder who they are. And why was it sealed in a bottle?"

"I don't know."

"Aren't you curious?"

The fact was that Theresa was indeed curious. Immediately after reading it, she had read it again, then a third time. What would it be like, she mused, to have someone love her that way?

"A little. But so what? There's no way we'll ever know."

"What are you going to do with it?"

"Keep it, I guess. I haven't really thought about it that much."

"Hmmm," Deanna said with an indecipherable smile. Then, "How was your jog?"

Theresa sipped a glass of juice she had poured. "It was good. The sun was really something when it came up. It looked like the world was glowing."

"That's just because you were dizzy from lack of oxygen. Jogging does that to you."

Theresa smiled, amused. "So, I take it you won't come with me this week."

Deanna reached for her cup of coffee with a doubtful look on her face. "Not a chance. My exercise is limited to vacuuming the house every weekend. Can you picture me out there, huffing and puffing? I'd probably have a heart attack."

"It's refreshing once you get used to it."

"That may be true, but I'm not young and svelte like you are. The only time I can remember running at all was when I was a kid and the neighbor's dog got out of the yard. I was running so fast, I almost wet my pants."

Theresa laughed out loud. "So, what's on the agenda today?"

"I thought we'd do a little shopping and have lunch in town. Are you up for something like that?"

"That's what I was hoping you'd say."

The two women talked about the places they might go. Then Deanna got up and went inside for another cup of coffee and Theresa watched her as she left.

Deanna was fifty-eight and round faced, with hair that was slowly turning to gray. She kept it cut short, dressed without an excess of vanity, and was, Theresa decided, easily the best person she knew. She was knowledgeable about music and art, and at work, the recordings of Mozart or Beethoven were always flooding out of her office into the chaos of the newsroom. She lived in a world of optimism and humor, and everyone who knew her adored her.

When Deanna came back to the table, she sat down and looked out across the bay. "Isn't this the most beautiful place you've ever seen?"

"Yes, it is. I'm glad you invited me."

"You needed it. You would have been absolutely alone in that apartment of yours."

"You sound like my mother."

"I'll take that as a compliment."

Deanna reached across the table and picked up the letter again. As she perused it her eyebrows raised, but she said nothing. To Theresa, it looked as though the letter had triggered something in her memory.

"What is it?"

"I just wonder . . . ," she said quietly.

"Wonder what?"

"Well, when I was inside, I got to thinking about this letter. I'm wondering if we should run this in your column this week."

"What are you talking about?"

Deanna leaned across the table. "Just what I said—I think we should run this letter in your column this week. I'm sure other people would love to read it. It really is unusual. People need to read something like this every once in a while. And this is so touching. I can picture a hundred women cutting it out and taping it to their refrigerators so their husbands can see it when they get home from work."

"We don't even know who they are. Don't you think we should get their permission first?"

"That's just the point. We can't. I can talk to the attorney at the paper, but I'm sure it's legal. We won't use their real names, and as long as we don't take credit for writing it or divulge where it might be from, I'm sure there wouldn't be a problem."

"I know it's probably legal, but I'm not sure if it's right. I mean, this is a very personal letter. I'm not sure it should be spread around so that everyone can read it."

"It's a human interest story, Theresa. People love those sorts of things. Besides, there's nothing in there that might be embarrassing to someone. This is a beautiful letter. And remember, this Garrett person sent it in a *bottle* in the *ocean*. He had to know it would wash up somewhere."

Theresa shook her head. "I don't know, Deanna . . ."

"Well, think about it. Sleep on it if you have to. I think it's a great idea."

                          ✳      ✳      ✳

Theresa did think about the letter as she undressed and got in the shower. She found herself wondering about the man who wrote it—Garrett, if that was his real name. And who, if anyone, was Catherine? His lover or his wife, obviously, but she wasn't around anymore. Was she dead, she wondered, or did something else happen that forced them apart? And why was it sealed in a bottle and set adrift? The whole thing was strange. Her reporter's instincts took over then, and she suddenly thought that the message might not mean anything. It could be someone who wanted to write a love letter but didn't have anyone to send it to. It could even have been sent by someone who got some sort of vicarious thrill by making lonely women cry on distant beaches. But as the words rolled through her head again, she realized that those possibilities were unlikely. The letter obviously came from the heart. And to think that a man wrote it! In all her years, she had never received a letter even close to that. Touching sentiments sent her way had always been emblazoned with Hallmark greeting card logos. David had never been much of a writer, nor had anyone else she had dated. What would such a man be like? she wondered. Would he be as caring in person as the letter seemed to imply?

She lathered and rinsed her hair, the questions slipping from her mind as the cool water rolled down her body. She washed the rest of her body with a washcloth and moisturizing soap, spent longer in the shower than she had to, and finally stepped out of the stall.

She looked at herself in the mirror as she toweled off. Not too bad for a thirty-six-year-old with an adolescent son, she thought to herself. Her breasts had always been smallish, and though it had bothered her when she was younger, she was glad now because they hadn't started to sag or droop like those of other women her age. Her stomach was flat, and her legs were long and lean from all the exercise over the years. Nor did the crow's-feet around the corners of her eyes seem to show as much, though that didn't make any sense. All in all, she was pleased with how she looked this morning, and she attributed her unusually easy acceptance of herself to being on vacation.

After putting on a little makeup, she dressed in beige shorts, a sleeveless white blouse, and brown sandals. It would be hot and humid in another hour, and she wanted to be comfortable as she walked around Provincetown. She looked out the bathroom window, saw that the sun had risen even higher, and made a note to pick up some sunscreen. Her skin would burn if she didn't, and she'd learned from experience that a sunburn was one of the quickest ways to ruin a beach trip.

Outside on the deck, Deanna had set breakfast on the table. There was cantaloupe and grapefruit, along with toasted bagels. After taking her seat, she spread some low-fat cream cheese on them—Deanna was on one of her endless diets again—and the two of them talked for a long while. Brian was out golfing, as he would be every day this week, and he had to go in the early morning because he was on some sort of medication that Deanna said "does awful things to his skin if he spends too much time in the sun."

Brian and Deanna had been together thirty-six years. College sweethearts, they'd married the summer after graduation, right after Brian accepted a job with an accounting firm in downtown Boston. Eight years later Brian became a partner and they bought a spacious house in Brookline, where they had lived alone for the past twenty-eight years.

They had always wanted children, but after six years of marriage Deanna had yet to become pregnant. They went to see a gynecologist and discovered that Deanna's fallopian tubes had been scarred and that having a child was impossible. They tried to adopt for several years, but the list seemed never-ending, and they eventually gave up hope. Then came the dark years, she once confided to Theresa, a time when the marriage almost failed. But their commitment, though shaken, remained solid, and Deanna turned to work to fill the void in her life. She started at the *Boston Times* when women were rare and gradually worked her way up the corporate ladder. When she became managing editor ten years ago, she began to take women reporters under her wing. Theresa had been her first student.

After Deanna had gone upstairs to shower, Theresa looked through the paper briefly, then checked her watch. She rose from her seat and went to the phone to dial David's number. It was still early there, only seven o'clock, but she knew the whole family would be awake by now. Kevin always rose at the crack of dawn, and for once she was thankful that someone else had to share in that wonderful experience. She paced back and forth as the phone rang a few times before Annette picked up. Theresa could hear the TV in the background and the sound of a crying baby.

"Hi. It's Theresa. Is Kevin around?"

"Oh, hi. Of course he's here. Hold on for just a second."

The phone clunked down on the counter and Theresa listened as Annette called for him: "Kevin, it's for you. Theresa's on the phone."

The fact that she wasn't referred to as Kevin's mom hurt more than she expected, but she didn't have time to dwell on it.

Kevin was out of breath when he reached the phone.

"Hey, Mom. How're you doing? How's your vacation?"

She felt a pang of loneliness at the sound of his voice. It was still high, childlike, but she knew it was only a matter of time before it changed.

"It's beautiful, but I only got here yesterday night. I haven't done much except for jogging this morning."

"Were there a lot of people on the beach?"

"No, but I saw a few people heading out as I finished. Hey, when do you take off with your dad?"

"In a couple days. His vacation doesn't start until Monday, so that's when we leave. Right now he's getting ready to go into the office to do some work so that he'll be free and clear by the time we go. Do you want to talk to him?"

"No, I don't have to. I was just calling to tell you that I hope you'll have a good time."

"It's going to be a blast. I saw a brochure on the river trip. Some of the rapids look pretty cool."

"Well, you be careful."

"Mom, I'm not a kid anymore."

"I know. Just reassure your old-fashioned mother."

"Okay, I promise. I'll wear my life jacket the whole time." He paused for a moment. "You know, we're not going to have a phone, though, so we won't be able to talk until I get back."

"I figured as much. It should be a lot of fun, though."

"It'll be awesome. I wish that you could come with us. We'd have a great time."

She closed her eyes for a moment before responding, a trick her therapist had taught her. Whenever Kevin said something about the three of them being together again, she always tried to make sure she said nothing that she'd later regret. Her voice sounded as optimistic as she could make it.

"You and your dad need some time alone. I know he's missed you a lot. You've got some catching up to do, and he's been looking forward to this trip as long as you have." *There, that wasn't so hard.*

"Did he tell you that?"

"Yes. A few times."

Kevin was quiet.

"I'll miss you, Mom. Can I call you as soon as I get back to tell you about the trip?"

"Of course. You can call me anytime. I'd love to hear all about it." Then, "I love you, Kevin."

"I love you too, Mom."

She hung up the phone, feeling both happy and sad, which was how she usually felt whenever they talked on the phone when he was with his father.

"Who was that?" Deanna said from behind her. She had come down the stairs wearing a yellow tiger-striped blouse, red shorts, white socks, and a pair of Reeboks. Her outfit screamed "I'm a tourist!" and Theresa did her best to keep a straight face.

"It was Kevin. I gave him a call."

"Is he doing okay?" She opened the closet and grabbed a camera to complete the ensemble.

"He's fine. He leaves in a couple of days."

"Good, that's good." She draped the camera around her neck. "And now that that's taken care of, we have some shopping to do. We've got to get you looking like a new woman."

Shopping with Deanna was an experience.

Once they got to Provincetown, they spent the rest of the

morning and early afternoon in a variety of shops. Theresa bought three new outfits and a new swimsuit before Deanna dragged her into a place called Nightingales, a lingerie shop.

Deanna went absolutely wild in there. Not for herself, of course, but for Theresa. She would pick up lacy, see-through underwear and matching bras off the racks and hold them up for Theresa to evaluate. "This looks pretty steamy," she'd say, or, "You don't have any this color, do you?" Naturally there would be others around as she blurted these things out, and Theresa couldn't help but laugh whenever she did it. Deanna's lack of inhibition was one of the things that Theresa loved most about her. She really didn't care what other people thought, and Theresa often wished she could be more like her.

After taking two of Deanna's suggestions—she was on vacation, after all—the two spent a couple of minutes in the record store. Deanna wanted the latest CD from Harry Connick Jr.— "He's cute," she said in explanation—and Theresa bought a jazz CD of one of John Coltrane's earlier recordings. When they returned to the house, Brian was reading the paper in the living room.

"Hey there. I was beginning to get worried about you two. How was your day?"

"It was good," Deanna answered. "We had lunch in Provincetown, then did a little shopping. How did your game go today?"

"Pretty well. If I hadn't bogeyed the last two holes, I would have shot an eighty."

"Well, you're just going to have to play a little more until you get it right."

Brian laughed. "You won't mind?"

"Of course not."

Brian smiled as he rustled the paper, content with the fact that he could spend a lot of time on the course this week. Recognizing his signal that he wanted to get back to reading, Deanna whispered in Theresa's ear, "Take it from me. Let a man play golf and he'll never raise a fuss about anything."

Theresa left the two of them alone for the rest of the afternoon. Since the day was still warm, she changed into the new suit she had bought, grabbed a towel and small fold-up chair and *People* magazine, then went to the beach.

She thumbed idly through *People*, reading a few articles here and there, not really interested in what was happening to the rich and famous. All around her she could hear the laughter of children as they splashed in the water and filled their pails with sand. Off to one side of her were two young boys and a man, presumably their father, building a castle near the water's edge. The sound of the lapping waves was soothing. She put down the magazine and closed her eyes, angling her face toward the sun.

She wanted a little color by the time she got back to work, if for no other reason than to look as though she had taken some time to do absolutely nothing. Even at work she was regarded as the type who was always on the go. If she wasn't writing her weekly column, she was working on the column for the Sunday editions, or researching on the Internet, or poring over child development journals. She had subscriptions at work to every major parenting magazine and every childhood magazine, as well as others devoted to working women. She also subscribed to medical journals, scanning them regularly for topics that might be suitable.

The column itself was never predictable—perhaps that was

one of the reasons it was so successful. Sometimes she responded to questions, other times she reported on the latest child development data and what it meant. A lot of columns were about the joys that came with raising children, while others described the pitfalls. She wrote of the struggles of single motherhood, a subject that seemed to touch a nerve in the lives of Boston women. Unexpectedly, her column had turned her into a local celebrity of sorts. But even though it was fun in the beginning to see her picture above her column, or to receive invitations to private parties, she always had so much going on, she didn't seem to have time to enjoy it. Now she regarded it as just another feature of the job—one that was nice but didn't really mean much to her.

After an hour in the sun, Theresa realized she was hot and walked to the water. She waded in to her hips, then went under as a small wave approached. The cool water made her gasp when her head came up, and a man standing next to her chuckled.

"Refreshing, isn't it?" he said, and she agreed with a nod as she crossed her arms.

He was tall with dark hair the same color as hers, and for a second she wondered if he was flirting with her. But the children nearby quickly ended that illusion with shouts of "Dad!" and after a few more minutes in the water, she got out and walked back to her chair. The beach was clearing out. She packed up her things as well and started back.

At the house, Brian was watching golf on television and Deanna was reading a novel with a picture of a young, handsome lawyer on the cover. Deanna looked up from her book.

"How was the beach?"

"It was great. The sun felt wonderful, but the water kind of shocks you when you go under."

"It always does. I don't see how people can stand to be in it for more than a few minutes."

Theresa hung the towel on a rack by the door. She spoke over her shoulder. "How's the book?"

Deanna turned the book over in her hands and glanced at the cover. "Wonderful. It reminds me of how Brian used to look a few years back."

Brian grunted without looking away from the television. "Huh?"

"Nothing, sweetheart. Just reminiscing." She turned her attention back to Theresa. Her eyes were shining. "Are you up for some gin rummy?"

Deanna loved card games of any kind. She was in two bridge clubs, played hearts like a champion, and kept a record of every time she won a game of solitaire. But gin rummy had always been the game that she and Theresa played when they had time, because it was the only game that Theresa actually stood a chance of winning.

"Sure."

Deanna folded the page with glee, put down her book, and rose from her seat. "I hoped you'd say that. The cards are on the table outside."

Theresa wrapped the towel around her suit and went outside to the table where they had eaten breakfast earlier. Deanna followed shortly with two cans of diet Coke and sat across from her as she picked up the deck. She shuffled the cards and dealt them. Deanna looked up from her hand.

"It looks like you got a little color in your cheeks. The sun must have been pretty intense."

Theresa started organizing her cards. "I felt like I was baking."

"Did you meet anyone interesting?"

"Not really. Just read and relaxed in the sun. Most everyone there was with their families."

"That's too bad."

"Why do you say that?"

"Well, I was kind of hoping you'd meet someone special this week."

"You're special."

"You know what I mean. I was kind of hoping you'd find yourself a man this week. One that took your breath away."

Theresa looked up in surprise. "What brought that on?"

"The sun, the ocean, the breezes. I don't know. Maybe it's the extra radiation soaking through my brain."

"I haven't really been looking, Deanna."

"Never?"

"Not much, anyway."

"Ah ha!"

"Don't make a big deal out of it. It hasn't been that long since the divorce."

Theresa put down the six of diamonds, and Deanna picked it up before discarding the three of clubs. Deanna spoke in the same tone her mother did when they talked about the same thing.

"It's been almost three years. Don't you have anyone on the back burner that you've been hiding from me?"

"No."

"No one?"

Deanna picked from the stack of cards and discarded a four of hearts.

"Nope. But it's not only me, you know. It's hard to meet people these days. It's not like I have time to go out and socialize."

"I know that, I really do. It's just that you've got so much to offer someone. I know there's someone out there for you somewhere."

"I'm sure there is. I just haven't met him yet."

"Are you even looking?"

"When I can. But my boss is a real stickler, you know. Won't give me a moment's rest."

"Maybe I should talk to her."

"Maybe you should," Theresa agreed, and they both laughed.

Deanna picked from the stack and discarded a seven of spades. "Have you been dating at all?"

"Not really. Not since Matt What's-his-name told me he didn't want a woman with children."

Deanna scowled for a moment. "Sometimes men can be real jerks, and he was a perfect example. He's the kind of guy whose head belongs mounted on a wall with a plaque that reads 'Typical Egocentric Male.' But they aren't all like that. There are lots of real men out there—men who could fall in love with you at the drop of a hat."

Theresa picked up the seven and discarded a four of diamonds. "That's why I like you, Deanna. You say the sweetest things."

Deanna picked from the stack. "It's true, though. Believe me. You're pretty, you're successful, you're intelligent. I could find a dozen men who would love to go out with you."

"I'm sure you could. But that doesn't mean that I would like them."

"You're not even giving it a chance."

Theresa shrugged. "Maybe not. But that doesn't mean I'll die alone in some boardinghouse for old maids later in life. Believe me, I'd love to fall in love again. I'd love to meet a wonderful guy and live happily ever after. I just can't make it a priority right now. Kevin and work take all my time as it is."

Deanna didn't reply for a moment. She threw down a two of spades.

"I think you're scared."

"Scared?"

"Absolutely. Not that there's anything wrong with that."

"Why do you say that?"

"Because I know how much David hurt you, and I know I'd be frightened of the same thing happening again if it were me. It's human nature. Once burned, twice shy, the old saying goes. There's a lot of truth in that."

"There probably is. But I'm sure if the right man comes along, I'll know it. I have faith."

"What kind of man are you looking for?"

"I don't know. . . ."

"Sure you do. Everyone knows a little bit about what they want."

"Not everyone."

"Sure you do. Start with the obvious, or if you can't do that, start with what you don't want—like . . . is it all right if he's in a motorcycle gang?"

Theresa smiled and picked from the stack. Her hand was

coming together. Another card and she'd be done. She threw down the jack of hearts.

"Why are you so interested?"

"Oh, just humor an old friend, will you?"

"Fine. No motorcycle gang, that's for sure," she said with a shake of her head. She thought for a moment. "Um . . . I guess most of all, he'd have to be the kind of man who would be faithful to me, faithful to *us*, throughout our relationship. I've already had another kind of man, and I can't go through something like that again. And I think I'd like someone my own age or close to it, if possible, as well." Theresa stopped there and frowned a little.

"And?"

"Give me a second—I'm thinking. This isn't as easy as it sounds. I guess I'd go with the standard clichés—I'd like him to be handsome, kind, intelligent, and charming—you know, all those good things that women want in a man."

Again she paused. Deanna picked up the jack. Her expression showed her pleasure at putting Theresa on the spot.

"And?"

"He would have to spend time with Kevin as if he were his own son—that's really important to me. Oh—and he'd have to be romantic, too. I'd love to receive some flowers now and then. And athletic, too. I can't respect a man if I could beat him in arm wrestling."

"That's it?"

"Yep, that's all."

"So, let me see if I've got this right. You want a faithful, charming, handsome, thirty-something-year-old man, who's also intelligent, romantic, and athletic. And he has to be good with Kevin, right?"

"You got it."

She took a deep breath as she laid her hand on the table.

"Well, at least you're not picky. Gin."


After losing decisively in gin rummy, Theresa went inside to start one of the books she'd brought with her. She sat in the window seat along the back side of the house while Deanna went back to her own book. Brian found yet another golf tournament and spent the afternoon watching it avidly, making comments to no one in particular whenever something caught his interest.

At six that evening—and, more important, after the golf tournament had ended—Brian and Deanna went for a walk along the beach. Theresa stayed behind and watched from the window as they strolled hand in hand along the water's edge. They had an ideal relationship, she thought as she watched them. They had completely different interests, yet that seemed to keep them together instead of driving them apart.

After the sun went down, the three of them drove to Hyannis and had dinner at Sam's Crabhouse, a thriving restaurant that deserved its reputation. It was crowded and they had to wait an hour for seats, but the steamed crabs and drawn butter were worth it. The butter had been flavored with garlic, and among the three of them they went through six beers in two hours. Toward the end of dinner, Brian asked about the letter that had washed up.

"I read it when I got back from golfing. Deanna had pinned it to the refrigerator."

Deanna shrugged and laughed. She turned to Theresa with an "I told you someone would do that" look in her eyes but said nothing.

"It washed up on the beach. I found it when I was jogging."

Brian finished his beer and went on. "It was quite a letter. It seemed so sad."

"I know. That's how I felt when I read it."

"Do you know where Wrightsville Beach is?"

"No. I've never heard of it."

"It's in North Carolina," Brian said as he reached into a pocket for a cigarette. "I had a golf trip down there once. Great courses. A little flat, but playable."

Deanna chimed in with a nod. "With Brian, everything is somehow connected to golf."

Theresa asked, "Where in North Carolina?"

Brian lit his cigarette and inhaled. As he exhaled, he spoke.

"Near Wilmington—or actually, it might even be a part of it—I'm not exactly sure about the boundaries. If you're driving, it's about an hour and a half north of Myrtle Beach. Have you ever heard of the movie *Cape Fear*?"

"Sure."

"The Cape Fear River is in Wilmington, and that's where both of the movies were set. Actually, a lot of movies are filmed there. Most of the major studios have a presence in town. Wrightsville Beach is an island right off the coast. Very developed—it's almost a resort community now. It's where a lot of the stars stay while they're on location filming."

"How come I've never heard of it?"

"I don't know. I guess it doesn't get much attention because of Myrtle Beach, but it's popular down south. The beaches are beautiful—white sand, warm water. It's a great place to spend a week if you ever get the chance."

Theresa didn't respond, and Deanna spoke again with a hint of mischief in her tone.

"So, now we know where our mystery writer is from."

Theresa shrugged. "I suppose so, but there's still no way to tell for sure. It could have been a place where they vacationed or visited. It doesn't mean he lives there."

Deanna shook her head. "I don't think so. The way the letter was written—it just seemed like his dream was too real to include a place he had only been to once or twice."

"You've really given this some thought, haven't you?"

"Instincts. You learn to go with them, and I'd be willing to bet that Wrightsville Beach or Wilmington is his home."

"So what?"

Deanna reached over to Brian's hand, took the cigarette, breathed deeply, and kept it as her own. She had done this for years. In her mind, because she didn't light it, she wasn't officially addicted. Brian, without seeming to notice what she had done, lit another. Deanna leaned forward.

"Have you given any more thought to having the letter published?"

"Not really. I still don't know if it's a good idea."

"How about if we don't use their names—just their initials? We can even change the name of Wrightsville Beach, if you want to."

"Why is this so important to you?"

"Because I know a good story when I see one. More than that, I think that this would be meaningful to a lot of people. Nowadays, people are so busy that romance seems to be slowly dying out. This letter shows that it's still possible."

Theresa absently reached for a strand of hair and began to twist it. A habit since childhood, it was what she did whenever she was thinking about something. After a long moment, she finally responded.

"All right."

"You'll do it?"

"Yes, but like you said, we'll use only their initials and we'll omit the part about Wrightsville Beach. And I'll write a couple of sentences to introduce it."

"I'm so glad," Deanna cried with girlish enthusiasm. "I knew you would. We'll fax it in tomorrow."

Later that night, Theresa wrote out the beginning of the column in longhand on some stationery she found in the desk drawer in the den. When she was finished, she went to her room, set the two pages on the bedstand behind her, then crawled into bed. That night she slept fitfully.

The following day, Theresa and Deanna went into Chatham and had the letter typed in a print shop. Since neither of them had brought their portable computers and Theresa was insistent that the column not include certain information, it seemed like the most logical thing to do. When the column was ready, they faxed it in. It would run in the next day's paper.

The rest of the morning and afternoon were spent like the day before—shopping, relaxing at the beach, easy conversation, and a delicious dinner. When the paper arrived early the next morning, Theresa was the first to read it. She woke early, finished her run before Deanna and Brian were up, then opened the paper and read the column.

> Four days ago, while I was on vacation, I was listening to some old songs on the radio and heard Sting singing "Message in a Bottle." Spurred to action by his impassioned crooning, I raced to the beach to find a bottle of my own. Within minutes I found one, and sure enough, it had a message inside. (Actually, I didn't hear the song first: I made that up for dramatic effect. But I did find a bottle the other morning with a deeply moving message inside.) I haven't been able to get it off my mind, and although it isn't something I'd normally write about, in a time where everlasting love and commitment seem to be in such short supply, I was hoping you would find it as meaningful as I did.

The rest of the column was devoted to the letter. When Deanna joined Theresa for breakfast, she read the column as well before looking at anything else. "Marvelous," she said when she finished. "It looks even better in print than I thought it would. You're going to get a lot of mail from this column."

"Do you think so?"

"Absolutely. I'm sure of it."

"Even more than usual?"

"Tons more. I can feel it. In fact, I'm going to call John today. I'm going to have him place this on the wire a couple times this week. You may even get some Sunday runs with this one."

"We'll see," Theresa said as she ate a bagel, not really sure whether to believe Deanna or not, but curious nonetheless.

CHAPTER  3

On Saturday, eight days after she'd arrived, Theresa returned to Boston.

She unlocked the door to her apartment and Harvey came
running from the back bedroom. He rubbed against her leg,
purring softly, and Theresa picked him up and brought him to
the refrigerator. She took out a piece of cheese and gave it to
Harvey while she stroked his head, grateful that her neighbor
Ella had agreed to look after him while she was away. After he
finished the cheese, he jumped from her arms and ambled toward the sliding glass doors that led to the back patio. The
apartment was stuffy from being closed up, and she slid the
doors open to air it out.

After unpacking her bags and picking up her keys and mail

from Ella, she poured herself a glass of wine, went to the stereo, and popped in the John Coltrane CD she had bought. As the sound of jazz filtered through the room, she sorted through the mail. As usual, it was mainly bills, and she put them aside for another time.

There were eight messages on her recorder when she checked it. Two were from men she had dated in the past, asking her to call if she had a chance. She thought about it briefly, then decided against it. Neither of them was attractive to her, and she didn't feel like going out just because she had a break in her schedule. She also had calls from her mother and sister, and she made a note to call them sometime this week. There were no calls from Kevin. By now he was rafting and camping with his father somewhere in Arizona.

Without Kevin, the house seemed strangely silent. It was tidy as well, though, and this somehow made it a little easier. It was nice to come home to a house and only have to clean up after herself once in a while.

She thought about the two weeks of vacation she still had left this year. She and Kevin would spend some time at the beach because she had promised him they would. But that left another week. She could use it around Christmas, but this year Kevin would be at his father's, so there didn't seem to be much point in that. She hated spending Christmas alone—it had always been her favorite holiday—but she didn't have a choice, and she decided that dwelling on that fact was useless. Maybe she could go to Bermuda or Jamaica or somewhere else in the Caribbean—but then, she didn't really want to go alone, and she didn't know who else would go with her. Janet might be able to, but she doubted it. Her three kids kept her busy, and Edward most likely couldn't get the time off work. Perhaps she could use the week to do the things around the house she had been meaning to do . . . but that seemed like a waste. Who wanted to spend their vacation painting and hanging wallpaper?

She finally gave up and decided that if nothing exciting came to mind, she would just save it for the following year. Maybe she and Kevin would go to Hawaii for a couple of weeks.

She got into bed and picked up one of the novels she had started at Cape Cod. She read quickly and without distraction and finished almost a hundred pages before she was tired. At midnight she turned off the light. That night, she dreamed she was walking along a deserted beach, though she didn't know why.

The mail on her desk Monday morning was overwhelming. There were almost two hundred letters there when she arrived, and another fifty arrived later that day with the postman. As soon as she walked into the office, Deanna had pointed proudly at the stack. "See, I told you so," she had said with a smile.

Theresa asked that her calls be put on hold, and she started opening the mail right away. Without exception, they were responses to the letter she had published in her column. Most were from women, though a few men wrote in as well, and their uniformity of opinion surprised her. One by one, she read how much they had been touched by the anonymous letter. Many asked if she knew who the writer was, and a few women suggested that if the man was single, they wanted to marry him.

She discovered that almost every Sunday edition across the country had run the column, and the letters came from as far away as Los Angeles. Six men claimed they had written the letter themselves, and four of them wanted royalties for it—one even threatened legal action. But when she examined their handwriting, none of them even remotely resembled the letter's.

At noon she went to lunch at her favorite Japanese restaurant, and a couple of people who were dining at other tables mentioned that they had read the column as well. "My wife taped it to the refrigerator door," one man said, which made Theresa laugh out loud.

By the end of the day she had worked through most of the stack, and she was tired. She hadn't worked on her next column at all, and she felt the pressure building behind her neck, as it usually did when her deadline approached. At five-thirty she started working on a column about Kevin being away and what that was like for her. It was going better than she expected and she was almost finished when her phone rang.

It was the newspaper's receptionist.

"Hey, Theresa, I know you asked me to hold your calls, and I have been," she started. "It wasn't easy, by the way—you got about sixty calls today. The phone has been ringing off the hook."

"So what's up?"

"This woman keeps calling me. This is the fifth time she's called today, and she called twice last week. She won't give her name, but I recognize the voice by now. She says she's got to talk to you."

"Can't you just take a message?"

"I've tried that, but she's persistent. She keeps asking to be put on hold until you have a minute. She says she's calling long distance, but that she has to talk to you."

Theresa thought for a moment as she stared at the screen in front of her. Her column was almost done—just another couple of paragraphs to go.

"Can't you ask for a phone number where I can reach her?"

"No, she won't give me that, either. She's very evasive."

"Do you know what she wants?"

"I don't have any idea. But she sounds coherent—not like a lot of people who've been calling today. One guy asked me to marry him."

Theresa laughed. "Okay, tell her to hold on. I'll be there in a couple of minutes."

"Will do."

"What line is she on?"

"Five."

"Thanks."

Theresa finished the column quickly. She would go over it again as soon as she got off the phone. She picked up the receiver and pressed line five.

"Hello."

The line was silent for a moment. Then, in a soft, melodic voice, the caller asked, "Is this Theresa Osborne?"

"Yes, it is." Theresa leaned back in her chair and started twirling her hair.

"Are you the one that wrote the column about the message in a bottle?"

"Yes. How can I help you?"

The caller paused again. Theresa could hear her breathing, as if she were thinking about what to say next. After a moment, the caller asked:

"Can you tell me the names that were in the letter?"

Theresa closed her eyes and stopped twirling. *Just another curiosity seeker*, she thought. Her eyes went back to the screen and she began to look over the column.

"No, I'm sorry, I can't. I don't want that information made public."

The caller was silent again, and Theresa began to grow impatient. She started reading the first paragraph on the screen. Then the caller surprised her.

"Please," she said, "I've got to know."

Theresa looked up from the screen. She could hear an absolute earnestness in the caller's voice. There was something else there, too, but she couldn't put her finger on it.

"I'm sorry," Theresa said finally, "I really can't."

"Then can you answer a question?"

"Maybe."

"Was the letter addressed to Catherine and signed by a man named Garrett?"

The caller had Theresa's full attention and she sat up higher in her seat.

"Who is this?" she asked with sudden urgency, and by the time the words were out, she knew the caller would know the truth.

"It is, isn't it?"

"Who is this?" Theresa asked again, this time more gently. She heard the caller take a deep breath before she answered.

"My name is Michelle Turner and I live in Norfolk, Virginia."

"How did you know about the letter?"

"My husband is in the navy and he's stationed here. Three years ago, I was walking along the beach here, and I found a letter just like the one you found on your vacation. After reading your column, I knew it was the same person who wrote it. The initials were the same."

Theresa stopped for a moment. It couldn't be, she thought. Three years ago?

"What kind of paper was it written on?"

"The paper was beige, and it had a picture of a sailing ship in the upper right hand corner."

Theresa felt her heart pick up speed. It still seemed unbelievable to her.

"Your letter had a picture of a ship, too, didn't it?"

"Yes, it did," Theresa whispered.

"I knew it. I knew it as soon as I read your column." Michelle sounded as if a load had been lifted from her shoulders.

"Do you still have a copy of the letter?" Theresa asked.

"Yes. My husband's never seen it, but I take it out every now and then just to read it again. It's a little different from the letter you copied in your column, but the feelings are the same."

"Could you fax me a copy?"

"Sure," she said before pausing. "It's amazing, isn't it? I mean, first me finding it so long ago, and now you finding one."

"Yes," Theresa whispered, "it is."

After giving the fax number to Michelle, Theresa could barely proofread her column. Michelle had to go to a copy store to fax the letter, and Theresa found herself pacing from her desk to the fax machine every five minutes as she waited for the letter to arrive. Forty-six minutes later she heard the fax machine come to life. The first page through was a cover letter from National Copy Service, addressed to Theresa Osborne at the *Boston Times*.

She watched it as it fell to the tray beneath and heard the sound of the fax machine as it copied the letter line for line. It went quickly—it took only ten seconds to copy a page—but even that wait seemed too long. Then a third page started printing, and she realized that, like the letter she had found, this one too must have covered both sides.

She reached for the copies as the fax machine beeped, signaling an end to the transmission. She took them to her desk without reading them and placed them facedown for a couple of minutes, trying to slow her breathing. It's only a letter, she told herself.

Taking a deep breath, she lifted the cover page. A quick glance at the ship's logo proved to her that it was indeed the same writer. She put the page into better light and began to read.

*March 6, 1994*

*My Darling Catherine,*

*Where are you? And why, I wonder as I sit alone in a darkened house, have we been forced apart?*

*I don't know the answer to these questions, no matter how hard I try to understand. The reason is plain, but my mind forces me to dismiss it and I am torn by anxiety in all my waking hours. I am lost without you. I am soulless, a drifter without a home, a solitary bird in a flight to nowhere. I am all these things, and I am nothing at all. This, my darling, is my life without you. I long for you to show me how to live again.*

*I try to remember the way we once were, on the breezy deck of Happenstance. Do you recall how we worked on her together? We became a part of the ocean as we rebuilt her, for we both knew it was the ocean that brought us together. It was times like those that I understood the meaning of true happiness. At night, we sailed on blackened water and I watched as the moonlight reflected your beauty. I would* watch you with awe and know in my heart that we'd be to-gether forever. Is it always that way, I wonder, when two peo-ple are in love? I don't know, but if my life since you were taken from me is any indication, then I think I know the an-swers. From now on, I know I will be alone.

I think of you, I dream of you, I conjure you up when I need you most. This is all I can do, but to me it isn't enough. It will never be enough, this I know, yet what else is there for me to do? If you were here, you would tell me, but I have been cheated of even that. You always knew the proper words to ease the pain I felt. You always knew how to make me feel good inside.

Is it possible that you know how I feel without you? When I dream, I like to think you do. Before we came to-gether, I moved through life without meaning, without rea-son. I know that somehow, every step I took since the moment I could walk was a step toward finding you. We were destined to be together.

But now, alone in my house, I have come to realize that destiny can hurt a person as much as it can bless him, and I find myself wondering why—out of all the people in all the world I could ever have loved—I had to fall in love with someone who was taken away from me.

Garrett

~

After reading the letter, she leaned back in her chair and brought her fingers to her lips. The sounds from the newsroom seemed to be coming from someplace far away. She reached for her purse, found the initial letter, and laid the two next to each other on her desk. She read the first letter, followed by the second one, then read them in reverse order, feeling almost like a voyeur of sorts, as if she were eavesdropping on a private, secret-filled moment.

She got up from her desk, feeling strangely unraveled. At the vending machine she bought herself a can of apple juice, trying to comprehend the feelings inside her. When she returned, however, her legs suddenly seemed wobbly and she plopped down in her chair. If she hadn't been standing in exactly the right place, she felt that she would have hit the floor.

Hoping to clear her mind, she absently began to clean up the clutter on her desk. Pens went in the drawer, articles she'd used in research were filed away, the stapler was reloaded, and pencils were sharpened and set in a coffee cup on her desk. When she finished, nothing was out of place except for the two letters, which she hadn't moved at all.

A little more than a week ago she'd found the first letter, and the words had left a deep impression, though the pragmatist inside her forced her to try to put it behind her. But now that seemed impossible. Not after finding a second letter, written by presumably the same person. Were there more? she wondered. And what type of man would send them in bottles? It seemed miraculous that another person, three years ago, had stumbled across a letter and had kept it hidden away in her drawer because it had touched her as well. Yet it *had* happened. But what did it all mean?

She knew it shouldn't really matter much to her, but all at once it did. She ran her hand through her hair and looked around the room. Everywhere people were on the move. She opened her can of apple juice and took a swallow, trying to fathom what was going through her head. She wasn't exactly sure yet, and her only wish was that no one would walk up to her desk in the next couple of minutes until she had a better grasp of things. She slipped the two letters back into her purse while the opening line of the second one rolled through her head.

*Where are you?*

She exited the computer program she used to write her column, and in spite of her misgivings, she chose a program that allowed her to access the Internet.

After a moment's hesitation, she typed the words

## WRIGHTSVILLE BEACH

into the search program and hit the return key. She knew something would probably be listed, and in less than five seconds she had a number of different topics she could choose from.

**Found 3 matches containing Wrightsville Beach. Displaying matches 1-3.**

---

**Locator Categories–Locator Sites–Mariposa Web Pages**

---

**Locator Categories**

**Regional: U.S. States:North Carolina:Cities:Wrightsville Beach**

**Locator Sites**

**Regional: U.S. States:North Carolina:Cities:Wilmington: Real Estate-Ticar Real Estate Company**—also offices in Wrightsville Beach and Carolina Beach

**Regional:U.S. States:North Carolina:Cities:Wrightsville Beach:Lodging**

    -**Cascade Beach Resort**

As she sat staring at the screen, she suddenly felt ridiculous. Even if Deanna had been right and Garrett lived somewhere in the Wrightsville Beach area, it would still be nearly impossible to locate him. Why, then, was she trying to do so?

She knew the reason, of course. The letters were written by a man who loved a woman deeply, a man who was now alone. As a girl, she had come to believe in the ideal man—the prince or knight of her childhood stories. In the real world, however, men like that simply didn't exist. Real people had real agendas, real demands, real expectations about how other people should behave. True, there were good men out there—men who loved with all their hearts and remained steadfast in the face of great obstacles—the type of man she'd wanted to meet since she and David divorced. But how to find such a man?

Here and now, she knew such a man existed—a man who was now alone—and knowing that made something inside her tighten. It seemed obvious that Catherine—whoever she was—was probably dead, or at least missing without explanation. Yet Garrett still loved her enough to send love letters to her for at least three years. If nothing else, he had proven that he was capable of loving someone deeply and, more important, remaining fully committed—even long after his loved one was gone.

*Where are you?*

It kept ringing through her head, like a song she heard on early morning radio that kept repeating itself the entire afternoon.

*Where are you?*

She didn't know exactly, but he did exist, and one of the things she had learned early in her life was that if you discovered something that made you tighten inside, you had better try to learn more about it. If you simply ignored the feeling, you would never know what might happen, and in many ways that was worse than finding out you were wrong in the first place. Because if you were wrong, you could go forward in your life without ever looking back over your shoulder and wondering what might have been.

But where would this all lead? And what did it mean? Had the discovery of the letter been somehow fated, or was it simply a coincidence? Or maybe, she thought, it was simply a reminder of what she was missing in her life. She twirled her hair absently as she pondered the last question. Okay, she decided. I can live with that.

But she *was* curious about the mysterious writer, and there was no sense in denying it—at least to herself. And because no one else would understand it (how could they, if she didn't?), she resolved then and there not to tell anyone about what she was feeling.

*Where are you?*

Deep down she knew the computer searches and fascination with Garrett would lead to nothing at all. It would gradually pass into some sort of unusual story that she would retell time and time again. She would go on with her life—writing her column, spending time with Kevin, doing all the things a single parent had to do.

And she was almost right. Her life would have proceeded exactly as she imagined. But something happened three days later that caused her to charge into the unknown with only a suitcase full of clothes and a stack of papers that may or may not have meant anything.

She discovered a third letter from Garrett.

CHAPTER 4

*T*he day she discovered the third letter, she had of course expected nothing unusual. It was a typical midsummer day in Boston—hot, humid, with the same news that usually accompanied such weather—a few assaults brought on by aggravated tensions and two early afternoon murders by people who had taken it too far.

Theresa was in the newsroom, researching a topic on autistic children. The *Boston Times* had an excellent database of articles published in previous years from a variety of magazines. Through her computer she could also access the library at Harvard University or Boston University, and the addition of literally hundreds of thousands of articles they had at their disposal made any search much easier and less time-consuming than it had been even a few years ago.

In a couple of hours she had been able to find almost thirty articles written in the last three years that had been published in journals she had never heard of, and six of the titles looked interesting enough to possibly use. Since she would be passing by Harvard on the way home, she decided to pick them up then.

As she was about to turn off her computer, a thought suddenly crossed her mind and she stopped. *Why not?* she asked herself. *It's a long shot, but what can I lose?* She sat down at her desk, accessed the database at Harvard again, and typed in the words

MESSAGE IN A BOTTLE

Because articles in the library system were indexed by subject or headline, she chose to scan by headlines to speed up the search. Subject searches usually produced more articles, but weeding through them was a laborious process, and she didn't have time to do it now. After hitting the return key, she leaned back and waited for the computer to retrieve the information she requested.

The response surprised her—a dozen different articles had been written on the subject in the last few years. Most of those were published by scientific journals, and their titles seemed to suggest that bottles were being used in various endeavors to learn about ocean currents.

Three articles seemed interesting, though, and she jotted down the titles, deciding to pick those up as well.

Traffic was heavy and slow, and it took longer than she thought it would to get to the library and copy the nine articles she was looking for. She got home late, and after ordering in from the local Chinese restaurant, she sat on the couch with the three articles on messages in bottles in front of her.

An article published in *Yankee* magazine in March of the previous year was the first one she picked up. It related some history about messages in bottles and chronicled stories about bottles that had washed up in New England over the past few years. Some of the letters that had been found were truly memorable. She especially enjoyed reading about Paolina and Ake Viking.

Paolina's father had found a message in a bottle that had been sent by Ake, a young Swedish sailor. Ake, who had grown bored during one of his many trips at sea, asked for any pretty woman who found it to write back. The father gave it to Paolina, who in turn wrote to Ake. One letter led to another, and when Ake finally traveled to Sicily to meet her, they realized how much they were in love. They married soon after.

Toward the end of the article, she came across two paragraphs that told of yet another message that had washed up on the beaches of Long Island:

Most messages sent by bottle usually ask the finder to respond once with little hope of a lifelong correspondence. Sometimes, however, the senders do not want a response. One such letter, a moving tribute to a lost love, was discovered washed up on Long Island last year. In part it read:

*"Without you in my arms, I feel an emptiness in my soul. I find myself searching the crowds for your face—I know it is an impossibility, but I cannot help myself. My search for*

*you is a never-ending quest that is doomed to fail. You and I
had talked about what would happen if we were forced
apart by circumstance, but I cannot keep the promise I made
to you that night. I am sorry, my darling, but there will never
be another to replace you. The words I whispered to you were
folly, and I should have realized it then. You—and you
alone—have always been the only thing I wanted, and now
that you are gone, I have no desire to find another. Till death
do us part, we whispered in the church, and I've come to believe that the words will ring true until the day finally
comes when I, too, am taken from this world."*

She stopped eating and abruptly put down her fork.

*It can't be!* She found herself staring at the words. *It's simply not
possible. . . .*

*But . . .*

*but . . . who else could it be?*

She wiped her brow, aware that her hands were suddenly
shaking. *Another letter?* She flipped to the front of the article and
looked at the author's name. It had been written by Arthur
Shendakin, Ph.D., a professor of history at Boston College,
meaning . . .

*he must live in the area.*

She jumped up and retrieved the phone book on the stand
near the dining room table. She thumbed through it, looking for
the name. There were fewer than a dozen Shendakins listed, although only two seemed like a possibility. Both had "A" listed as
the first initial, and she checked her watch before dialing. Nine-
thirty. Late, but not too late. She punched in the numbers. The

first call was answered by a woman who said she had the wrong number, and when she put down the phone, she noticed her throat had gone dry. She went to the kitchen and filled a glass with water. After taking a long drink, she took a deep breath and went back to the phone.

She made sure she dialed the correct number and waited as the phone started to ring.

Once.

Twice.

Three times.

On the fourth ring she began to lose hope, but on the fifth ring she heard the other line pick up.

"Hello," a man said. By the sound of his voice, she thought he must be in his sixties.

She cleared her throat.

"Hello, this is Theresa Osborne of the *Boston Times*. Is this Arthur Shendakin?"

"Yes, it is," he answered, sounding surprised.

*Keep calm*, she told herself.

"Oh, hi. I was just calling to find out if this is the same Arthur Shendakin who had an article published last year in *Yankee* magazine about messages in bottles."

"Yes, I wrote that. How can I help you?"

Her hands felt sweaty on the receiver. "I was curious about one of the messages you said had washed up on Long Island. Do you remember which letter I'm talking about?"

"Can I ask why you're interested?"

"Well," she began, "the *Times* is thinking of doing an article on the same topic, and we were interested in obtaining a copy of the letter."

She winced at her own lie, but telling the truth seemed worse. How would that have sounded? *Oh, hi, I'm infatuated with a mysterious man who sends messages in bottles, and I'm wondering if the letter that you found was written by him as well. . . .*

He answered slowly. "Well, I don't know. That was the letter that inspired me to write the articles . . . I'd have to think about it."

Theresa's throat tightened. "So, you have the letter?"

"Yes. I found it a couple of years ago."

"Mr. Shendakin, I know this is an unusual request, but I can tell you that if you let us use the letter, we'd be happy to pay you a small sum. And we don't need the actual letter. A copy of it will do, so you really wouldn't be giving anything up."

She could tell the request surprised him.

"How much are we talking about?"

*I don't know, I'm making all this up on the fly. How much do you want?*

"We're willing to offer three hundred dollars, and of course, you'll be properly credited as the person who found it."

He paused for a moment, considering. Theresa chimed back in before he could formulate a rejection.

"Mr. Shendakin, I'm sure there's a part of you that's worried about the similarity between your article and what the newspaper intends to print. I can assure you that they will be very different. The article that we're doing is mainly about the direction that bottles travel—you know, ocean currents and all that. We just want some actual letters that will provide some sort of human interest to our readers."

*Where did that come from?*

"Well . . ."

"Please, Mr. Shendakin. It would really mean a lot to me."

He was silent for a moment.

"Just a copy?"

*Yes!*

"Yes, of course. I can give you a fax number, or you can send it. Should I make the check out to you?"

He paused again before answering. "I . . . I suppose so." He sounded as though he'd been somehow maneuvered into a corner and didn't know how to get out.

"Thanks, Mr. Shendakin." Before he could change his mind, Theresa gave him the fax number, took his address, and made a note to pick up a money order the following day. She thought it might look suspicious if she sent one of her personal checks.

The next day, after calling the professor's office at Boston College to leave a message for him that the payment had been sent, she went to work with her head spinning. The possible existence of a third letter made it difficult to think of anything else. True, there still wasn't any guarantee that the letter was from the same person, but if it was, she didn't know what she would do. She'd thought about Garrett almost all night, trying to picture what he looked like, imagining things he liked to do. She didn't understand quite what she was feeling, but in the end she finally decided to let the letter decide things. If it wasn't from Garrett, she would end all this now. She wouldn't use her computer to search for him, she wouldn't look for evidence of any other letters. And if she found herself continuing to obsess, she would throw the two letters away. Curiosity was fine as long as it didn't take over your life—and she wouldn't let that happen.

But, on the other hand, if the letter *was* from Garrett . . .

She still didn't know what she would do then. Part of her hoped it wouldn't be, so she wouldn't have to make that decision.

When she got to her desk, she purposely waited before going to the fax machine. She turned on her computer, called two physicians she needed to speak with about the column she was writing, and jotted a few notes on possible other topics. By the time she had finished her busywork, she had almost convinced herself that the letter wouldn't be from him. There are probably thousands of letters floating around in the ocean, she told herself. Odds are it's someone else.

She finally went to the fax machine when she couldn't think of anything else to do and began to look through the stack. It hadn't been sorted yet, and there were a few dozen pages addressed to various people. In the middle of the stack, she found a cover letter addressed to her. With it were two more pages, and when she looked more closely at them, the first thing she noticed—as she had with the other two letters—was the sailing ship embossed in the upper right corner. But this one was shorter than the other letters, and she read it before she got back to her desk. The final paragraph was the one she had seen in Arthur Shendakin's article.

September 25, 1995

Dear Catherine,

A month has passed since I've written, but it has seemed to pass much more slowly. Life passes by now like the scenery outside a car window. I breathe and eat and sleep as I always did, but there seems to be no great purpose in my life that requires active participation on my part. I simply drift along like the messages I write you. I do not know where I am going or when I will get there.

Even work does not take the pain away. I may be diving for my own pleasure or showing others how to do so, but when I return to the shop, it seems empty without you. I stock and order as I always did, but even now, I sometimes glance over my shoulder without thinking and call for you. As I write this note to you, I wonder when, or if, things like that will ever stop.

Without you in my arms, I feel an emptiness in my soul. I find myself searching the crowds for your face—I know it is an impossibility, but I cannot help myself. My search for you is a never-ending quest that is doomed to fail. You and I had talked about what would happen if we were forced apart by circumstance, but I cannot keep the promise I made to you that night. I am sorry, my darling, but there will never be another to replace you. The words I whispered to you were folly, and I should have realized it then. You—and you alone—have always been the only thing I wanted, and now that you are gone, I have no desire to find another. Till death do us part, we whispered in the church, and I've come to believe that the words will ring true until the day finally comes when I, too, am taken from this world.

Garrett

"Deanna, do you have a minute? I need to talk to you."

Deanna looked up from her computer and took off her reading glasses. "Of course I do. What's up?"

Theresa laid the three letters on Deanna's desk without speaking. Deanna picked them up one by one, her eyes widening in surprise.

"Where did you get these other two letters?"

Theresa explained how she'd come across them. When she finished her story, Deanna read the letters in silence. Theresa sat in the chair opposite her.

"Well," she said, putting down the last letter, "you've certainly been keeping a secret, haven't you?"

Theresa shrugged, and Deanna went on. "But there's more to this than just finding the letters, isn't there?"

"What do you mean?"

"I mean," Deanna said with a sly smile, "you didn't come in here because you found the letters. You came in here because you're interested in this Garrett fellow."

Theresa's mouth opened, and Deanna laughed.

"Don't look so surprised, Theresa. I'm not a complete idiot. I knew something was going on these last few days. You've been so distracted around here—it's like you've been a hundred miles away. I was going to ask you about it, but I figured you'd talk to me when you were ready."

"I thought I was keeping things under control."

"Perhaps for other people. But I've known you long enough to know when something's up with you." She smiled again. "So tell me, what's going on?"

Theresa thought for a moment.

"It's been really strange. I mean, I can't stop thinking about

him, and I don't know why. It's like I'm in high school again and
I have a crush on someone I've never met. Only this is worse—
not only have we never spoken, but I've never even seen him. For
all I know, he could be a seventy-year-old man."

Deanna leaned back in her chair and nodded thoughtfully.
"That's true . . . but you don't think that's the case, do you?"

Theresa slowly shook her head. "No, not really."

"Neither do I," Deanna said as she picked up the letters again.
"He talks about how they fell in love when they were young, he
hasn't mentioned any children, he teaches diving, and writes
about Catherine as if he had only been married a few years. I
doubt if he's that old."

"That's what I thought, too."

"Do you want to know what I think?"

"Absolutely."

Deanna spoke the words carefully. "I think you should go to
Wilmington to try to find Garrett."

"But it seems so . . . so ridiculous, even to me—"

"Why?"

"Because I don't know anything about him."

"Theresa, you know a good deal more about Garrett than I
did about Brian before I met him. And besides, I didn't tell you
to marry him, I just told you to go find him. You may find out
that you don't like him at all, but at least you'll know, won't you?
I mean, what can it hurt?"

"What if . . ." She paused, and Deanna finished her statement.

"What if he's not what you imagine? Theresa, I can guarantee he's not what you're imagining already. No one ever is. But
to my mind, that shouldn't make any difference in your decision.

If you think you want to find out more, just go. The worst thing that can happen is you find out he's not the kind of man you're looking for. And what would you do then? You'd come back to Boston, but you'd come back with your answer. How bad would that be? Probably no worse than what you're going through now."

"You don't think this whole thing is crazy?"

Deanna shook her head thoughtfully. "Theresa, I've wanted you to start looking for another man for a long time. Like I told you when we were on vacation, you deserve to find another person to share your life with. Now, I don't know how this whole thing with Garrett will work out. If I had to bet, I'd say it's probably not going to lead to anything. But that doesn't mean you shouldn't try. If everyone who thought they might fail didn't even try, where would we be today?"

Theresa was silent for a moment. "You're being much too logical about this whole thing. . . ."

Deanna shrugged off her protests. "I'm older than you, and I've gone through a lot. One of the things I've learned in my life is that sometimes you've got to take a chance. And to me, this one isn't all that large. I mean, you're not leaving your husband and family to go find this person, you're not giving up your job and moving across the country. You're really in a wonderful situation. There's no downside for you to go, so don't blow this out of proportion. If you feel like you should go, go. If you don't want to go, don't. It's really as simple as that. Besides, Kevin isn't around and you have plenty of vacation left this year."

Theresa began twisting a strand of hair around her finger.

"And my column?"

"Don't worry about it. We still have the one column you

wrote that we didn't use because we published the letter instead. After that, we can run a couple of repeats from past years. Most papers hadn't picked up your column then, so they probably won't know the difference."

"You make this sound so easy."

"It is easy. The hard part is going to be finding him. But I think these letters have some information we can use to help you. What do you say we make a few phone calls and do a little hunting on the computer?"

They were both silent for a long time.

"Okay," Theresa said finally. "But I hope I don't end up regretting this."

"So," Theresa asked Deanna, "where do we begin?"

She pulled her chair around to the other side of Deanna's desk.

"First off," Deanna began, "let's begin with what we're pretty sure about. First, I think it's fair to say that his name actually is Garrett. That's how he signed all the letters, and I don't think he would have bothered using a name other than his own. He might have done so if it was only one letter, but with three letters, I'm fairly confident that it's either his first name, or even his middle name. Either way, it's the name he's called by."

"And," Theresa added, "he's probably in Wilmington or Wrightsville Beach, or another community close by."

Deanna nodded. "All his letters talk about the ocean or ocean themes, and of course, that's where he throws the bottles. From the tone of the letters, it sounds like he writes them when he gets lonely or when he's thinking about Catherine."

"That's what I thought. He didn't seem to mention any special occasions in the letters. They talked about his day-to-day life, and what he was going through."

"Okay, good," Deanna said, nodding. She was getting more excited as they went on. "There was a boat that was mentioned . . ."

"*Happenstance,*" Theresa said. "The letter said that they restored the boat and used to sail together. So, it's probably a sailboat."

"Write that down," Deanna said. "We may be able to find out more about that with a couple of calls from here. Maybe there's a place that registers boats by name. I think I can call the paper down there to find out. Was there anything else in the second letter?"

"Not that I can tell. But the third letter has a little bit more information. From what he writes, two things stand out."

Deanna chimed in. "One, that Catherine has indeed passed away."

"And also that it looks like he owns a scuba-diving shop where he and Catherine used to work."

"That's another thing to write down. I think we can find out more about that from up here as well. Anything else?"

"I don't think so."

"Well, it's a good beginning. This might be easier than we think. Let's start making some calls."

The first place Deanna called was the *Wilmington Journal,* the newspaper that served the area. She identified herself and asked to speak with someone who was familiar with boating. After a couple of transfers, she found herself speaking with Zack Norton, who covered sportfishing and other ocean sports. After explaining that she wanted to know if there was a place that kept a registry of boat names, she was told that there wasn't.

"Boats are registered with an identification number, almost like cars," he said in a slow drawl, "but if you have the name of the person, you might be able to find out the name of the boat on the form if it's listed. It's not a required piece of information, but a lot of people put it down anyway." Deanna scribbled the words "Boats not registered by name" on the pad in front of her and showed it to Theresa.

"That was a dead end," Theresa said quietly.

Deanna put her hand over the receiver and whispered, "Maybe, maybe not. Don't give up so easily."

After thanking Zack Norton for his time and hanging up, Deanna looked over the list of clues again. She thought for a moment, then decided to call information for the phone numbers of scuba-diving shops in the Wilmington area. Theresa watched as Deanna wrote down the names and numbers of the eleven shops that were listed. "Is there anything else I can do for you, ma'am?" the operator asked.

"No, you've been more than helpful. Thank you."

She hung up the phone, and Theresa looked at her curiously. "What are you going to ask them when you call?"

"I'm going to ask for Garrett."

Theresa's heart skipped a beat. "Just like that?"

"Just like that," Deanna said, smiling as she dialed. She motioned for Theresa to pick up the other extension, "just in case it's him," and they both waited quietly for someone to answer at Atlantic Adventures, the first name they were given.

When the phone finally picked up, Deanna took a deep breath and asked pleasantly if Garrett was available to teach any classes. "I'm sorry, I think you have the wrong number," the voice said quickly. Deanna apologized and hung up.

They received the same answer on the next five calls. Unswayed, Deanna went down the list to the next name and dialed again. Expecting the same answer, she was surprised when the person on the line hesitated for a moment.

"Are you talking about Garrett Blake?"

*Garrett.*

Theresa nearly fell from the chair at the sound of his name. Deanna said yes, and the man who answered went on.

"He's with Island Diving. Are you sure we can't help you? We've got some classes starting soon."

Deanna quickly excused herself. "No, I'm sorry. I really need to work with Garrett. I promised him I would." When she put the phone back in the cradle, she was smiling broadly.

"So, we're getting close now."

"I can't believe it was that easy. . . ."

"It wasn't that easy, if you think about it, Theresa. Unless a person found more than one letter, it wouldn't have been possible."

"Do you think it's the same Garrett?"

She cocked her head and raised an eyebrow. "Don't you?"

"I don't know yet. Maybe."

Deanna shrugged off the reply. "Well, we'll find out soon enough. This is getting fun."

Deanna then called information again and got the number for the ship registry of Wilmington. After dialing, she told the voice on the line who she was and asked for someone who could help her verify some information. "My husband and I were vacationing down there," she told the woman who answered the phone, "when our boat broke down. This nice gentleman found us and helped us get back to shore. His name was Garrett Blake, and I think the name of his boat was *Happenstance*, but I want to be sure when I write the story."

Deanna went on, refusing to let the woman get a word in edgewise. She told her how scared she had been and how much it had meant when Garrett had come to their rescue. Then, after flattering the woman about how nice people were in the South and Wilmington in particular and how she wanted to do a story on southern hospitality and the kindness of strangers, the woman was more than willing to help. "Since you're just verifying the information and not asking for anything you don't know, I'm sure it won't be a problem. Hold on for a second."

Deanna drummed her fingers on the desk while the sounds of Barry Manilow wafted through the receiver. The woman picked up again.

"Okay. Let's see now . . ." Deanna heard tapping on a keyboard, then a strange beep. After a moment, the woman said the words that both Deanna and Theresa hoped she would.

"Yes, here it is. Garrett Blake. Um . . . you got the name right, at least according to the information we have. It says here that the boat is named *Happenstance*."

Deanna thanked her profusely and asked for the lady's name, "so she could write about another person who epitomized hospitality." After spelling it back to the woman, she hung up the phone, beaming.

"Garrett Blake," she said with a victorious smile. "Our mysterious writer is named Garrett Blake."

"I can't believe you found him."

Deanna nodded as if she'd accomplished something even she doubted she could do. "Believe it. This old woman still knows how to research information."

"That you do."

"Anything else that you want to know more about?"

Theresa thought for a moment. "Can you find out anything about Catherine?"

Deanna shrugged and readied herself for the task. "I don't know, but we can give it a try. Let's call the paper to see if anything is in their records. If the death was accidental, it may have been written up."

Again, Deanna called the paper and asked for the news department. Unfortunately, after speaking with a couple of people, she was told that newspapers from a few years back were recorded on microfiche and couldn't be accessed easily without a specific date. Deanna asked for and received a name that Theresa should contact when she got down there, in case she wanted to look up the information on her own.

"I think that's about all we can do from here. The rest is up to you, Theresa. But at least you know where to find him."

Deanna held out the slip of paper with the name. Theresa hesitated. Deanna looked at her for a moment, then set the paper on the desk. She picked up the phone one more time.

"Now who're you calling?"

"My travel agency. You're going to need a flight and a place to stay."

"I haven't even said I was going yet."

"Oh, you're going."

"How can you be so sure?"

"Because I'm not going to have you sitting around the newsroom for the next year wondering what might have been. You don't work well when you're distracted."

"Deanna . . ."

"Don't 'Deanna' me. You know the curiosity would drive you crazy. It's already driving me crazy."

"But—"

"But nothing." She paused for a moment, and her words came softer. "Theresa, remember—you've got nothing to lose. The worst that could possibly happen is that you fly home in a couple of days. That's all. You're not going on a quest to search for a tribe of cannibals. You're just going to find out if your curiosity was warranted."

They were both silent as they stared at each other. Deanna had a slight smirk on her face, and Theresa felt her pulse quicken as the finality of the decision hit her. *My God, I'm actually going to do this. I can't believe I'm going along with this.*

Still, she gave one last halfhearted attempt at denial.

"I don't even know what I would say if I finally met him. . . ."

"I'm sure you'll think of something. Now, let me take care of this call. Go get your purse. I'm going to need a credit card number."

Theresa's mind was a whirl as she started back to her desk. *Garrett Blake. Wilmington. Island Diving. Happenstance.* The words kept rolling through her head, as if she were rehearsing for a part in a play.

She unlocked the bottom drawer where she kept her purse and paused for a second before going back. But something else had taken hold of her, and in the end she handed Deanna a credit card. The following evening she would leave for Wilmington, North Carolina.

Deanna told her to take the rest of that day and the following off, and on her way out of the office, Theresa sort of felt as if she had been cornered into something in the same way she had cornered old Mr. Shendakin.

But unlike Mr. Shendakin, deep down she was pleased about it, and when the plane touched down in Wilmington the following day, Theresa Osborne checked into a hotel, wondering where all this would lead.

$\mathcal{T}$heresa woke early, as was her custom, and rose from the bed to look out the window. The North Carolina sun was casting golden prisms through an early morning haze, and she slid open the balcony door to freshen the room.

In the bathroom, she slipped out of her pajamas and started a shower. Stepping into the stall, she thought about how easy it had been to get here. A little less than forty-eight hours ago she had been sitting with Deanna, studying the letters, making phone calls, and searching for Garrett. Once she got home, she had spoken to Ella, who again agreed to watch Harvey and pick up her mail.

The next day she went to the library and read up on scuba diving. It seemed like the logical thing to do. Her years as a reporter had taught her to take nothing for granted, to make a plan, and to do her best to prepare for anything.

The plan she finally came up with was simple. She would go to Island Diving and browse around the store, with the hope of getting a look at Garrett Blake. If he turned out to be a seventy-year-old man or a twenty-year-old student, she would simply turn around and go home. But if their instincts were right and he seemed to be approximately her age, she decided she would try to speak with him. That was why she had taken the time to learn something about scuba diving—she wanted to sound as if she knew something about it. And she would probably be able to learn more about him if she could talk to him about something he was interested in, without having to tell him too much about herself. Then she'd have a better grasp on things.

But after that? That was the part she wasn't exactly sure about. She didn't want to tell Garrett the complete truth about why she came—that would sound crazy. *Hi, I read your letters to Catherine, and knowing how much you loved her, I just thought you might be the man I've been looking for.* No, that was out of the question, and the other option didn't seem much better—*Hi, I'm from the* Boston Times *and I found your letters. Could we do a story on you?* That didn't seem right, either. Nor did any of the other ideas that filtered through her mind.

But she hadn't come this far to give up now, despite the fact she didn't know what to say. Besides, as Deanna had said, if it didn't work out, she would simply return to Boston.

She stepped out of the shower, dried off before putting some lotion on her arms and legs, and dressed in a short-sleeved white blouse, denim shorts, and a pair of white sandals. She wanted to look casual, and she did. What she didn't want was to be noticed right off the bat. After all, she didn't know what to expect, and she wanted the opportunity to evaluate the situation on her own terms, without having to deal with anyone else.

When she was finally ready to leave, she found the phone book, thumbed through it, and scribbled the address of Island Diving on a piece of paper. Two deep breaths later, she was walking down the hall. Again she repeated Deanna's mantra.

Her first stop was at a convenience store, where she bought a map of Wilmington. The clerk had also given her directions, and she found her way easily, despite the fact that Wilmington was larger than she had imagined. The streets were packed with cars, especially as she passed by the bridges that led to the islands right off the coast. Kure Beach, Carolina Beach, and Wrightsville Beach were reached by bridges that crossed from the city, and that was where most of the traffic seemed to be headed.

Island Diving was located near the marina. Once she made her way through town, the traffic became a little less congested, and after reaching the road she needed, she slowed the car and looked for the shop.

From where she had turned, it wasn't far. Just as she had hoped, a few other cars were parked on the side of the building. She pulled into a space a few spots from the entrance.

It was an older wooden building, faded from the salt air and sea breezes, with one side of the store facing the Atlantic Intracoastal Waterway. The hand-painted sign hung on two rusty metal chains, and the windows had the dusty look of a thousand rainstorms.

She stepped out of her car, brushed the hair from her face, and started toward the entrance. She paused before opening the door to take a deep breath and collect her thoughts, then stepped inside, doing her best to pretend she was there for ordinary reasons.

She browsed through the store, walking among the aisles, watching assorted customers pull and replace items from the racks. She kept an eye out for anyone who appeared to work there. She glanced furtively at every man in the store, wondering, *Are you Garrett?* Most, however, appeared to be customers.

She worked her way to the back wall and found herself staring at a series of newspaper and magazine articles, framed and laminated, hanging above the racks. After a quick glance, she leaned forward for a closer look and suddenly realized she had stumbled across the answer to the first question she had about the mysterious Garrett Blake.

She finally knew what he looked like.

The first article, reprinted from the newspaper, was about scuba diving, and the caption beneath the photo read simply "Garrett Blake of Island Diving, readying his class for its first ocean dive."

In it, he was adjusting the straps that held the tank to one of the student's back, and she could tell from the photo that Deanna and she had been right about him. He looked to be in his thirties, with a lean face and short brown hair that seemed to have bleached a little from hours spent in the sun. He was taller than the student by a couple of inches, and the sleeveless shirt he was wearing showed well-defined muscles in his arms.

Because the picture was a little grainy, she couldn't make out the color of his eyes, though she could tell that his face was weathered as well. She thought she saw wrinkles around the corners of his eyes, though that could have been caused by squinting in the sun.

She read the article carefully, noting when he generally taught his classes and some facts about getting certification. The second article had no picture but talked about shipwreck diving, which was popular in North Carolina. North Carolina, it seemed, had more than five hundred wrecks charted off the coast and was called the Graveyard of the Atlantic. Because of the Outer Banks and other islands directly off the coast, ships had run aground for centuries.

The third article, again without a picture, concerned the *Monitor*, the first federal ironclad of the Civil War. En route to South Carolina, it had sunk off Cape Hatteras in 1862 while being towed by a steamer. The wreck had finally been discovered, and Garrett Blake, along with other divers from Duke Marine Institute, had been asked to dive to the ocean floor to explore the possibility of raising it.

The fourth article was about *Happenstance*. Eight pictures of the boat had been taken from various angles, inside and out, all detailing the restoration. The boat, she learned, was fairly unique in that it was made entirely of wood and had first been manufactured in Lisbon, Portugal, in 1927. Designed by Herreshoff, one of the most noted maritime engineers of that period, it had a long and adventurous history (including being used in the Second World War to study the German garrisons that lined the shores of France). Eventually the boat made its way to Nantucket, where it was bought by a local businessman. By the time Garrett Blake purchased it four years ago, it had fallen into disrepair, and the article said that he and his wife, Catherine, had restored it.

*Catherine . . .*

Theresa looked at the article's date. April 1992. The article didn't mention that Catherine had died, and because one of the letters she had was found three years ago in Norfolk, it meant that Catherine must have died sometime in 1993.

"Can I help you?"

Theresa turned instinctively toward the voice behind her. A young man was smiling behind her, and she was suddenly glad she had seen a picture of Garrett moments before. This person obviously wasn't he.

"Did I startle you?" he asked, and Theresa quickly shook her head.

"No . . . I was just looking at the pictures."

He nodded toward them. "She's something, isn't she?"

"Who?"

"*Happenstance.* Garrett—the guy that owns the shop—rebuilt her. She's a wonderful boat. One of the prettiest I've ever seen, now that she's done."

"Is he here? Garrett, I mean."

"No, he's down at the docks. He won't be in until later this morning."

"Oh . . ."

"Can I help you find something? I know the shop's kind of cluttered, but everything you need to go diving you can find here."

She shook her head. "No, I was just browsing, actually."

"Okay, but if I can help you find something, let me know."

"I will," she said, and the young man nodded cheerfully, then turned and started toward the counter at the front of the store. Before she could stop the words, she heard herself ask:

"You said Garrett was at the docks?"

He turned again and kept walking backward as he spoke. "Yeah—a couple blocks down the road. At the marina. Do you know where that is?"

"I think I passed it on the way here."

"He should be there for the next hour or so, but like I said, if you come back later, he'll be here. Do you want me to leave a message for him?"

"No, that's okay. It's not that important."

She spent the next three minutes pretending to look at different items on the racks, then walked out after waving good-bye to the young man.

But instead of going to her car, she headed in the direction of the marina.

When she reached the marina, she looked around, hoping to spot *Happenstance*. Because the vast majority of boats were white and *Happenstance* was natural wood, she found it easily and made her way to the appropriate ramp.

Although she felt nervous as she started down the ramp, the articles in the shop had given her a couple of ideas of what to talk about. Once she met him, she would simply explain that after reading the article about *Happenstance*, she wanted to see the boat up close. It would sound believable, and hopefully she could parlay that into a longer conversation. Then, of course, she'd have some idea of what he was like in person. And after that . . . well, then she'd see.

As she approached the boat, however, the first thing she noticed was that no one seemed to be around. There wasn't anyone on board, there wasn't anyone on the docks, and it appeared as if no one had been there all morning. The boat was locked down, the sail covered, and nothing seemed out of place. After looking around for any sign of him, she checked the name on the back of the boat. It was indeed *Happenstance*. She brushed aside some hair that had blown onto her face as she puzzled over it. Odd, she thought, the man at the store had said he was here.

Instead of returning to the shop right away, she took a moment to admire the boat. It was beautiful—rich and textured, unlike the boats that surrounded it. It had much more character than the other sailboats docked on either side of it, and she knew why the paper had done an article on it. In a way, it reminded her of a much smaller version of pirate ships she had seen in the movies. She paced back and forth for a few minutes, studying it from different angles, and wondered how run-down it had been prior to the restoration. Most of it looked new, though she assumed that they hadn't replaced all the wood. They had probably sanded her down, and as she looked closer, she saw nicks in the hull, lending credence to her theory.

She finally decided to try Island Diving a little later. It was obvious the man at the store was mistaken. After one last glance at the boat, she turned to leave.

A man stood on the ramp a few feet from her, watching her carefully.

*Garrett . . .*

He was sweating in the morning heat, and his shirt was soaked through in a couple of places. The sleeves had been torn off, revealing tight muscles in his arms and forearms. His hands were black with what appeared to be grease, and the diver's watch he had on his wrist looked scarred, as if he'd used it for years. He wore tan shorts and Top-Siders without socks and looked like someone who spent most, if not all, of his time near the ocean.

He watched her as she took an involuntary step backward. "Can I help you with something?" he asked. He smiled but didn't approach her, as if he were afraid she would feel trapped.

Which was exactly how she felt when their eyes met.

For a moment all she could do was stare at him. Despite the fact that she had seen a picture of him, he looked better than she expected, though she wasn't sure why. He was tall and broad shouldered. Though not strikingly handsome, his face was tan and rugged, as if the sun and sea had taken their toll. His eyes weren't nearly as hypnotic as David's had been, but there was something compelling about him for sure. Something masculine in the way he stood before her.

Remembering her plan, she took a deep breath. She motioned toward *Happenstance*.

"I was just admiring your boat. It's really beautiful."

Rubbing his hands together to remove some of the excess grease, he said politely, "Thank you, that's nice of you to say."

His steady gaze seemed to expose the reality of the situation, and suddenly everything came to her at once—finding the bottle, her growing curiosity, the research she had done, her trip to Wilmington, and finally this meeting, face-to-face. Overwhelmed, she closed her eyes and caught herself fighting for control. Somehow she hadn't expected this to happen so quickly. She suddenly felt a moment of pure terror.

He took a small step forward. "Are you okay?" he asked in a concerned voice.

Taking another deep breath and willing herself to relax, she said, "Yeah, I think so. I just got a little dizzy there for a second."

"You sure?"

She ran her hand through her hair, embarrassed. "Yeah. I'm fine now. Really."

"Good," he said as if waiting to see whether she was telling the truth. Then, after he was sure she was, he asked curiously: "Have we met before?"

Theresa shook her head slowly. "I don't think so."

"Then how did you know the boat was mine?"

Relieved, she answered, "Oh . . . I saw your picture down at the shop in the articles on the wall, along with the pictures of the boat. The young man in your shop said you would be here, and I thought that as long as you were, I'd come down to see for myself."

"He said I was here?"

She was silent as she remembered the exact words. "Actually, he told me you were at the docks. I just assumed that meant you were here."

He nodded. "I was at the other boat—the one we use for diving."

A small fishing boat blared its horn, and Garrett turned and waved to the man standing on the deck. After it had gone by, he faced her again and was struck by how pretty she was. She looked even better up close than she had when he'd seen her from across the marina. On impulse, he lowered his eyes and reached for the red bandanna he had in his back pocket. He wiped the sweat from his forehead.

"You did a wonderful job restoring it," Theresa said.

He smiled faintly as he put the bandanna away. "Thanks, that's kind of you to say."

Theresa glanced toward *Happenstance* as he spoke, then back to him. "I know it's not any of my business," she said casually, "but since you're here, would you mind if I asked you a little bit about it?"

She could tell by his expression that it wasn't the first time he'd been asked to talk about the boat.

"What would you like to know?"

She did her best to sound conversational. "Well, was it in as bad a condition when you first got it as the article implied?"

"Actually, it was in worse condition." He stepped forward and pointed to the various spots on the boat as he mentioned them. "A lot of the wood had rotted near the bow, there were a series of leaks along the side—it was a wonder she was still afloat at all. We ended up replacing a good portion of the hull and the deck, and what was left of her had to be sanded completely and then sealed and varnished again. And that was just the outside. We had to do the inside, too, and that took a great deal longer."

Though she noticed the word "we" in his answer, she decided not to comment on it.

"It must have been a lot of work."

She smiled as she said it, and Garrett felt something tighten inside. *Damn, she's pretty.*

"It was, but it was worth it. She's more fun to sail than other boats."

"Why?"

"Because she was built by people who used her to make their living. They put a lot of care into designing her, and that makes sailing a lot easier."

"I take it you've been sailing a long time."

"Ever since I was a kid."

She nodded. After a short pause, she took a small step toward the boat. "Do you mind?"

He shook his head. "No, go ahead."

Theresa stepped toward it and ran her hands along the side of the hull. Garrett noticed that she wasn't wearing a ring, though it shouldn't matter one way or the other. Without turning, Theresa asked: "What kind of wood is this?"

"Mahogany."

"The whole boat?"

"Most of it. Except for the masts and some of the interior."

She nodded again, and Garrett watched as she walked alongside *Happenstance*. As she stepped farther away, he couldn't help but notice her figure and how her straight, dark hair grazed her shoulders. But it wasn't only the way she looked that caught his eye—there was a confidence in the way she moved. It was as if she knew exactly what men were thinking as she stood near them, he realized suddenly. He shook his head.

"Did they really use this boat to spy on the Germans in World War Two?" she asked, turning to face him.

He laughed under his breath, doing his best to clear his mind. "That's what the previous owner told me, though I don't know if it was true or if he said it to get a higher price."

"Well, even if it wasn't, it's still a beautiful boat. How long did it take you to restore it?"

"Almost a year."

She peeked in one of the round windows, but it was too dark to make out much of the interior. "What did you sail on while you were fixing *Happenstance*?"

"We didn't. There wasn't enough time, not with working in the shop, teaching classes, and trying to get this one ready."

"Did you go through sailing withdrawals?" she asked with a smile, and for the first time, Garrett realized he was enjoying the conversation.

"Absolutely. But they all went away just as soon as we finished and got her out on the water."

Again, she heard the word "we."

"I'm sure they did."

After admiring the boat for another few seconds, she returned to his side. For a moment, neither of them spoke. Garrett wondered if she knew he was watching her from the corners of his eyes.

"Well," she finally said as she crossed her arms, "I've probably taken enough of your time."

"It's okay," he said, and again he felt the sweat on his forehead. "I love to talk about sailing."

"I would, too. It always looked like fun to me."

"You sound like you've never gone sailing before."

She shrugged. "I haven't. I've always wanted to go, but I've never actually had the chance."

She looked at him when she spoke, and when their eyes met, Garrett found himself reaching for the bandanna for the second time in a few minutes. *Damn, it's hot out here.* He wiped his forehead and heard the words coming out of his mouth before he could stop them.

"Well, if you'd like to go, I usually take her out after work. You're welcome to come along this evening."

Why he'd said that, he wasn't exactly sure. Maybe, he thought, it was a desire for female companionship after all these years, if only for a short time. Or maybe it had something to do with the way her eyes lit up whenever she talked. But no matter what the reason, he had just asked her to come with him, and there was nothing he could do to change it.

Theresa, too, was a little surprised, but she quickly decided to accept. It was, after all, the reason she'd come to Wilmington.

"I'd love to," she said. "What time?"

He put the bandanna away, feeling a little unsettled about what he'd just done. "How about seven o'clock? The sun begins to drop then, and it's the ideal time to go out."

"Seven o'clock is great for me. I'll bring along something to eat." To Garrett's surprise, she looked both pleased and excited about going.

"You don't have to do that."

"I know, but it's the least I can do. After all, you didn't have to offer to bring me along. Are sandwiches okay?"

Garrett took a small step backward, suddenly needing a little breathing space. "Yeah, that's fine. I'm not that picky."

"Okay," she said, then paused for a moment. She shifted her weight from one foot to the other, waiting to see if he'd say anything else. When he didn't, she absently adjusted the purse on her shoulder. "I guess I'll see you tonight. Here at the boat, right?"

"Right here," he said, and realized how tense he sounded. He cleared his throat and smiled a little. "It will be fun. You'll enjoy it."

"I'm sure I will. See you later."

She turned and started down the docks, her hair blowing in the breeze. As she was walking away, Garrett realized what he'd forgotten.

"Hey!" he shouted.

She stopped and turned to face him, using her hand to shield her eyes from the sun. "Yes?"

Even at a distance she was pretty.

He took a couple of steps in her direction. "I forgot to ask. What's your name?"

"I'm Theresa. Theresa Osborne."

"My name's Garrett Blake."

"Okay, Garrett, I'll see you at seven."

With that, she turned and walked briskly away. Garrett watched her retreating figure, trying to make sense of his conflicting emotions. Though part of him was excited about what had just happened, another part of him felt that there was something wrong with the whole thing. He knew there wasn't any reason to feel guilty, but the feeling was definitely there, and he wished there was something he could do about it.

But there wasn't, of course. There never was.

CHAPTER 6

The clock rolled past the dinner hour and onward toward seven, but for Garrett Blake, time had stopped three years ago when Catherine had stepped off the curb and was killed by an elderly man who lost control of his car and changed the lives of two separate families forever. In the ensuing weeks, his anger at the driver eventually gave way to plans of revenge that went unfulfilled, simply because his sorrow rendered him incapable of any action whatsoever. He couldn't sleep more than three hours a night, cried whenever he saw her clothes in the closet, and lost almost twenty pounds on a diet that consisted of coffee and Ritz crackers. The following month, he started smoking for the first time in his life and turned to alcohol on nights when the pain was too unbearable for him to face sober. His father temporarily took over the business while Garrett sat in silence on the back porch of his home, trying to imagine a world without her. He had neither the will nor the desire to exist anymore, and sometimes as he sat there, he hoped that the salty, humid air would swallow him up completely so he wouldn't have to face the future alone.

What made it so hard was that it seemed as though he couldn't remember a time when she wasn't around. They had known each other most of their lives and had attended the same schools throughout their younger years. In third grade they were best friends, and he gave her two cards on Valentine's Day, but after that, they drifted apart and simply coexisted as they progressed from one grade to the next. Catherine was gangly and thin, always the smallest in her class, and though Garrett always held a special place in his heart for her, he never noticed that she was slowly becoming an attractive young woman. They never went to a prom together or even to a movie, but after four years at Chapel Hill, where he majored in marine biology, he bumped into her at Wrightsville Beach and suddenly realized how foolish he had been. She was no longer the gangly girl he remembered. In a word, she was beautiful, with wonderful curves that made men and women alike turn their heads whenever she walked past them. Her hair was blond and her eyes held infinite mystery; and when he finally closed his gaping mouth and asked her what she was doing later, they started a relationship that eventually led to marriage and six wonderful years together.

On their wedding night, alone in a hotel room lit only by candles, she handed him the two valentines he'd once given her and laughed aloud when she saw the expression on his face when he realized what they were. "Of course I kept them," she whispered as she wrapped her arms around him. "It was the first time I ever loved someone. Love is love, no matter how old you are, and I knew that if I gave you enough time, you'd come back to me."

Whenever Garrett found himself thinking of her, he remembered either the way she looked that night or how she looked the very last time they went sailing. Even now he remembered that evening clearly—her blond hair blowing wildly in the breeze, her face rapturous as she laughed aloud.

"Feel the spray!" she cried exultantly as she stood at the bow of the boat. Holding on to a line, she leaned out into the wind, her profile outlined against the glittering sky.

"Be careful!" Garrett shouted back, holding the wheel steady.

She leaned out even farther, glancing back at Garrett with a mischievous smile.

"I'm serious!" he shouted again. For a moment it looked as if her grip were weakening. Garrett quickly stepped away from the wheel, only to hear her laugh again as she pulled herself upright. Ever light on her feet, she made her way back easily to the wheel and put her arms around him.

Kissing his ear, she whispered playfully, "Did I make you nervous?"

"You always make me nervous when you do things like that."

"Don't sound so gruff," she teased. "Not when I've finally got you all to myself."

"You have me all to yourself every night."

"Not like this," she said as she kissed him again. After a quick scan around them, she smiled. "Why don't we lower the sails and drop the anchor?"

"Now?"

She nodded. "Unless, of course, you'd rather sail all night." With a subtle look that betrayed nothing, she opened the door to the cabin and vanished from *sight. Four minutes later the boat was hastily stabilized and he opened the door to join her. . . .*

Garrett exhaled sharply, dispelling the memory like smoke. Though he could remember the events of that evening, he found that as time was rolling on, it was becoming more and more difficult to visualize exactly the way she looked. Little by little her features were beginning to vanish before his eyes, and though he knew that forgetting helped to deaden the pain, what he wanted most of all was to see her again. In three years he'd looked through the photo album only once, and that had hurt so much he'd sworn it was the last time he'd ever do it. Now he saw her clearly only at night, after he'd fallen asleep. He loved it when he dreamed of her because it seemed as though she were still alive. She would talk and move, and he would hold her in his arms, and for a moment it seemed that everything was suddenly right in the world. Yet the dreams took a toll as well, because upon waking, he always felt exhausted and depressed. Sometimes he'd go to the shop and lock himself in the office for the entire morning so he wouldn't have to talk to anyone.

His father tried to help as best he could. He, too, had lost a wife and so knew what his son was going through. Garrett still visited him at least once a week and always enjoyed the company his father provided. He was the one person Garrett shared a real understanding with, a feeling reciprocated by the old man. Last year his father had told him that he should start dating again. "It isn't right that you're always alone," he'd said. "It's almost like you've given up." Garrett knew there was a measure of truth to that. But the simple fact was that he had no desire to find anyone else. He hadn't made love to a woman since Catherine had died, and worse, he'd felt no desire for that, either. It was as if part of him were dead inside. When Garrett asked his father why he should take the advice when he himself had never re-married, his father simply looked away. But then his father said something else that haunted them both, something he later wished he hadn't said at all.

"Do you really think it's possible for me to find someone else who's good enough to take her place?"

In time, Garrett returned to the shop and started working again, doing his best to go on with his life. He stayed at the shop as late as he could, organizing files and rearranging his office, simply because it was less painful than going home. He found that if it was dark enough outside by the time he got back to his house and he turned on only a few lights, he didn't notice her things as much and her presence wasn't as strong. He got used to living alone again, cooking, cleaning, and doing his own laun-dry, and he even worked in the garden as she used to, though he didn't enjoy it as much as she did.

He thought he was getting better, but when the time came to pack up Catherine's things, he didn't have the heart to do it. His father eventually took matters into his own hands. After a week-end spent diving, Garrett came home to a house stripped of her belongings. Without her things, the house was empty; he no longer saw any reason to stay. He sold it within a month, moved to a smaller house on Carolina Beach, thinking that by leaving, he'd finally be able to move on. And he had, kind of, for over three years now.

His father hadn't found everything, though. In a small box that sat in his end table, he kept a few things that he couldn't bear to part with—the valentine cards he'd once given her, her wedding ring, and other things that people wouldn't understand. Late at night he liked to hold them in his hands, and even though his father sometimes commented that he seemed to be doing better, he would lie there thinking that no, he wasn't. To him, nothing would ever be the same again.

Garrett Blake went to the marina with a few minutes to spare so he could get *Happenstance* ready. He removed the sail cover, unlocked the cabin, and generally checked everything out.

His father had called just as he was stepping out the door on the way to the docks, and Garrett found himself remembering the conversation.

"Would you like to come for supper?" he'd asked.

Garrett had replied that he couldn't. "I'm going sailing with someone tonight."

His father had stayed quiet for a moment. Then: "With a woman?"

Garrett explained briefly how he and Theresa met.

"You sound like you're a little nervous about your date," his father remarked.

"No, Dad, I'm not nervous. And it's not a date. Like I said, we're just going sailing. She said she'd never gone before."

"Is she pretty?"

"What does that matter?"

"It doesn't. But it still sounds like a date to me."

"It's not a date."

"If you say so."

Garrett saw her walking up the dock a little after seven, dressed in shorts and a red sleeveless shirt, carrying a small picnic basket in one hand and a sweatshirt and light jacket in the other. She didn't look as nervous as he felt, nor did her expression betray what she was thinking as she approached him. When she waved, he felt some familiar pangs of guilt and quickly waved back before he finished untying the lines. He was mumbling to himself and doing his best to clear his mind when she reached the boat.

"Hi," she said easily. "I hope you haven't been waiting long."

He took off the gloves he was wearing as he spoke. "Oh, hi. And no—I haven't been waiting long at all. I came out here a little early to get her ready."

"Did you finish everything you needed?"

He glanced around to make sure. "Yeah, I think so. Can I help you up?"

He set aside the gloves and extended his arm. Theresa handed him her things, and he set them on one of the seats that ran along the deck. When he took her hands to pull her up, she felt the calluses on his palms. After she was safely aboard, he motioned toward the wheel, taking a small step backward.

"Are you ready to head out?"

"Whenever you are."

"Then go ahead and take a seat. I'm going to get us out onto the water. Do you want anything to drink before we get going? I have some soda in the refrigerator."

She shook her head. "No thanks. I'm fine right now."

She looked around the boat before finding a seat in the corner. She watched as he turned a key and the sound of an engine hummed to life. Then, stepping away from the wheel, he released the two lines that held the boat in place. Slowly *Happen-*

*stance* began to back out of its slip. A little surprised, Theresa said, "I didn't know there was an engine."

He turned and answered over his shoulder, speaking loudly enough so that she could hear him. "It's a small one—just enough power to get us in and out of the slip. We put a new one in when we rebuilt her."

*Happenstance* cleared the slip, then the marina. Once it was safely in the open water of the Intracoastal Waterway, Garrett turned into the wind and cut the engine. After putting on his gloves, he raised the sails quickly. *Happenstance* heeled to the breeze, and in one quick motion, Garrett was next to Theresa, leaning his body close.

"Watch your head—the boom is going to swing over you."

The next few actions came furiously. She ducked her head and watched as it all happened just the way he said it would. The boom moved above her, carrying the sail with it to capture the wind. When it was in the correct position, he used the lines to secure it again. Before she had time to blink, he was back at the wheel, making adjustments and looking over his shoulder at the sail, as if to be sure he had done everything correctly. The whole thing had taken less than thirty seconds.

"I didn't know you had to do everything so quickly. I thought sailing was a leisurely sport."

He looked over his shoulder again. Catherine used to sit in the same spot, and with the setting sun splitting the shadows, there was a brief moment when he thought it was her. He pushed the thought away and cleared his throat.

"It is, when you're out on the ocean with no one else around. But right now we're on the Intracoastal, and we have to do our best to set a course out of the way of the other boats."

He held the wheel almost perfectly still, and Theresa felt *Happenstance* gradually picking up speed. She got up from her seat and started back toward Garrett, stopping when she reached his side. The breeze was blowing, and though she could feel it on her face, it didn't seem strong enough to fill a sail.

"All right, I think we've got it," he said with an easy smile, glancing at her. "We should be able to make it without having to tack. Unless the wind changes, of course."

They moved toward the inlet. Because she knew he was concentrating on what he was doing, she kept quiet as she stood next to him. From the corner of her eye, she watched him—his strong hands on the wheel, his long legs shifting his weight as the boat heeled in the wind.

In the lull of conversation, Theresa looked around. Like most sailboats, this one had two levels—the lower outside deck, where they were standing, and the forward deck, about four feet higher, which stretched to the front of the boat. That was where the cabin was located, and there were two small windows, coated on the outside with a thin layer of salt that made it impossible to see inside. A small door led into the cabin, low enough that people had to duck their heads to keep from bumping them.

Turning back to him, she wondered how old Garrett was. In his thirties, probably—she couldn't pin it down any more than that. Looking at him closely didn't really help—his face was a little worn, almost windblown, giving him a distinctive appearance that no doubt made him appear older than he actually was.

She thought again that he wasn't the most handsome man she'd ever seen, but there was something arresting about him, something indefinable.

Earlier, when she'd spoken with Deanna on the phone, she'd

tried to describe him, but because he didn't look like most of the men she knew in Boston, she'd had a hard time. She'd told Deanna that he was about her age, handsome in his own way and fit, but that he looked natural, as if his strength were simply the result of the life he'd chosen to live. That was about as close as she could get at the time, though after seeing him up close again, she thought she wasn't so far off.

Deanna was thrilled when Theresa told her about going sailing later that evening, though Theresa had gone through a period of doubt immediately afterward. For a while she worried about being alone with a stranger—especially out in the open water—but she convinced herself that her worries were unfounded. *It's just like any other date*, she'd told herself most of the afternoon. *Don't make a big deal out of this.* When it was time for her to head to the docks, however, she almost didn't. In the end, she'd decided it was something she had to do, mainly for herself, but also because of the grief Deanna would have given her if she didn't.

As they approached the inlet, Garrett Blake turned the wheel. The sailboat responded and moved farther from the banks, toward the deep waters of the Intracoastal. Garrett looked from side to side, watching for other boats as he steadied the wheel. Despite the shifting wind, he seemed to be in absolute control of the boat, and Theresa could tell that he knew exactly what he was doing.

Terns circled directly overhead as the sailboat cut through the water, gliding on updrafts. The sails rumbled loudly as they moved with the wind. Water rushed along the side of the boat. Everything seemed to be in motion as they moved under the graying North Carolina sky.

Theresa crossed her arms and reached for the sweatshirt she had brought along. She slipped it on, glad that she had brought it. Already the air seemed a lot cooler than it had when they'd left. The sun was dropping faster than she expected, and the fading light reflected off the sails, casting shadows across most of the deck.

Directly behind the boat, the rushing water hissed and swirled, and she stepped closer to take a better look. Watching the churning water was hypnotic. Keeping her balance, she put her hand on the railing and felt something that had yet to be sanded. Looking carefully, she noticed an inscription carved into the railing. *Built in 1934—Restored in 1991.*

Waves from a larger boat passing in the distance made them bob, and Theresa made her way back toward Garrett. He was turning the wheel again, more sharply this time, and she caught a quick smile as he motioned toward the open sea. She watched him until the boat was safely clear of the inlet.

For the first time in what seemed like forever, she had done something completely spontaneous, something she couldn't have imagined doing less than a week ago. And now that it was done, she wasn't sure what to expect. What if Garrett turned out to be nothing like she had imagined? Granted, she would go home to Boston with her answer . . . but for now, she hoped she wouldn't have to leave right away. Too much had happened already—

Once there was enough distance between *Happenstance* and the other boats, Garrett asked Theresa to hold the wheel. "Just keep it steady," he said. Again he adjusted the sails, seemingly in less time than it had taken before. Taking over, he made sure the boat was headed up-weather, then tied a small loop in the jib line and looped it around the capstan in the wheel, leaving about an inch of slack.

"Okay, that should do it," he said, tapping the wheel, making sure it would stay in position. "We can take a seat if you want."

"You don't have to hold it?"

"That's what the loop is for. Sometimes—when the wind is really shifty—you have to hold the wheel the whole time. But we got lucky with the weather tonight. We could sail in this direction for hours."

With the sun descending slowly in the evening sky behind them, Garrett led the way back to where Theresa had been sitting earlier. After making sure there wasn't anything behind her that might snag her clothes, they sat in the corner—she on the side, he against the back—angled so that they could face each other. Feeling the wind in her face, Theresa pulled her hair back, looking out over the water.

Garrett watched her as she did it. She was shorter than he was—about five feet seven, he guessed—with a lovely face and a figure that reminded him of models he had seen in magazines. But even though she was attractive, there was something else about her that caught his eye. She was intelligent, he could sense that right away, and confident, too, as if she were able to move through life on her own terms. To him, these were the things that really mattered. Without them, beauty was nothing.

In a way, when he looked at her, he was reminded of Catherine. Especially her expression. She looked as though she were daydreaming as she watched the water, and he felt his thoughts wandering back to the last time they had sailed together. Again he felt guilty, though he did his best to push aside the feelings.

He shook his head and absently adjusted his watchband, first loosening it, then tightening it back in its original position.

"It's really beautiful out here," she finally said as she turned toward him. "Thanks for inviting me along."

He was glad when she broke the silence.

"You're welcome. It's nice to have some company once in a while."

She smiled at his answer, wondering if he meant it. "Do you usually sail alone?"

He leaned back as he spoke, stretching his legs out in front of him. "Usually. It's a good way to unwind after work. No matter how stressful the day is, once I get out here, the wind seems to blow it all away."

"Is diving that hard?"

"No, it's not the diving. That's the fun part. It's more or less everything else. The paperwork, dealing with people who cancel their lessons at the last minute, making sure the shop has the right amount of everything. It can make for a long day."

"I'm sure. But you like it, don't you?"

"Yeah, I do. I wouldn't trade what I do for anything." He paused and adjusted the watch on his wrist. "So, Theresa, what do you do?" It was one of the few safe questions he'd thought up during the course of the day.

"I'm a columnist for the *Boston Times*."

"Here on vacation?"

She paused only slightly before answering. "You could say that."

He nodded, expecting the answer. "What do you write about?"

She smiled. "I write about parenting."

She saw the surprised look in his eyes, the same look she saw whenever she dated someone new. *You may as well get this over with right away*, she thought to herself. "I have a son," she went on. "He's twelve."

He raised his eyebrows. "Twelve?"

"You look shocked."

"I am. You don't look old enough to have a twelve-year-old."

"I'll take that as a compliment," she said with a smirk, not rising to the bait. She wasn't quite ready to betray her age. "But, yes, he is twelve. Would you like to see a picture?"

"Sure," he said.

She found her wallet, took out the photo, and handed it to him. Garrett stared at it for a moment, then glanced at her.

"He has your coloring," he said, handing the picture back. "He's a good-looking boy."

"Thank you." As she was putting the picture away, she asked, "How about you? Do you have any children?"

"No." He shook his head. "No kids. At least none that I know of."

She chuckled at his answer, and he went on: "What's your son's name?"

"Kevin."

"Is he here in town with you?"

"No, he's with his father in California. We divorced a few years ago."

Garrett nodded without judgment, then looked over his shoulder at another sailboat passing in the distance. Theresa watched it for a moment as well, and in the silence, she noticed how peaceful it was on the ocean compared to the Intracoastal. The only sounds now came from the sail as the wind rippled through it and the water as *Happenstance* cut its way through the waves. She thought their voices sounded different from the way they had on the docks. Out here they sounded almost free, as if the open air would carry them forever.

"Would you like to see the rest of the boat?" Garrett asked.

She nodded. "I'd love to."

Garrett rose and checked the sails again before leading the way inside, Theresa one step behind him. When he opened the door he paused, suddenly overcome by the fragment of a memory, long buried but shaken loose, perhaps by the newness of this woman's presence.

*Catherine sat at the small table with a bottle of wine already open. In front of her, a vase with a single flower caught the light of a small burning candle. The flame swayed with the boat's motion, casting long shadows across the interior of the hull. In the semidarkness, he could just make out the ghost of a smile.*

*"I thought this would be a nice surprise," she said. "We haven't eaten by candlelight in a while."*

*Garrett looked to the small stove. Two foil-wrapped plates sat beside it.*

*"When did you get all this on the boat?"*

*"While you were at work."*

Theresa moved around him silently, leaving him to the privacy of his thoughts. If she had noticed his hesitation, she gave no sign, and for that, Garrett was grateful.

On Theresa's left, a seat ran along one side of the boat—wide and long enough for someone to sleep comfortably; directly opposite the seat on the other side was a small table with room enough for two people to sit. Near the door were a sink and stove burner with a small refrigerator underneath, and straight ahead was a door that led to the sleeping cabin.

He stood off to one side with his hands on his hips as she explored the interior, looking at everything. He didn't hover over her shoulder as some men would have but instead gave her space. Still, she could feel his eyes watching her, though he wasn't obvious about it. After a moment she said, "From the outside, you wouldn't think it's as large as it is."

"I know." Garrett cleared his throat awkwardly. "Surprising, isn't it?"

"Yeah, it is. It looks like it has everything you need, though."

"It does. If I wanted, I could sail her to Europe, not that I'd recommend it. But it's great for me."

He stepped around her and went to the refrigerator, bending over to pull a can of Coca-Cola from the refrigerator. "Are you up for something to drink yet?"

"Sure," she said. She ran her hands along the walls, feeling the texture of the wood.

"What would you like? I've got SevenUp or Coke."

"SevenUp's fine," she answered.

He stood and handed her the can. Their fingers touched briefly as she took it.

"I don't have any ice on board, but it's cold."

"I'll try to rough it," she said, and he smiled.

She opened it and took a swallow before setting it on the table.

As he opened his own can of soda, he looked at her, thinking about what she'd said earlier. She had a twelve-year-old son . . . and as a columnist, that meant she probably went to college. If she'd waited until after then to get married and have a child . . . that would make her about four or five years older than he was. She didn't look that much older—that much was certain—but she didn't act like most of the twenty-somethings he knew in town. There was a maturity to her actions, something that came only to those who had experienced their share of highs and lows in life.

Not that it mattered.

She turned her attention to a framed photograph that hung on the wall. In it, Garrett Blake was standing on a pier with a marlin he'd caught, looking much younger than he was now. In the photo he was smiling broadly, and his buoyant expression reminded her of Kevin whenever he scored a goal in soccer.

Into the sudden lull she said, "I see you like to fish." She pointed toward the picture. He stepped toward her, and once he was close, she felt the warmth radiating from him. He smelled like salt and wind.

"Yeah, I do," he said quietly. "My father was a shrimper, and I pretty much grew up on the water."

"How long ago was this taken?"

"That one's about ten years old—it was taken right before I went back to college for my senior year. There was a fishing contest, and my dad and I decided to spend a couple of nights out in the Gulf Stream and we caught that marlin about sixty miles off shore. It took almost seven hours to bring him in because my dad wanted me to learn how to do it the old-fashioned way."

"What does that mean?"

He laughed under his breath. "Basically it means that my hands were cut to pieces by the time I was finished, and I could barely move my shoulders the next day. The line we had hooked it on wasn't really strong enough for a fish that size, so we had to let the marlin run until it stopped, then slowly reel it in, then let it run again all day long until the thing was too exhausted to fight anymore."

"Kind of like Hemingway's *The Old Man and the Sea.*"

"Kind of, except that I didn't feel like an old man until the next day. My father, on the other hand, could have played the part in the movie."

She looked at the picture again. "Is that your father standing next to you?"

"Yeah, that's him."

"He looks like you," she said.

Garrett smiled a little, wondering whether or not it was a compliment. He motioned to the table, and Theresa sat down opposite him. Once she was comfortable, she asked:

"You said you went to college?"

He met her eyes. "Yeah, I went to UNC and majored in marine biology. Nothing else interested me much, and since my dad told me I couldn't come home without a degree, I thought I'd learn something that I might be able to use later."

"So you bought the shop. . . ."

He shook his head. "No, at least not right away. After graduating, I worked for the Duke Maritime Institute as a dive specialist, but there wasn't much money in that. So, I got a teaching certificate and started taking in students on the weekends. The shop came a few years later." He cocked an eyebrow. "How about you?"

Theresa took another drink of the SevenUp before she answered.

"My life isn't quite as exciting as yours. I grew up in Omaha, Nebraska, and went to school at Brown. After graduation, I bounced around in a couple of different places and tried a few different things, eventually settling down in Boston. I've been with the *Times* for nine years now, but only the last few as a columnist. Before that, I was a reporter."

"How do you like being a columnist?"

She thought about it for a moment, as if she were considering it for the first time.

"It's a good job," she finally said. "A lot better now than when I started. I can pick Kevin up after school, and I have the freedom to write whatever I want, as long as it's in line with my column. It pays fairly well, too, so I can't complain about that, but . . ."

She paused again. "It's not all that challenging anymore. Don't get me wrong, I like what I do, but sometimes I feel like I'm writing the same things over and over. Even that wouldn't be so bad, though, if I didn't have so many other things to do with Kevin. I guess that right now, I'm your typical, overworked single mother, if you know what I mean."

He nodded and spoke softly. "Life doesn't often turn out the way we think it will, does it?"

"No, I guess it doesn't," she said, and again she caught his gaze. His expression made her wonder if he'd said something he rarely said to anyone else. She smiled and leaned toward him.

"Are you ready for something to eat? I brought some things in the basket."

"Whenever you are."

"I hope you like sandwiches and cold salads. They were the only things I could think of that wouldn't spoil."

"It sounds better than what I would have had. If it was just me, I probably would have stopped for a burger before I went out tonight. Would you like to eat down here or outside?"

"Outside, definitely."

They picked up their cans of soda and left the cabin. On their way out, Garrett grabbed a raincoat from a peg near the door and motioned for her to go on without him. "Give me a minute to drop the anchor," he said, "so we can eat without having to check the boat every few minutes." Theresa reached her seat and opened the basket she had brought with her. On the horizon, the sun was sinking into a bank of cumulus clouds. She pulled out a couple of sandwiches wrapped in cellophane, as well as some Styrofoam containers of coleslaw and potato salad.

She watched as Garrett set aside the coat and lowered the sails, the boat slowing almost immediately. With his back to her as he worked, she again noticed how strong he looked. From where she was sitting, his shoulder muscles appeared larger than she had first realized, amplified by his small waist. She couldn't believe she was actually sailing with this man when only two days ago she was in Boston. The whole thing seemed unreal.

While Garrett worked steadily, Theresa looked upward. The breeze had picked up now that the temperature had dropped, and the sky was darkening slowly.

Once the boat had stopped completely, Garrett lowered the anchor. He waited about a minute, making sure the anchor would hold, and when he was satisfied, he took his seat next to Theresa.

"I wish there was something I could do to help you," Theresa said with a smile. She flipped her hair onto her shoulder the same way Catherine used to, and for a moment he didn't say anything.

"Is everything okay?" Theresa asked.

He nodded, suddenly uncomfortable again. "We're fine right here. But I was just thinking that if the wind keeps picking up, we'll have to tack a bit more often on our way back."

She put some potato salad and coleslaw along with his sandwich on his plate and handed it to him, conscious of the fact that he was sitting closer than he had before.

"Will it take longer to get back, then?"

Garrett reached for one of the white plastic forks and took a bite of coleslaw. It took a moment for him to answer.

"A little—but it won't be a problem unless the wind stops completely. If that happens, we'd be stuck."

"I take it that's happened to you before."

He nodded. "Once or twice. It's rare, but it does happen."

She looked confused. "Why is that rare? The wind doesn't always blow, does it?"

"On the ocean it usually does."

"How come?"

He smiled in amusement and set the sandwich on his plate. "Well, winds are driven by differences in temperature—when warm air rushes to cooler air. For the wind to stop blowing when you're out on the ocean, you'd need the air temperature to exactly equal the water temperature for miles around. Down here, the air is usually hot during the day, but as soon as the sun starts to set, the temperature drops quickly. That's why the best time to go out is at dusk. The temperature is changing constantly, and that makes for great sailing."

"What happens if the wind does stop?"

"The sails empty and the boat comes to a halt. You're absolutely powerless to do anything to make it move."

"And you said this has happened to you before?"

He nodded.

"What did you do?"

"Nothing, really. Just sat back and enjoyed the quiet. I wasn't in danger, and I knew that in time the air temperature would drop. So I just waited it out. After an hour or so, a breeze picked up and I made it back to port."

"Sounds like it ended up being an enjoyable day."

"It was." He looked away from her intent gaze and focused on the cabin door. After a moment he added, almost to himself, "One of the best."

*Catherine scooted over in her seat. "Come here and sit next to me."*

*Garrett closed the cabin door and made his way to her.*

*"This is the best day we've spent together in a long time," Catherine said softly.*

*"It seems like we've both been too busy lately, and . . . I don't know . . ."* *She trailed off. "I just wanted to do something special for us."*

*As she spoke, it seemed to Garrett that his wife wore the same tender expression she'd had on their wedding night.*

*Garrett sat beside her and poured the wine. "I'm sorry I've been so busy at the shop lately," he said quietly. "I love you, you know."*

*"I know." She smiled and covered his hand with her own.*

*"It'll be better soon, I promise."*

*Catherine nodded, reaching for her wine. "Let's not talk about that right now. Right now, I want to enjoy us, just the two of us. Without any distractions."*

"Garrett?"

Startled, Garrett looked at Theresa. "I'm sorry . . . ?" he began.

"Are you okay?" She was staring at him with a mixture of concern and puzzlement.

"I'm fine. . . . I was just remembering something I have to take care of," Garrett improvised. "Anyway," he said, straightening and folding his hands over one raised knee. "Enough about me. If you don't mind, Theresa . . . tell me something about yourself."

Puzzled and a little unsure about what he wanted to know exactly, she started from the beginning, touching on all the basic facts in a little more detail—her upbringing, her job, her hobbies. Mostly, though, she talked about Kevin and what a wonderful son he was and how she regretted not being able to spend more time with him.

Garrett listened as she spoke, not saying much. When she finished he asked, "And you said you were married once?"

She nodded. "For eight years. But David—that's his name—seemed to lose heart in the relationship, somehow . . . he ended up having an affair. I just couldn't live with that."

"I couldn't, either," Garrett said softly, "but it still doesn't make it any easier."

"No, it didn't." She paused and took a drink of her soda. "But we're on friendly terms, in spite of everything. He's a good father to Kevin, and that's all I want from him now."

A large swell passed beneath the hull, and Garrett turned his head to make sure the anchor would hold. When he turned back Theresa said: "Okay, your turn. Tell me about you."

Garrett also started from the beginning, talking about growing up in Wilmington as an only child. He told her that his mother had died when he was twelve, and because his father spent most of his time on the boat, he pretty much grew up on

the water. He spoke about his college days—omitting some of
the wilder stories that might provide a misleading impression—
and described what it had been like to start the shop and what
his typical days were like now. Strangely, he said nothing at all
about Catherine, over which Theresa could only wonder.

As they talked on, the sky turned to black and fog began to
settle in around them. With the boat rocking slightly in the
waves, a kind of intimacy descended upon them. The fresh air,
the breeze in their faces, and the gentle movement of the boat
all conspired to ease their earlier nervousness.

Afterward Theresa tried to remember the last time she'd had
a date like this. Not once did she feel any pressure from Garrett
to see him again, nor did he seem to expect something more
from her this evening. Most of the men she met in Boston
seemed to share the attitude that if they went out of their way
to have a pleasant evening, then something was owed in return.
It was an adolescent attitude—but typical nonetheless—and she
found the change refreshing.

When they reached a quiet point in the conversation, Garrett
leaned back and ran his hands through his hair. He closed his
eyes and seemed to be savoring a silent moment for himself.
While he was doing that, Theresa quietly put the used plates
and napkins back into the basket to keep them from blowing
into the ocean. When Garrett was ready, he rose from his seat.

"I think it's about time we start back," he said, almost as if regretting that the trip was coming to an end.

A few minutes later the boat was under way again, and she
noticed that the wind was much stronger than it had been earlier. Garrett stood at the wheel, keeping *Happenstance* on course.
Theresa stood next to him with her hand on the railing, running

through their conversation again and again in her head. Neither of them spoke for a long while, and Garrett Blake found himself wondering why he felt so off balance.

*On their last sail together, Catherine and Garrett talked quietly for hours, enjoying the wine and dinner. The sea was calm, and the gentle rise and fall of the swells were comforting in their familiarity.*

*Later that night, after making love, Catherine lay by Garrett's side, skimming her fingers across his chest, saying nothing.*

*"What are you thinking?" he asked finally.*

*"Just that I didn't think it was possible to love someone as much as I love you," she whispered.*

*Garrett ran his finger down her cheek. Catherine's eyes never left his.*

*"I didn't think it was possible, either," he answered softly. "I don't know what I'd ever do without you."*

*"Will you make me a promise?"*

*"Anything."*

*"If anything ever does happen to me, promise me that you'll find someone else."*

*"I don't think I could love anyone except you."*

*"Just promise me, okay?"*

*It took a moment to answer. "All right—if it makes you happy, I promise." He smiled tenderly.*

*Catherine snuggled into him. "I'm happy, Garrett."*

When the memory finally faded, Garrett cleared his throat and touched Theresa's arm with his hand to get her attention. He pointed toward the sky. "Look at all this," he said finally, doing his best to keep the conversation neutral. "Before they had sextants and compasses, they used the stars to navigate the seas. Over there, you can see Polaris. It always points due north."

Theresa looked up into the sky. "How do you know which star it is?"

"You use marker stars. Can you see the Big Dipper?"

"Sure."

"If you draw a straight line from the two stars that make up the tip of the spoon, they'll point to the North Star."

Theresa watched as he pointed out the stars he was talking about, musing about Garrett and the things that interested him. Sailing, diving, fishing, navigation by stars—anything to do with the ocean. Or anything, it seemed, that would enable him to be alone for hours on end.

With one hand, Garrett reached for the navy blue raincoat he'd left near the wheel earlier and slipped it on. "The Phoenicians were probably the greatest ocean explorers in history. In 600 B.C. they claimed to have sailed around the continent of Africa, but no one believed that they had done it because they swore that the North Star disappeared halfway through their voyage. But it had."

"Why?"

"Because they entered the southern hemisphere. That's how historians know they actually did it. Before then, no one had ever seen that happen before, or if they had, they'd never recorded it. It took almost two thousand years before they were proved right."

She nodded, imagining their faraway voyage. She wondered why she never learned such things growing up and wondered about the man who had. And suddenly she knew exactly why Catherine had fallen in love with him. It wasn't that he was unusually attractive, or ambitious, or even charming. He was partly those things, but more important, he seemed to live life on his own terms. There was something mysterious and different about the way he acted, something masculine. And that made him unlike anyone she'd ever met before.

Garrett glanced at her when she didn't respond and again noticed how lovely she was. In the darkness her pale skin looked ethereal, and he found himself picturing what it would feel like to lightly trace the outline of her cheek. He shook his head then, trying to push the thought away.

But he couldn't. The breeze was blowing through her hair, and the sight of it made something tighten in his stomach. How long had it been since he'd felt this way? Too long, for sure. But there wasn't anything he could, or would, do about it. He knew that too as he watched her. It was neither the right time nor the right place . . . nor was it the right person. Deep down, he wondered if anything would ever be right again.

"I hope I'm not boring you," he said finally, with forced calmness. "I've always been interested in those types of stories."

She faced him and smiled. "No, it's not that. Not at all. I liked the story. I was just imagining what those men must have gone through. It's not easy to head into something completely foreign."

"No, it's not," he said, feeling as if she'd somehow read his mind.

The lights from the buildings along the shore seemed to flicker in the slowly thickening fog. *Happenstance* rocked slightly in the rising swells as it approached the inlet, and Theresa looked over her shoulder for the things she had brought with her. Her jacket had blown into the corner near the cabin. She made a note not to forget it when she got back to the marina.

Even though Garrett had said he usually sailed alone, she wondered if he had brought anyone out besides Catherine and herself. And if he never had, what did that mean? She knew he had watched her carefully this evening, though he'd never been obvious. But even if he was curious about her, he'd kept his feelings well hidden. He hadn't pressed her for information she wasn't willing to give, he hadn't questioned her about whether she was involved with someone else. He hadn't done anything this evening that could be interpreted as being more than casually interested.

Garrett turned a switch, and a series of small lights came on around the boat. Not enough to see each other well, but enough so that other boats would see them approaching. He pointed toward the blackness of the coast—"The inlet is right over there, between the lights"—and turned the wheel in that direction. The sails rippled and the beam shifted for a moment before returning to its original position.

"So," he finally asked, "did you enjoy your first time sailing?"

"I did. It was wonderful."

"I'm glad. It wasn't a trip to the southern hemisphere, but it's about all I could do."

They stood beside each other, both seemingly lost in thought. Another sailboat appeared in the darkness a quarter mile away, making its way back to the marina as well. Giving it a wide berth, Garrett looked from side to side, making sure nothing else would appear. Theresa noticed that the fog had made the horizon invisible.

Turning toward him, she saw that his hair had been blown

back by the wind. The coat he was wearing hung to midthigh, unzipped. Worn and weathered, it looked as though he'd used it for years. It made him seem larger than he really was, and it would be this image of him that she could imagine remembering forever. This, and the first time she had seen him.

As they moved closer to shore, Theresa suddenly doubted that they would see each other again. In a few minutes they'd be back at the docks and they would say good-bye. She doubted he would ask her to join him again, and she wasn't going to ask him herself. For some reason it didn't seem like the right thing to do.

They made their way through the inlet, turning toward the marina. Again he kept the boat in the center of the waterway, and Theresa saw a series of triangular signs marking the channel. He kept the sails up until approximately the same spot he'd first raised them, then lowered them with the same intensity he had used to guide the boat all evening. The engine kicked to life, and within a few minutes they had made their way past the boats that had been moored all evening. When they reached his dock, she stood on the deck while Garrett jumped off and secured *Happenstance* with the lines.

Theresa walked to the stern to get the basket and her jacket, then stopped. Thinking for a moment, she picked up the basket, but instead of grabbing her jacket, she pushed it partway under the seat cushion with her free hand. When Garrett asked if everything was okay, she cleared her throat and said, "I'm just getting my things." She walked to the side of the boat, and he offered his hand. Again she felt the strength in it as she took it, and she stepped down from *Happenstance* onto the dock.

They stared at each other for just a moment, as if wondering what would come next, before Garrett finally motioned toward the boat. "I've got to close her up for the night, and it's going to take a little while."

She nodded. "I thought you might say that."

"Can I walk you to your car first?"

"Sure," she said, and he started down the dock with Theresa beside him. When they reached her rental car, Garrett watched as she fished through the basket for her keys. After finding them, she unlocked the car door and opened it.

"Like I said earlier, I had a wonderful time tonight," she said.

"So did I."

"You should take more people out. I'm sure they would enjoy it."

Grinning, he answered, "I'll think about it."

For a moment their eyes met, and for a moment he saw Catherine in the darkness.

"I'd better get back," he said quickly, slightly uncomfortable. "I've got an early morning tomorrow." She nodded, and not knowing what else to do, Garrett held out his hand. "It was nice to have met you, Theresa. I hope you enjoy the rest of your vacation."

Shaking his hand felt a little strange after the evening they'd just spent, but she would have been surprised if he'd done anything different.

"Thanks for everything, Garrett. It was nice meeting you, too."

She took her seat behind the steering wheel and turned the ignition. Garrett shut the door for her and listened as she put the car into gear. Smiling at him one last time, she glanced in the rearview mirror and slowly backed the car out. Garrett waved as she began to pull away and watched as her car finally left the marina. When she was safely on her way, he turned and walked back up the docks, wondering why he felt so unsettled.

Twenty minutes later, just as Garrett was finishing up with *Happenstance*, Theresa unlocked the door to her hotel room and stepped inside. She tossed her things on the bed and made her way to the bathroom. She splashed cold water on her face and brushed her teeth before undressing. Then, lying in bed with only the bedside lamp on, she closed her eyes, thinking about Garrett.

David would have done everything so differently had he been the one who had taken her sailing. He would have tailored the evening to suit the charming image he wanted to project—"I just happen to have some wine, would you care for a glass?"— and he definitely would have talked a little more about himself. But it would have been subtle—David was good at anticipating when confidence crossed the line to arrogance—and he'd have made sure not to cross that line right away. Until you knew him better, you didn't know it was a carefully orchestrated plan designed to make the best impression. With Garrett, though, she knew right away that he wasn't acting—there was something sincere about him—and she found herself intrigued by his manner. Yet had she done the right thing? She still wasn't sure about that yet. Her actions seemed almost manipulative, and she didn't like to think of herself that way.

But it was already done. She'd made her decision, and there wasn't any turning back now. She turned off the lamp, and once her eyes adjusted to the darkness, she looked toward the space between the loosely drawn curtains. The crescent moon had finally risen, and a little moonlight spilled onto the bed. Staring at it, she found herself unable to turn away until her body finally relaxed and her eyes closed for the night.

## CHAPTER 7

*A*nd then what happened?"

Jeb Blake leaned over his cup of coffee, speaking in a raspy voice. Nearly seventy, he was lean and tall—almost too thin—and his face was deeply wrinkled. The thinning hair on his head was almost white, and his Adam's apple protruded from his neck like a small prune. His arms were tattooed and scarred, covered with sun spots, and the knuckles on his hands were permanently swollen from years of wear and tear as a shrimper. If not for his eyes, a person would think he was frail and sick when looking at him, but in truth he was far from it. He still worked almost every day, though only part-time now, always leaving the house before daybreak and returning around noon.

"Nothing happened. She got into her car and drove away."

Rolling the first of the dozen cigarettes he would smoke a day, Jeb Blake stared at his son. For years his doctor told him he was killing himself by smoking, but because the doctor died of a heart attack at sixty, his father didn't put much faith in medical advice. As it was, Garrett assumed the old man would probably outlive him as well.

"Well, that's kind of a waste, isn't it?"

Garrett was surprised by his bluntness. "No, Dad, it wasn't a waste. I had a good time last night. She was easy to talk to, and I enjoyed her company."

"But you're not going to see her again."

Garrett took a drink of coffee and shook his head. "I doubt it. Like I said, she's here on vacation."

"For how long?"

"I don't know. I didn't ask."

"Why not?"

Garrett reached for another packet of cream and added it to his coffee. "Why are you so interested, anyway? I went out sailing with someone and had a good time. There's not much more I can say about it."

"Sure there is."

"Like what?"

"Like whether you enjoyed your date enough to start seeing other people again."

Garrett stirred his coffee thinking, So that was it. Though he'd grown used to his father's interrogations over the years, he wasn't in the mood to cover old ground this morning. "Dad, we've gone over this before."

"I know, but I'm worried about you. You spend too much time alone these days."

"No, I don't."

"Yes," his father said with surprising softness, "you do."

"I don't want to argue about it, Dad."

"I don't, either. I've already tried that, and it doesn't work." He smiled. After a moment of silence, Jeb Blake tried another approach.

"So, what was she like?"

Garrett thought for a moment. Despite himself, he'd thought about her for a long time before finally turning in for the night.

"Theresa? She's attractive and intelligent. Very charming, too, in her own way."

"Is she single?"

"I think so. She's divorced, and I don't think she would have come along if she were seeing someone else."

Jeb studied his son's expression carefully as Garrett answered. When he finished, he leaned over his coffee again. "You liked her, didn't you."

Looking his father in the eyes, Garrett knew he couldn't hide the truth. "Yeah, I did. But like I said, I probably won't see her again. I don't know where she's staying, and for all I know, she could be leaving town today."

His father watched him in silence for a moment before asking the next question carefully. "But if she were still here and you knew where she was, do you think you would?"

Garrett looked away without answering, and Jeb reached across the table, taking his son's arm. Even at seventy his hands were strong, and Garrett felt him applying just enough pressure to get his attention.

"Son, it's been three years now. I know you loved her, but it's okay to let it go now. You know that, don't you? You've got to be able to let it go."

It took a moment for him to answer. "I know, Dad. But it's not that easy."

"Nothing that's worthwhile is ever easy. Remember that."

A few minutes later they finished their coffee. Garrett tossed a couple of dollars onto the table and followed his father out of the diner, toward his truck in the parking lot. When Garrett finally got to the shop, a dozen different things were going through his head. Unable to concentrate on the paperwork he needed to do, he decided to go back to the docks to finish working on the engine he had started repairing the day before. Though he definitely had to spend some time in the shop today, at the moment he needed to be alone.

Garrett pulled his toolbox from the back of his truck and carried it to the boat he used when he taught scuba diving. An older Boston Whaler, it was large enough to carry up to eight students and the necessary gear needed for underwater dives.

Working on the engine was time-consuming but not difficult, and he'd made good headway the day before. As he removed the engine casing, he thought about the conversation he'd had with his father. He'd been right, of course. There wasn't any reason to continue feeling the way he did, but—as God was his witness— he didn't know how to stop it. Catherine had meant everything to him. All she'd had to do was look at him and he'd feel as if everything were suddenly right in the world. And when she smiled . . . Lord, that was something he'd never been able to find in anyone else. To have something like that taken away . . . it just wasn't fair. And more than that, it just seemed *wrong*. Why her, of all people? And why him? For months he had lain awake at night, asking himself "What if." What if she'd waited an extra second before crossing the street? What if they had lingered at breakfast for another few minutes? What if he'd gone with her that morning instead of going straight to the shop? A thousand what ifs, and he was no closer to understanding the whole thing than he had been when it first happened.

Trying to clear his mind, he concentrated on the task at hand. He removed the bolts that held the carburetor in place and removed it from the engine. Carefully he began to take it apart, making sure nothing was too worn inside. He didn't think that this was the source of the problem, though he wanted a closer look just to make sure.

The sun rose overhead as he worked steadily, and he found himself wiping the sweat as it formed on his forehead. Yesterday at about this time, he remembered, he'd watched as Theresa walked down the docks toward *Happenstance*. He'd noticed her right away, if for no other reason than she was alone. Women who looked as she did almost never came down to the docks alone. Usually they were accompanied by wealthy, older gentlemen who owned the yachts that were moored on the other side of the marina. When she stopped at his boat, he'd been surprised, though he'd expected her to pause for only a moment before moving on to her final destination. That's what most people usually did. But after watching her for a little while, he realized that she had come to the docks to see *Happenstance*, and the way she kept pacing around made it seem as if she were there for something else as well.

His curiosity aroused, he'd gone over to speak with her. At the time, he didn't notice it, but when he was closing up the boat later in the evening, he realized there was something odd in the way she had first looked at him. It was almost as if she *recognized* something about him that he usually kept buried deep within himself. More than that, it was as if she knew more about him than she was willing to admit.

He shook his head then, knowing that didn't make any sense. She said she'd read the articles in the shop—maybe that's where the strange look came from. He thought about it, finally deciding that had to be the case. He knew he'd never met her before—he would have remembered something like that—and besides, she was vacationing from Boston. It was the only plausible explanation he could come up with, but even now there was something that didn't sit quite right about the whole situation.

Not that it mattered.

They'd gone sailing, enjoyed each other's company, and said good-bye. That was the end of it. As he'd told his father, he couldn't reach her again even if he wanted to. Right now she was probably on her way back to Boston, or she would be in a few days, and he had a hundred things to do this week. Summer was a popular season for diving classes, and he was booked up every weekend until late August. He had neither the time nor the energy to call every hotel in Wilmington to find her, and even if he did, what would he say? What *could* he say that wouldn't sound ridiculous?

With these questions rolling through his mind, he worked on the engine. After finding and replacing a leaking clamp, he reinstalled the carburetor and the engine casing and cranked the motor. The engine sounding much better, he freed the boat from its lines and took the Boston Whaler out for forty minutes. He ran it through a series of speeds, started and stopped the engine more than once, and when satisfied, returned the boat to its slip. Pleased that it had taken less time than he'd thought it would, he collected his tools, returned them to his truck, and drove the couple of blocks to Island Diving.

As usual, there were papers stacked in the in-box on his desk, and he took a moment to review them. Most were order forms, already filled out, for items that were needed in the shop. There were a few bills as well, and settling himself in his chair, he worked quickly through the stack.

Just before eleven, he finished most of what he needed to do and headed toward the front of the shop. Ian, one of his summertime employees, was on the phone when Garrett walked up and handed him three slips of paper. The first two were from distributors, and from the short messages scrawled, it seemed likely there had been a mix-up with some of the orders they had placed recently. Another thing to take care of, he thought, starting back toward the office.

He read the third message as he was walking and stopped when he realized who it was from. Making sure it wasn't a mistake, he entered his office and closed the door behind him. He dialed the number and asked for the proper extension.

Theresa Osborne was reading the paper when the phone rang and picked up on the second ring.

"Hey, Theresa, this is Garrett. There's a message here that you called."

She sounded pleased to hear from him. "Oh, hi, Garrett. Thanks for returning my call. How are you?"

Hearing her voice brought back memories of the evening before. Smiling to himself, he imagined what she looked like as she sat in her hotel room. "I'm fine, thanks. I was just going through some paperwork and I got your message. What can I do for you?"

"Well, I left my jacket on the boat last night and I was wondering if you found it."

"I didn't, but I really wasn't looking that closely. Did you leave it in the cabin?"

"I'm not sure."

Garrett paused for a moment. "Well, let me run down there and take a look. I'll call you back and let you know whether I found it."

"Is that too much trouble?"

"Not at all. It should just take a few minutes. Will you be there for a little while?"

"I should be."

"Okay, I'll call you right back."

Garrett said good-bye and left the shop, walking quickly back to the marina. After stepping aboard *Happenstance*, he unlocked the cabin and went below. Not finding the jacket, he turned and glanced up the deck, finally spotting it near the stern, partially hidden under one of the seat cushions. He picked it up, made sure it wasn't stained, then returned to the shop.

In his office again, he dialed the number written on the slip. This time Theresa picked up on the first ring.

"This is Garrett again. I found your jacket."

She sounded relieved. "Thanks. I appreciate your looking for it."

"It wasn't a problem at all."

She was quiet for a moment, as if deciding what to do. Finally: "Could you hold it for me? I can be down at your shop in about twenty minutes to pick it up."

"I'd be glad to," he answered. After hanging up the phone, he leaned back in his chair, thinking about what had just happened. She hasn't left town yet, he thought, and I'm going to get to see her again. Though he couldn't understand how she could have forgotten her jacket since she'd brought only a couple of things with her, one thing had just made itself abundantly clear: he was definitely glad it had happened.

Not, of course, that it mattered.

Theresa arrived twenty minutes later, dressed in shorts and a low-necked sleeveless blouse that did wonderful things for her figure. When she entered the shop, both Ian and Garrett stared at her as she glanced around. Finally spotting him, she smiled and called out, "Hi," from where she was standing, and Ian raised his eyebrow at Garrett, as if to ask "What haven't you been telling me?" Garrett ignored the expression and moved toward Theresa with her jacket in hand. He knew that Ian would scrutinize everything he did and badger him about it later, though he wasn't planning on saying anything.

"Good as new," he said, offering it to her when she stepped close enough to take it. While she was on her way, Garrett had washed the grease off his hands and changed into one of the new T-shirts his store offered for sale. It wasn't spectacular, but it was better than the way he'd looked before. At least now he looked clean.

"Thanks for picking it up for me," she said, and there was something in her eyes that made the initial attraction he'd felt the day before begin to rise again. Absently he scratched the side of his face.

"I was glad to do it. I guess the wind must have forced it from plain view."

"I guess so," she said with a slight shrug, and Garrett watched as she adjusted the shoulder of her blouse with her hand. He didn't know if she was in a hurry, and he wasn't sure he wanted her to leave yet. He said the first words that came to mind:

"I had a good time last night."

"So did I."

Her eyes caught his as she said it, and Garrett smiled softly. He didn't know what else to say—it had been a long time since he'd been in a situation like this. Though he was always good with customers and strangers in general, this was completely different. He found himself shifting his weight from one leg to the other, feeling as if he were sixteen again. Finally it was she who spoke.

"I feel like I owe you something for taking the time to do this."

"Don't be ridiculous. You don't owe me anything."

"Maybe not for picking up my jacket, but for last night as well."

He shook his head. "Not for that, either. I was glad you came."

*I was glad you came.* The words rolled through his head immediately after he spoke them. Two days ago he couldn't have imagined himself saying them to anyone.

In the background the phone rang, and the sound of it broke him from his thoughts. Buying time, he asked: "Did you come all the way down here just for your jacket, or were you going to do a little sight-seeing as well?"

"I hadn't really planned on that. It's about lunchtime, and I

was going to get a quick bite to eat." She looked at him expectantly. "Any recommendations?"

He thought for a moment before responding. "I like Hank's,
down at the pier. The food is fresh, and the view is out of this
world."

"Where is it, exactly?"

He motioned over his shoulder. "On Wrightsville Beach. You
take the bridge over to the island and turn right. You can't miss
it—just look for the signs to the pier. The restaurant is located
right there."

"What kind of food do they have?"

"Mainly seafood. They have great shrimp and oysters, but if
you want something other than seafood, they have burgers and
things like that as well."

She waited to see if he would add anything else, and when he
didn't, she glanced away, looking toward the windows. Still she
stood there, and for the second time in a couple of minutes,
Garrett felt awkward in her presence. What was it about her that
made him feel this way? Finally, gathering himself, he spoke.

"If you'd like, I could show you the place. I'm getting kind of
hungry myself, and I'd be happy to take you there if you want
some company."

She smiled. "I'd like that, Garrett."

He looked relieved. "My truck is out back. Do you want me
to drive?"

"You know the way better than I do," she replied, and Garrett pointed the way, leading her through the shop and out the
back door. Walking slightly behind him so that he couldn't see
her expression, Theresa couldn't help but smile to herself.

*    *    *

Hank's had been in business since the pier was built and was frequented by locals and tourists alike. Low in ambience but high in character, it was similar to the pier restaurants they had on Cape Cod—wooden floors scraped and scuffed by years of sandy shoes, large windows offering a view of the Atlantic Ocean, pictures of trophy fish on the walls. Off to one side was a door that led to the kitchen, and Theresa saw plates of fresh seafood loaded on trays, carried by waiters and waitresses dressed in shorts and blue T-shirts emblazoned with the name of the restaurant. The tables and chairs were wooden, sturdy looking, and decorated by the carvings of hundreds of former visitors. It wasn't a place that required more than casual beachwear, and Theresa noticed that most of the people there looked as though they had been lying in the sun most of the morning.

"Trust me," he said as they were walking to a table. "The food is great, no matter what this place looks like."

They took their seats at a table near the corner, and Garrett pushed aside two bottles of beer that hadn't yet been cleared. The menus were stacked between a series of condiments including ketchup, Tabasco, tartar sauce, and cocktail sauce in squeeze bottles, as well as another sauce labeled simply "Hank's." Cheaply laminated, the menus looked as though they hadn't been replaced in years. Glancing around, Theresa saw that nearly every table was occupied.

"It's crowded," she said, making herself comfortable.

"It always is. Even before Wrightsville Beach got popular with tourists, this place was kind of a legend. You can't even get in here on Friday or Saturday nights, unless you're willing to wait for a couple of hours."

"What's the draw?"

"The food and the prices. Every morning Hank gets a load of fresh fish and shrimp, and you can usually get out of here without spending more than ten dollars, including the tip. And that's with a couple of beers."

"How does he do it?"

"Volume, I guess. Like I said, this place is always crowded."

"Then we were lucky to get a table."

"Yeah, we were. But we got here before the locals come in, and the beach crowd never lingers. They just pop in for a quick bite and head back out into the sun."

She looked around the restaurant one last time before glancing at the menu. "So what do you recommend?"

"Do you like seafood?"

"I love it."

"Then go with the tuna or the dolphin. They're both delicious."

"Dolphin?"

He laughed under his breath. "Not Flipper. It's dolphin-fish. That's what we call it around here."

"I think I'll go with the tuna," she said with a wink, "just to make sure."

"You think I'd make up something like that?"

She spoke in a teasing voice. "I don't know what to think. We just met yesterday, remember. I don't know you well enough to be completely sure what you're capable of."

"I'm hurt," he said in the same voice, and she laughed. He laughed, too, and after a moment she surprised him by reaching across the table and touching his arm briefly. Catherine, he suddenly realized, used to do the same thing to get his attention.

"Look over there," she said, nodding toward the windows,

and Garrett turned his head. On the pier an older man carried his fishing gear, looking completely normal except for the large parrot that was perched on his shoulder.

Garrett shook his head and smiled, still feeling the remnants of her touch lingering on his arm. "We get all kinds around here. It's not quite California, but give us a few years."

Theresa kept watching as the man with the bird wandered down the pier. "You should get yourself one of those to keep you company when you go sailing."

"And ruin my peace and quiet? Knowing my luck, the thing wouldn't talk. It would just squawk the whole time and probably bite off part of my ear the first time the wind shifted."

"But you'd look like a pirate."

"I'd look like an idiot."

"Oh, you're no fun," Theresa said with a mock frown. After a brief pause, she looked around. "So do they have anyone to serve you here, or do we have to catch and cook our own fish?"

"Damn Yankees," he mumbled while shaking his head, and she laughed again, wondering if he was having as much fun as she was, knowing somehow that he probably was.

A few moments later the waitress arrived and took their orders. Both Theresa and Garrett ordered beers, and after putting the order into the kitchen, the waitress brought two bottles to the table.

"No glasses?" she asked with a raised eyebrow after the waitress had left.

"Nope. This place is nothing if not classy."

"I can see why you like it so much."

"Is that a comment about my lack of taste?"

"Only if you're insecure about it."

"Now you sound like a psychiatrist."

"I'm not, but I am a mother, and that makes me something of an expert in human nature."

"Is that so?"

"It's what I tell Kevin."

Garrett took a sip of his beer. "Did you talk to him today?"

She nodded and took a drink as well. "Just for a few minutes. He was on his way to Disneyland when I called. He had early morning passes, so he couldn't talk that long. He wanted to be one of the first in line at the Indiana Jones ride."

"Is he having a good time with his father?"

"He's having a great time. David's always been good with him, but I think he tries to make up for the fact that he doesn't see Kevin that often. Whenever Kevin goes out there, he expects something fun and exciting."

Garrett looked at her curiously. "You sound like you're not so sure about it."

She hesitated before continuing. "Well, I just hope it doesn't lead to disappointment later. David and his new wife have started a family, and as soon as the baby gets a little older, I think it's going to be a lot harder for David and Kevin to be alone together."

Garrett leaned forward as he spoke. "It's impossible to protect your kids against disappointment in life."

"I know that, I really do. It's just that . . ."

She stopped, and Garrett gently finished her thoughts for her. "He's your son and you don't want to see him hurt."

"Exactly." Beads of condensation had formed on the outside of her bottle of beer, and Theresa began to peel off the label. Again, it was the same thing Catherine used to do, and Garrett took another drink of beer and forced his mind back to the conversation at hand.

"I don't know what to say except that if Kevin's anything like you, I'm sure he'll end up all right."

"What do you mean?"

He shrugged. "No one's life is easy—yours included. You've had some tough times, too. I think that by watching you overcome adversity, he'll learn how to do it as well."

"Now you're the one sounding like a psychiatrist."

"I'm just telling you what I learned growing up. I was about Kevin's age when my mom died of cancer. Watching my dad taught me that I had to go on with my life, no matter what happens."

"Did your dad ever remarry?"

"No," he said, shaking his head. "I think there were a few times that he wished he had, but he never got around to it."

So that's where it comes from, she thought. Like father, like son.

"Does he still live in town?" she asked.

"Yeah, he does. I see him a lot these days. We try to get together at least once a week. He likes to keep me on the straight and narrow."

She smiled. "Most parents do."

The food arrived a few minutes later, and they continued their conversation as they ate. This time Garrett spoke more than she did, telling her what it was like growing up in the South, and why he'd never leave given the choice. He also told her about some of the adventurous things that had happened while sailing or scuba diving. She listened, fascinated. Compared with the stories that the men told up in Boston—which usually focused on business accomplishments—his stories were completely new to her. He spoke about the thousands of different sea creatures he had seen on his dives and what it was like to sail through a storm that had come up unexpectedly and nearly capsized his boat. One time he'd even been chased by a hammerhead shark and was forced to take cover in the wreck he'd been exploring. "I almost ran out of air before I could come up," he said, shaking his head at the memory.

Theresa watched him closely as he spoke, pleased that he had loosened up compared with the evening before. She still noticed the things she had last night—the lean face, his light blue eyes, and the easy way he moved. Yet there was energy in the way he spoke to her now, and she found the change appealing. No longer did he seem to be measuring every word he said.

They finished their lunch—he was right, the food was delicious—and went through a second beer each as the ceiling fans whirred overhead. With the sun rising steadily in the sky, it was hot in the restaurant now, but no less crowded. After the bill arrived, Garrett put some money on the table and motioned for them to leave.

"Are you ready?"

"Whenever you are. And thanks for lunch. It was great."

As they walked out the front door, she fully expected that Garrett would want to return to the shop right away, but he surprised her by suggesting something different.

"How about a walk along the beach? It's usually a little cooler down by the water." When she said yes, he led her to the side of the pier and started down the steps, walking beside Theresa. The steps were slightly warped and thinly layered with sand, forcing them to hold the railings as they made their way down. Once they reached the beach, they turned toward the water, walking beneath the pier. The shade was refreshing in the midday heat, and when they reached the compact sand at the edge of the tide, both of them stopped for a moment to remove their shoes. All around them, families were crowded onto towels and splashing in the water.

They began to walk in silence, strolling beside each other as Theresa looked around, taking in the sights.

"Have you spent a lot of time on the beaches while you've been here?" Garrett asked.

Theresa shook her head. "No. I only got here the day before yesterday. This is the first time I've been on the beach here."

"How do you like it?"

"It's beautiful."

"Is it like the beaches up north?"

"Some of them, but the water's a lot warmer here. Haven't you ever been to the coast up north?"

"I've never been outside North Carolina."

She smiled at him. "A real world traveler, huh?"

He laughed under his breath. "No, but I don't feel like I'm missing that much. I like it here and couldn't imagine a prettier place. There's no place I'd rather be." After a few steps, he glanced at her and changed the subject: "So, how long are you staying in Wilmington?"

"Until Sunday. I have to go back to work on Monday."

Five more days, he thought.

"Do you know anyone else in town?"

"No. I came down here on my own."

"Why?"

"I just wanted to visit. I'd heard some good things about the place, and I wanted to see it for myself."

He wondered about her answer. "Do you usually take vacations alone?"

"Actually, this is my first time."

A female jogger appeared, moving quickly toward them with a black Labrador retriever by her side. The dog looked spent in the heat, his tongue hanging out too far. Oblivious of the dog's condition, she kept going, eventually veering around Theresa. Garrett almost said something to the woman about it as she passed but didn't think it was his business.

It was a few moments before Garrett spoke again. "Can I ask you a personal question?"

"It depends on the question."

He stopped walking and picked up a couple of small seashells that caught his eye. After turning them over a few times, he handed them to her. "Are you seeing anyone up in Boston?"

She took the shells as she answered. "No."

Lapping waves collected at their feet as they stood in the shallow water. Though he had expected the answer, he couldn't understand why someone like her would spend most of her evenings alone.

"Why not? A woman like you should have your pick of men."

She smiled at that, and they slowly started walking again. "Thanks, that's nice of you to say. But it's not that easy, especially when you have a son. There are a lot of things I have to consider when I meet someone." She paused. "But what about you? Are you seeing anyone right now?"

He shook his head. "No."

"Then it's my turn to ask—why not?"

Garrett shrugged. "I guess I haven't met anyone I'd really like to see on a regular basis."

"Is that all?"

It was a moment of truth, and Garrett knew it. All he had to do was affirm his earlier statement and that would be the end of it. But for a few steps he didn't say anything.

The beach crowd had thinned as they moved farther away from the pier, and the only sound now was that of the crashing waves. Garrett saw a group of terns standing near the water's edge, already moving out of their path. The sun, almost directly overhead now, reflected off the sand and made them both squint a little as they strolled along. Garrett didn't look at her as he spoke, and Theresa moved closer so that she could hear him over the roar of the ocean.

"No, that's not all. It's more of an excuse than anything. To be honest, I haven't even tried to find someone."

Theresa watched him carefully as he spoke. He was looking straight ahead as if gathering his thoughts, but she could sense his reluctance as he went on.

"There was something I didn't tell you last night."

She felt something tighten inside, knowing exactly what was coming. Keeping her face neutral, she said simply: "Oh?"

"I was married once, too," he finally said. "For six years." He turned to her with an expression that made her flinch. "But she passed away."

"I'm sorry," she said quietly.

Again he stopped and picked up some seashells, only this time he didn't hand them to Theresa. After inspecting them casually, he threw one into the oncoming waves. Theresa watched it disappear into the ocean.

"It happened three years ago. Ever since then, I haven't been interested in dating, or even looking." He stopped for a moment, uncomfortable.

"It must get lonely sometimes."

"It does, but I try not to think about that too much. I keep busy at the shop—there's always something to do there—and it helps the days go by. Before I know it, it's time for me to go to bed and I start the whole thing over the next day."

When he finished, he glanced at her with a weak smile. There, he'd said it. He'd wanted to tell someone other than his father for years, and he'd ended up telling it to a woman from Boston he barely knew. A woman who had somehow been able to open doors that he himself had nailed shut.

She said nothing. When he didn't add anything else, she asked: "What was she like?"

"Catherine?" Garrett's throat went dry. "Do you really want to know?"

"Yeah, I do," she said in a gentle voice.

He threw another shell into the surf, gathering his thoughts. How could he hope to describe her in words? Yet part of him wanted to try, wanted Theresa of all people to understand. Despite himself, he was drawn back in time once more.

*"Hey, sweetheart," Catherine said as she looked up from the garden. "I didn't expect you home so soon."*

*"It's been pretty slow in the shop this morning, and I thought I'd pop home for lunch to see how you were doing."*

*"I'm feeling a lot better."*

*"You think it was the flu?"*

*"I don't know. It was probably something I ate. About an hour after you left, I felt good enough to do a little gardening."*

*"I can see that."*

*"How do you like the flowers?" She gestured at a freshly turned patch of soil.*

*Garrett surveyed the freshly planted pansies lining the porch. He smiled. "They're great, but don't you think you should have left some of the dirt in the flower bed?"*

*She wiped her forehead with the back of her hand and stood, squinting up at him in the bright sunlight. "Do I look that bad?"*

*Her knees were dark from kneeling in the dirt, and a streak of mud ran across her cheek. Her hair was escaping from a messy ponytail, and her face was red and sweating from exertion.*

*"You look perfect."*

*Catherine took off her gloves and tossed them on the porch. "I'm not perfect, Garrett, but thanks. C'mon, let me get you some lunch. I know you've got to get back to the shop."*

He sighed and finally turned his head. Theresa was staring at him, waiting. He spoke softly.

"She was everything I ever wanted. She was beautiful and charming, with a quick sense of humor, and she supported me in everything I did. I'd known her practically my whole life—we went to school together. We got married a year after I graduated from UNC. We were married for six years before the accident, and they were the best six years I ever had. When she was taken away . . ." He paused as if he were at a loss for words. "I don't know whether I'll ever get used to being without her."

The way he spoke about Catherine made Theresa hurt for

him more than she would have imagined. It wasn't just his voice, but the look on his face before he described her—as if torn between the beauty of his memories and the pain of remembering. Though the letters had been touching, they hadn't prepared her for this. *I shouldn't have brought it up,* she thought. *I already knew how he felt about her. There wasn't any reason to make him talk about it.*

*But there was,* another voice in her head suddenly chimed in. *You had to see his reaction for yourself. You had to find out whether he was ready to put the past behind him.*

After a few moments, Garrett absently tossed the remaining shells into the water. "I'm sorry about that," he said.

"What?"

"I shouldn't have told you about her. Or so much about me."

"It's okay, Garrett. I wanted to know. I asked you about her, remember?"

"I didn't mean to come off sounding like I did." He spoke as if he'd done something wrong. Theresa's reaction was almost instinctive.

Stepping toward him, she reached for his hand. Taking it slowly in hers, she squeezed it gently. When she looked at him, she saw surprise in his eyes, though he didn't try to pull away.

"You lost a wife—something that most people our age don't know anything about." He lowered his eyes as she struggled for the right words.

"Your feelings say a lot about you. You're the kind of person who loves someone forever. . . . That's nothing to be ashamed of."

"I know. It's just that it's been three years . . ."

"Someday you'll find someone special again. People who've been in love once usually do. It's in their nature."

She squeezed his hand again, and Garrett felt her touch warm him. For some reason he didn't want to let go.

"I hope you're right," he said finally.

"I am. I know these things. I'm a mother, remember?"

He laughed under his breath, trying to release the tension he felt. "I remember. And you're probably a good one."

They turned around and started back to the pier, talking quietly about the last three years, still holding hands. By the time they reached his truck and headed back to the shop, Garrett was more confused than ever. The events of the past two days were just so unexpected. Theresa wasn't just a stranger anymore, nor was she just a friend. There was no question he was drawn to her. But then again, she'd be gone in a few days, and he knew that it was probably better that way.

"What are you thinking?" she asked. Garrett shifted the truck into a higher gear as they made their way over the bridge toward Wilmington and Island Diving. Go ahead, he thought. Tell her what's really going through your head.

"I was thinking," he finally said, surprising himself, "that if you don't have plans tonight, I'd like to have you over for supper."

She smiled. "I was hoping you'd say that."

He was still surprised at himself for asking as he turned left onto the road that led to his shop.

"Can you come by my place about eight? I have some things I have to do at the shop, and I probably won't be able to finish until late."

"That's fine. Where do you live?"

"On Carolina Beach. I'll give you directions when we get to the shop."

They pulled into the lot and Theresa followed Garrett into the office. He scribbled the directions on a slip of paper. Trying not to look as confused as he felt, he said:

"You shouldn't have any trouble finding the place—just look for my truck out front. But if you have any problems, my number's at the bottom."

After she left, Garrett found himself thinking about the upcoming evening. As he sat in his office, two questions plagued him without answer. First, why was he so attracted to Theresa? And second, why did he suddenly feel as if he were betraying Catherine?

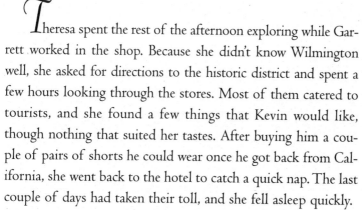

CHAPTER 8

*T*heresa spent the rest of the afternoon exploring while Garrett worked in the shop. Because she didn't know Wilmington well, she asked for directions to the historic district and spent a few hours looking through the stores. Most of them catered to tourists, and she found a few things that Kevin would like, though nothing that suited her tastes. After buying him a couple of pairs of shorts he could wear once he got back from California, she went back to the hotel to catch a quick nap. The last couple of days had taken their toll, and she fell asleep quickly.

Garrett, on the other hand, faced one small crisis after another. A shipment of new equipment arrived just after he got back, and after packing up what he didn't need, he called the company to make arrangements to send back the rest. Later in the afternoon he found out that three people who had been scheduled for dive classes this weekend would be out of town and had to cancel. A quick check of the waiting list proved fruitless.

By six-thirty he was tired, and he breathed a sigh of relief when he finally closed up for the night. After work he drove first to the grocery store and picked up the items he needed for dinner. He showered and put on a pair of clean jeans and a light cotton shirt, then went to the refrigerator to get a beer. After opening it, he stepped out onto the back deck and sat in one of the wrought-iron chairs. Checking his watch, he realized that Theresa would be here soon.

Garrett was still sitting on the back porch when he finally heard the sound of a slowly idling motor making its way down the block. He stepped off the deck and went around the side of the house, watching as Theresa parked on the street, right behind his truck.

She stepped out wearing jeans and the same blouse she had worn earlier, the one that did wonderful things for her figure. She looked relaxed as she walked toward him, and when she smiled warmly at him, he realized that his attraction had grown stronger since their lunch this afternoon, and it made him a little uneasy for a reason he didn't want to admit.

He walked toward her as casually as he could, and Theresa met him halfway, carrying a bottle of white wine. When he got close to her, he smelled the scent of perfume, something she hadn't worn before.

"I brought some wine," she said, handing it to him. "I

thought it might go well with dinner." Then, after a short pause: "How was your afternoon?"

"It was busy. Customers kept coming in until we closed, and I had a load of paperwork I had to get through. In fact, I just got home a little while ago." He started toward the front door, Theresa right beside him. "How about you? What did you end up doing the rest of the day?"

"I got to take a nap," she said as if teasing him, and he laughed.

"I forgot to ask you earlier, but do you want anything special for dinner?" he asked.

"What were you planning on?"

"I was thinking of cooking some steaks on the grill, but then I got to wondering if you ate things like that."

"Are you kidding? You forget I grew up in Nebraska. I love a good steak."

"Then you're in for a pleasant surprise."

"What?"

"I happen to make the best steaks in the world."

"Oh, you do, huh?"

"I'll prove it to you," he said, and she laughed, a melodic sound.

As they approached the door, Theresa looked at the house for the first time. It was relatively small—one story and rectangular shaped—with painted wooden siding that was peeling badly in more than one place. Unlike the homes on Wrightsville Beach, this home sat directly on the sand. When she asked him why it wasn't raised like the other houses, he explained that the house was built before the hurricane building codes went into effect. "Now the houses have to be elevated so that the tidal surge can

pass under the main structure. The next big hurricane will probably wash this old house out to sea, but I've been fortunate so
far."

"Don't you worry about that?"

"Not really. There's not much to the place, and that's the only
reason I could afford it. I think the former owner finally got
tired of all the stress every time a big storm started moving
across the Atlantic."

They reached the cracked front steps and walked inside. The
first thing Theresa noticed upon entering was the view from the
main room. The windows extended from the floor to the ceiling
and ran along the entire back side of the house, overlooking the
back deck and Carolina Beach.

"This view is incredible," she said, surprised.

"It is, isn't it? I've been here for a few years now, but I still
don't take it for granted."

Off to one side was a fireplace, surrounded by a dozen underwater photographs. She moved toward them. "Do you mind
if I look around?"

"No, go ahead. I have to get the grill out back ready anyway.
It needs a bit of cleaning."

Garrett left through the sliding glass door.

After he left, Theresa looked at the pictures for a while, then
toured the rest of the house. Like many beach houses she had
seen, there wasn't room for more than one or two people to live
here. There was only one bedroom, reached by a door off the
living room. Like the main room, it also had floor-to-ceiling
windows that overlooked the beach. The front portion of the
house—the side closest to the street—contained a kitchen, a
small dining area (not quite a room), and the bathroom. Though

everything was tidy, the house looked as though it hadn't been updated in years.

Returning to the main room, she stopped at his bedroom and glanced inside. Again she saw underwater photographs decorating the walls. In addition, there was a large map of the North Carolina coast that hung directly over his bed, documenting the location of almost five hundred shipwrecks. When she looked toward his nightstand, she saw a framed picture of a woman. Making sure that Garrett was still outside cleaning the grill, she stepped in to take a closer look.

Catherine must have been in her mid-twenties when it was taken. Like the photos on the walls, it looked as though Garrett had taken it himself, and she wondered whether it had been framed before or after the accident. Picking it up, she saw that Catherine was attractive—a little more petite than she was—with blond hair that hung to midshoulder. Even though the picture was slightly grainy and looked as if it had been reproduced from a smaller photo, she still noticed Catherine's eyes. Deep green and almost catlike, they gave her an exotic look and almost seemed as if they were staring back at her. She put the photo down gently, making sure it was set in the same angle it was before. Turning around, she continued to feel as if Catherine were watching her every move.

Ignoring the sensation, she looked at the mirror attached to his chest of drawers. Surprisingly, there was only one more photo that included Catherine. It was a picture of Garrett and Catherine smiling broadly, standing on the deck of *Happenstance*. Because the boat looked as if it had already been restored, she assumed the picture must have been taken only a few months before she died.

Knowing he could enter the house at any time, she left his bedroom, feeling a little guilty about poking around in the first place. She walked to the sliding glass doors that led from the main room onto the deck and opened them. Garrett was cleaning the grill top and smiled at her when he heard her come out. She strolled to the edge of the deck where he was working and leaned against one of the rails, one leg over the other.

"Did you take all the photos on the walls?" she asked.

He used the back of his hand to wipe the hair from his face. "Yeah. For a while there, I took my camera out on most of my dives. I hung most of them at the shop, but because I had so many, I thought I'd put some up here as well."

"They look professional."

"Thanks. But I think their quality had more to do with the sheer volume I took. You should have seen all the ones that didn't come out."

As he spoke, Garrett held up the grill top. Although it was charred black in places, it looked ready, and he set it off to one side. He reached for a bag of charcoal and dumped some into a grill that looked thirty years old, using his hand to make sure they were spread evenly. Then he added a bit of lighter fluid, soaking each briquette for just a moment.

She spoke in the same teasing voice she had used before. "You know, they have propane grills now."

"I know, but I like to do it the way we did it growing up. Besides, it tastes better this way. Cooking with propane is just like cooking inside."

She smiled. "And you did promise me the best steak I've ever had."

"And you'll get it. Trust me."

He finished with the lighter fluid and set it by the bag of charcoal. "I'm going to let this soak for a couple of minutes. Do you want anything to drink?"

Theresa asked, "What do you have?"

Garrett cleared his throat. "Beer, soda, or the wine you brought."

"A beer sounds good."

Garrett picked up the charcoal and lighter fluid and put them in an old sea chest that sat next to the house. After dusting the sand off the bottoms of his shoes, he went inside, leaving the sliding glass door open.

While he was gone, Theresa turned and looked up and down the beach. Now that the sun was going down, most of the people were gone, and the few that were left were jogging or walking. Even though the beach wasn't crowded, more than a dozen people went past the house in the short time he was gone.

"Do you ever get tired of having all these people around?" she asked when he returned.

He handed her the beer. "Not really. I'm not here all that much anyway. Usually by the time I get home, the beach is pretty much deserted. And in the winter, no one is out here at all."

For just a moment, she imagined him sitting on his deck, watching the water, alone as always. Garrett reached into his pocket and took out a box of matches. He lit the charcoals, stepping back when the flames shot up. The light breeze made the fire dance in circles.

"Now that the coals are started, I'm going to get supper going."

"Can I give you a hand with something?"

"There's not much to do," he answered. "But if you're lucky, maybe I'll share my secret recipe with you."

She cocked her head and looked at him slyly. "You know you're setting a pretty high standard for these steaks."

"I know. But I have faith."

He winked at her and she laughed before following him inside, to the kitchen. Garrett opened one of the cabinets and pulled out a couple of potatoes. Standing in front of the sink, he washed his hands first and then the potatoes. After turning on the oven, he wrapped the potatoes in foil and set them on the rack.

"What can I do?"

"Like I said, not much. I think I've got it pretty much in control. I bought one of those prepackaged salads, and there's not anything else on the menu."

Theresa stood off to one side as Garrett put the last of the potatoes in the oven and got the salad out of the refrigerator. From the corner of his eye, he glanced at her as he emptied the salad into a bowl. What was it about her that made him suddenly want to be as close to her as possible? Wondering, he opened the refrigerator and pulled out the steaks he'd had the store cut just for tonight. He opened the cabinet next to the refrigerator and found the rest of the items he needed. After collecting them, he set everything down next to Theresa.

She shot him a challenging smile. "So, what's so special about these steaks?"

Clearing his mind, he poured some brandy into a shallow bowl. "There's a few things. First, you get a couple of thick filets like these. The store doesn't usually cut them this thick, so you have to ask for it special. Then you season them with a little salt, pepper, and garlic powder, and you let them soak in the brandy while the coals are turning white."

He did this as he spoke, and for the first time since she'd met him, he looked his age. Based on what he'd told her, he was at least four years younger than she was.

"That's your secret?"

"It's only the beginning," he promised, suddenly aware of how beautiful she looked. "Right before they go on the grill, I'll add some tenderizer. The rest of it involves *how* you cook them, not what they're flavored with."

"You sound like you're quite a cook."

"No, not really. I'm good with a few things, but I don't prepare many meals these days. By the time I get home, I'm usually in the mood for something that doesn't take much effort."

"That's how I am. If it wasn't for Kevin, I don't think I'd cook very much at all anymore."

Since he was finished with the steaks for now, he went to the drawer again and found a knife, returning to her side. He reached for a couple of tomatoes that were on the counter and began dicing.

"It sounds like you have a great relationship with Kevin."

"I do. I just hope it continues. He's almost a teenager now, and I worry that when he gets older, he's going to want to spend less time with me."

"I wouldn't worry too much. From the way you talk about him, I would think that you two will always be close."

"I hope so. Right now, he's all I have—I don't know what I'd do if he started to shut me out of his life. I have some friends with boys a little older than he is, and they tell me it's inevitable."

"I'm sure he's going to change somewhat. Everyone does, but that doesn't mean he won't talk to you."

She looked over at him. "Are you talking from experience or just telling me what I want to hear?"

He shrugged, again noticing her perfume. "I'm just remembering what I went through with my father. We'd always been close growing up, and it didn't change when I started high school. I started doing different things and seeing my friends more, but we still talked all the time."

"I hope it's the same way for me," she said.

With the preparation under way, a peaceful silence descended upon them. The simple act of cutting tomatoes with her by his side eased some of the anxiety he'd felt up to this point. Theresa was the first woman he'd invited to this house, and Garrett realized there was something comfortable about having her here.

When he finished, Garrett put the tomatoes in the salad bowl and wiped his hands on a paper towel. Then he bent over to remove his second beer.

"Are you up for another?"

She drained the last of her bottle, surprised she had finished so quickly. She nodded, setting the empty bottle on the counter. Garrett twisted off the bottlecap and handed her another, opening one for himself. Theresa was relaxing against the counter, and when she took the bottle, something about the way she was standing struck him as familiar: the smile playing across her lips, maybe, or the slant of her gaze as she watched him lift his own bottle to his mouth. He was reminded again of that lazy summer afternoon with Catherine, when he'd come home to surprise her for lunch—a day that in retrospect seemed so fraught with signs . . . yet how could he have foreseen everything that would happen? They had stood in the kitchen, just as he and Theresa were doing now.

*"I take it you've already eaten," Garrett said as Catherine stood in front of the open refrigerator.*

*Catherine glanced at him. "I'm not very hungry," she said. "But I am thirsty. Do you want some iced tea?"*

*"Tea sounds great. Do you know if the mail came in yet?"*

*Catherine nodded as she pulled the pitcher of tea from the top shelf. "It's on the table."*

*She opened the cupboard and reached for two glasses. After setting the first glass on the counter, she was pouring the second when it slipped from her hand.*

*"Are you all right?" Garrett dropped the mail, concerned.*

*Catherine ran her hand through her hair, embarrassed, then bent to pick up the glass shards. "I just got a little woozy there for a second. I'll be okay."*

*Garrett moved toward her and began to help clean up. "Are you feeling sick again?"*

*"No, but maybe I spent too much time outside this morning."*

*He was quiet for a moment as he picked up the glass.*

*"Are you sure I should go back to work? This last week's been pretty tough on you."*

*"I'll be fine. Besides, I know you've got a lot to do there."*

*Though she was right, when he finally started back to work, he got the feeling that maybe he shouldn't have listened to her.*

He swallowed hard, suddenly aware of the stillness in the kitchen. "I'm going to check the coals to see how they're doing," he said, needing something, anything, to do. "Hopefully, they're getting close."

"Can I set the table while you're checking?"

"Sure. Most of the things you'll need are right over here."

After showing her where to find what she needed, he headed outside, forcing himself to relax and clearing his mind of the ghostly memories. Once he reached the grill, he checked the coals, putting his mind to the task at hand. Almost white, they had another few minutes, he figured. Again he went to the sea chest, and this time he removed a small, handheld bellows. He set it on the railing next to the grill and took a deep breath. The ocean air was fresh, almost intoxicating, and for the first time, he suddenly realized that despite his vision of Catherine just moments ago, he was still pleased that Theresa was here. In fact, he felt happy, something he hadn't felt in a long time.

It wasn't only in the way they got along, but it was little things Theresa did. The way she smiled, the way she looked at him, even the way she'd taken his hand earlier this afternoon—it was already beginning to feel as if he knew her longer than he actually did. He wondered whether it was because she was similar to Catherine in so many ways or whether his father had been right about him needing to spend some time with another person.

While he was outside, Theresa set the table. She put a wineglass beside each plate and sorted through the drawer for some silverware. Beside the utensils were two candles with small holders for each. After wondering whether it would be too much, she decided to put them on the table as well. She would leave it to him whether or not to light them. Garrett came in just as she was finishing up.

"We've got a couple of minutes. Would you like to sit outside while we wait?"

Theresa picked up her beer and followed him out. As it had the night before, the breeze was blowing, but it wasn't nearly as strong. She sat in one of the chairs, Garrett right beside her, his legs crossed at the ankles. His light shirt brought out his deeply tanned skin, and Theresa watched him as he stared out over the water. She closed her eyes for a moment, feeling more alive than she had in a long time.

"I bet you don't have a view like this from where you live in Boston," he said into the sudden silence.

"You're right," she said, "I don't. I live in an apartment. My parents think I'm crazy for living downtown. They think I should live in the suburbs."

"Why don't you?"

"I used to, before the divorce. But now, it's just a lot easier. I can get to work in just a few minutes, Kevin's school is right down the block, and I never have to take the highway unless I'm going out of town. Besides, I wanted something different after my marriage ended. I just couldn't handle the looks my neighbors gave me after they found out that David had left."

"What do you mean?"

She shrugged, and her voice softened. "I never told any of them why David and I separated. I just didn't think it was any of their business."

"It wasn't."

She paused for a moment, remembering. "I know that, but in their minds, David was a wonderful husband. He was handsome and successful, and they didn't want to believe that he did anything wrong. Even when we were together, he acted as if everything were perfect. I didn't have any idea he was having an affair until the very end."

She turned toward him, a rueful look on her face. "As they say, the wife is always the last to know."

"How did you find out?"

She shook her head. "I know it sounds like a cliché, but I found out from the dry cleaner, of all people. When I picked up his clothes, the cleaner handed me some receipts that had been in his pocket. One was from a hotel downtown. And I knew from the date that he had been home that evening, so it must have been for just an afternoon. He denied it when I confronted him, but by the way he looked at me, I knew he was lying. Eventually, the whole story came out, and I filed for divorce."

Garrett listened quietly, letting her finish, wondering how she could have fallen in love with someone who would do that to her. As if reading his mind, she went on:

"You know, David was one of those men who could say anything and make you believe it. I think he even believed most of the things he told me. We met in college, and I was overwhelmed by how much he had going for him. He was smart and charming, and I was flattered that he was interested in someone like me. Here I was, a young girl straight from Nebraska, and he was unlike anyone I'd ever met before. And when we got married, I thought I'd have a storybook life. But I guess it was the furthest thing from his mind. I found out later that he had his first affair only five months after we were married."

She stopped for a moment, and Garrett looked toward his beer. "I don't know what to say."

"There's nothing you can say," she said with finality. "It's over, and like I said yesterday, the only thing I want from him now is for him to be a good father to Kevin."

"You make it sound so easy."

"I don't mean to. David hurt me pretty badly, and it took me a couple of years and more than a few sessions with a good therapist to get to this point. I learned a lot from my therapist, and I learned a lot about myself along the way. Once, when I was babbling about what a jerk he had been, she pointed out that if I kept holding on to my anger, he'd still be controlling me, and I wasn't willing to accept that. So I let it go."

She took another sip of her beer. Garrett asked: "Did your therapist say anything else that you remember?"

She thought for a moment, then smiled faintly. "As a matter of fact, she did. She said that if I ever came across someone who reminded me of David that I should turn around and run for the hills."

"Do I remind you of David?"

"Not in the slightest. You're about as different from David as a man can get."

"That's good," he said with mock seriousness. "There aren't many hills in this part of the country, you know. You'd have to run a mighty long way."

She giggled, and Garrett looked over at the grill. Seeing that the coals were ready, he asked, "Are you ready to start the steaks?"

"Will you show me the rest of your secret recipe?"

"With pleasure," he said as they rose from their seats. In the kitchen he found the tenderizer and sprinkled some on the top of the steaks. Then, removing both filets from the brandy, he added some to the other sides as well. He opened the refrigerator and pulled out a small plastic bag.

"What's that?" Theresa asked.

"It's tallow—the fatty part of the steak that's usually trimmed off. I had the butcher save some when I bought the steaks."

"What's it for?"

"You'll see," he said.

After returning to the grill with the steaks and a pair of tongs, he set them on the railing beside the bellows. Then, taking the bellows he'd removed earlier, he began to blow the ashes off the briquettes, explaining to her what he was doing.

"Part of cooking a great steak is making sure the coals are hot. You use the bellows to blow off the ashes. That way, you don't have anything blocking the heat."

He put the grill top back on the barbecue, let it heat for about a minute, then used the tongs to put on the steaks. "How do you like your steak?"

"Medium rare."

"With steaks this size, that's about eleven minutes on each side."

She raised her eyebrows. "You're very precise about all this, aren't you?"

"I promised you a good steak, and I intend to deliver."

In the little while it took to cook the steaks, Garrett watched Theresa out of the corner of his eye. There was something sensual about her figure, outlined against the setting sun. The sky was turning orange, and the warm light made her look especially beautiful, darkening her brown eyes. Her hair lifted tantalizingly in the evening breeze.

"What are you thinking?"

He tensed at the sound of her voice, suddenly realizing he hadn't said anything since he'd started cooking.

"I was just thinking about what a jerk your ex-husband was," he said, turning toward her, and he saw her smile. She patted his shoulder gently.

"But if I was still married, I wouldn't be here with you."

"And that," he said, still feeling her touch, "would be a shame."

"Yes, it would," she echoed, their eyes lingering for a moment. Finally Garrett turned away and reached for the tallow. Clearing his throat:

"I think we're ready for this now."

He took the tallow, which had been cut into smaller pieces, and put the pieces on the briquettes, directly beneath the steaks. Then, he leaned over and blew on them until they burst into flame.

"What are you doing?"

"The flames from the tallow will sear in the juices and keep the steak tender. That's the same reason you use tongs instead of a fork."

He threw a few more pieces of tallow onto the briquettes and repeated the process. Looking around, Theresa commented:

"It's so peaceful out here. I can see why you bought the place."

He finished what he was doing and took another drink of beer, wetting his throat. "There's something about the ocean that does that to people. I think that's why so many people come here to relax."

She turned toward him. "Tell me, Garrett, what do you think about when you're out here alone?"

"A lot of things."

"Anything in particular?"

I think about Catherine, he wanted to say but didn't.

He sighed. "No, not really. Sometimes I think about work, sometimes I think about the new places I want to explore on my dives. Other times, I dream about sailing away and leaving every-thing behind."

She watched him carefully as he spoke the last words. "Could you really do that? Sail away and never come back?"

"I'm not sure, but I like to think I could. Unlike you, I don't have any family except for my father, and in a way, I think he'd understand. He and I are a lot alike, and I think that if it wasn't for me, he would have taken off a long time ago."

"But that would be like running away."

"I know."

"Why would you want to do that?" she pressed, somehow knowing the answer. When he didn't respond, she leaned close to him and spoke gently.

"Garrett, I know it's not any of my business, but you can't run away from what you're going through." She gave him a reassur-ing smile. "And besides, you've got so much to offer someone."

Garrett stayed silent, thinking about what she'd said, won-dering how she seemed to know exactly what to say to make him feel better.

For the next few minutes, the only sounds around them came from elsewhere. Garrett turned the steaks, and they sizzled on the grill. The gentle evening breeze made a distant wind chime sing. Waves rolled up on the shore, a soothing, continuous roar.

Garrett's mind drifted through the last two days. He thought about the moment he'd first seen her, the hours they'd spent on *Happenstance*, and their walk on the beach earlier in the day when he'd first told her about Catherine. The tension he'd felt earlier in the day was almost gone now, and as they stood beside each other in the deepening twilight, he sensed that there was some-thing more to this evening than either of them wanted to admit.

Just before the steaks were ready, Theresa went back inside to get the rest of the table ready. She pulled the potatoes out of the oven, unwrapped the foil, and placed one on each plate. The salad came next, and she set it in the middle of the table, along with a couple of different dressings she had found in the refrigerator door. Last, she put down salt, pepper, butter, and a couple of napkins. Because it was getting dark inside the house, she turned on the kitchen light, but that seemed too bright. She switched it off again. On impulse, she went ahead and lit the candles, standing back from the table to see if it was too much. Thinking it looked about right, she picked up the bottle of wine and was placing it on the table just as Garrett came inside.

After closing the sliding glass door, Garrett saw what she had done. It was dark in the kitchen except for the small flames pointing upward, and the glow made Theresa look beautiful. Her dark hair looked mysterious in the candlelight, and her eyes seemed to capture the moving flames. Unable to speak for a long moment, all Garrett could do was stare at her, and it was in that moment that he knew exactly what he'd been trying to deny to himself all along.

"I thought these would be a nice touch," she said quietly.

"I think you're right."

They continued to watch each other from across the room, both frozen for a moment by the shadow of distant possibilities. Then Theresa glanced away.

"I couldn't find a wine opener," she said, grasping for something to say.

"I'll get it," he said quickly. "I don't use it very often, so it's probably buried in one of the drawers."

He carried the plate of steaks to the table, then went to the drawer. After sorting through the utensils toward the back, he found the opener and brought it to the table. In a couple of easy moves, he opened the bottle and poured just the right amount into each glass. Then, sitting down, he used the tongs to put the steaks on each of their plates.

"It's the moment of truth," she said right before taking her first bite. Garrett smiled as he watched her try it. Theresa was pleasantly surprised to find out that he had been right all along.

"Garrett, this is delicious," she said earnestly.

"Thank you."

The candles burned lower as the evening wore on, and Garrett twice told her how glad he was that she had come this evening. Both times Theresa felt something tingle in the back of her neck and had to take another sip of wine just to make the feeling go away.

Outside, the ocean slowly rose toward high tide, driven by a crescent moon that had seemingly come from nowhere.

After dinner, Garrett suggested another walk along the beach. "It's really beautiful at night," he said. When she agreed, he picked up the plates and silverware from the table and put them in the sink.

They left the kitchen and walked outside, Garrett closing the door behind him. The night was mild. They stepped off the deck, making their way over a small sand dune and onto the beach itself.

When they reached the water's edge, they repeated their actions of earlier that day, slipping off their shoes and leaving them on the beach, since no one else was around. They walked slowly, close to each other. Surprising her, Garrett reached for her hand. Feeling his warmth, Theresa wondered for just a moment what it would be like to have him touch her body, lingering over her skin. The thought made something inside her tighten, and when she glanced over at him, she wondered if he knew what she'd been thinking.

They continued strolling, both of them taking in the evening. "I haven't had a night like this in a long time," Garrett said finally, his voice sounding almost like a remembrance.

"Neither have I," she said.

The sand was cool beneath their feet. "Garrett, do you remember when you first asked me to go sailing?" Theresa asked.

"Yes."

"Why did you ask me to go with you?"

He looked at her curiously. "What do you mean?"

"I mean that you looked almost like you regretted it the moment you said it."

He shrugged. "I'm not sure that regret is the word I'd use. I think I was surprised that I asked, but I didn't regret it."

She smiled. "Are you sure?"

"Yeah, I'm sure. You have to remember that I haven't asked anyone out in over three years. When you said that you had never gone sailing before—I think it just sort of hit me that I was tired of always being alone."

"You mean I was in the right place at the right time?"

He shook his head. "I didn't mean it to sound like that. I wanted to take you out with me—I don't think I would have offered if it had been someone else. Besides, this whole thing has turned out much better than I thought it would. These last couple of days have been the best days I've had in a long time."

She felt warm inside at what he'd said. As they walked, she

felt him slowly moving his thumb, tracing small circles on her skin. He went on.

"Did you think your vacation would be anything like this?"

She hesitated, deciding it wasn't the right time to tell him the truth.

"No."

They walked together quietly. There were a few others on the beach, though they were far enough away that Theresa couldn't make out anything but shadows.

"Do you think you'll ever come back here again? I mean for another vacation?"

"I don't know. Why?"

"Because I was kind of hoping you would."

In the distance, she could see lights along a faraway pier. Again she felt his hand moving against hers.

"Would you make dinner for me again if I did?"

"I'd cook you anything you want. As long as it's a steak."

She laughed under her breath. "Then I'll consider it. I promise."

"How about if I threw in a few scuba lessons as well?"

"I think Kevin would enjoy that more than me."

"Then bring him along."

She glanced over at him. "You wouldn't mind?"

"Not at all. I'd love to meet him."

"I bet you'd like him."

"I know I would."

They walked along in silence, until Theresa blurted out, "Garrett—can I ask you something?"

"Sure."

"I know this is going to sound strange, but . . ."

She paused for a moment, and he looked at her quizzically. "What?"

"What's the worst thing you've ever done?"

He laughed aloud. "Where did that come from?"

"I just want to know. I always ask people that question. It lets me know what people are really all about."

"The worst thing?"

"The absolute worst."

He thought for a moment. "I guess I would say that the worst thing I've ever done is when a bunch of my friends and I went out one night in December—we were drinking and raising hell when we ended up driving by a street that was totally decorated in Christmas lights. Well, we parked and right there and then proceeded to unscrew and steal every light bulb we could."

"You didn't!"

"We did. There were five of us, and we filled the back of the truck with stolen Christmas lights. And we left the strands— that was the worst part. It looked like the Grinch had come wandering down the street. We were out there for almost two hours, laughing uproariously about what we were doing. The street had been featured in the newspaper as one of the most decorated streets in the city, and when we were done . . . I can't imagine what those people thought. They must have been furious."

"That's terrible!"

He laughed again. "I know. Thinking back, I know it was terrible. But at the time, it was hilarious."

"And here I was, thinking you're such a nice guy. . . ."

"I am a nice guy."

"You were the Grinch." She pressed on, curious. "So what else did you and your friends do?"

"Do you really want to know?"

"Yeah, I do."

He began to regale her then with tales of other teenage mis-adventures—from soaping car windows to tepeeing the houses of former girlfriends. Once, he claimed, he saw one of his friends driving alongside him while he was on a date. After his friend motioned for him to roll down the window, he did—and his friend promptly launched a bottle rocket into his car that ex-ploded at his feet.

Twenty minutes later he was still telling stories, much to her amusement. When he finally finished, he asked her the same question that had originally started the conversation.

"Oh, I've never done anything like you," she said almost coyly. "I've always been a good girl."

He laughed again then, feeling as if he'd been manipulated—not that he minded—and knowing full well that she wasn't telling the truth.

They walked the full length of the beach, exchanging addi-tional stories from childhood. Theresa tried to imagine him as a young man while he spoke, wondering what she would have thought about him had she met him while she was in college. Would she have found him as compelling as she did now, or would she have fallen for David again? She wanted to believe that she would have appreciated the differences between them, but would she? David had seemed so perfect back then.

They stopped for a moment and looked out over the water. He stood close to her, their shoulders barely touching.

"What are you thinking?" Garrett asked.

"I was just thinking how nice the silence is with you."

He smiled. "And I was just thinking that I've told you a lot of things I don't tell anyone."

"Is that because you know I'm going back to Boston and I won't tell anyone?"

He chuckled. "No, it's not that at all."

"Then what is it?"

He looked at her curiously. "You don't know?"

"No."

She smiled when she said it, almost daring him to continue. He wondered how to explain something he had difficulty understanding himself. Then, after a long moment in which he gathered his thoughts, he spoke quietly:

"I guess it's because I wanted you to know who I really am. Because if you really know me, and still want to spend time with me . . ."

Theresa said nothing but knew exactly what he was trying to say. Garrett looked away.

"I'm sorry about that. I didn't mean to make you feel uncomfortable."

"It didn't make me feel uncomfortable," Theresa began. "I'm glad you said it. . . ."

She paused. After a moment they slowly started walking again.

"But you don't feel the same way I do."

She looked over at him. "Garrett . . . I . . ." She trailed off.

"No, you don't have to say anything—"

She didn't let him finish. "Yes, I do. You want an answer, and I want to tell you." She paused, thinking of the best way to say

it. Then, taking a deep breath: "After David and I split up, I
went through an awful period. And just when I thought I was
getting over it, I started to date again. But the men I met . . . I
don't know, it just seemed like the world changed while I was
married. They all wanted things, but none of them wanted to
give. I guess I got jaded about men in general."

"I don't know what to say. . . ."

"Garrett, I'm not telling you this because I think you're like
that. I think you're the furthest thing from it. And it scares me
a little. Because if I tell you how much I care for you . . . in a
way, I'm telling myself the same thing. And if I do that, then I
guess I'm opening up myself to get hurt again."

"I'd never hurt you," he said gently.

She stopped walking and made him face her. She spoke
quietly.

"I know you believe that, Garrett. But you've been dealing
with your own demons for the past three years. I don't know if
you're ready to go on yet, and if you're not, then I'm going to be
the one who gets hurt."

The words hit hard, and it took a moment for him to respond. Garrett willed her to meet his eyes.

"Theresa . . . since we met . . . I don't know . . ."

He stopped, realizing that he wasn't able to put into words
the way he was feeling.

Instead he raised his hand and touched the side of her face
with his finger, tracing so lightly that it felt almost like a feather
against her skin. The moment he touched her, she closed her
eyes and despite her uncertainty let the tingling feeling travel
through her body, warming her neck and breasts.

With that, she felt everything begin to slip away, and suddenly it felt right to be here. The dinner they had shared, their walk on the beach, the way he was looking at her now—she couldn't imagine anything better than what was happening at this very moment.

Waves rolled up on the beach, wetting their feet. The warm summer breeze blew through her hair, heightening the sensation of his touch. The moonlight lent an ethereal sheen to the water, while the clouds cast shadows along the beach, making the landscape seem almost unreal.

They gave in then to everything that had been building since the moment they met. She sank into him, feeling the warmth of his body, and he released her hand. Then, slowly wrapping both arms around her, he drew her against him and kissed her softly on the lips. After pulling back slightly to look at her, he gently kissed her again. She kissed him back, feeling his hand run up along her back and settle into her hair, burying his fingers in it.

They stood with their arms around each other, kissing in the moonlight for a long time, neither of them caring if anyone could see them. They had both waited too long for this moment, and when they finally pulled back, they stared at each other. Then, taking his hand again, Theresa slowly led him back to his house.

It seemed like a dream as they moved inside. Garrett kissed her again immediately after closing the door, more passionately this time, and Theresa felt her body tremble with anticipation. She walked to the kitchen, picked up the two candles from the table, and led him to the bedroom. She put the candles on his bureau, and he pulled the matches from his pocket, lighting them as she walked to the windows and began to close the curtains.

Garrett was standing by the bureau when she returned to him. Standing close again, she ran her hands over his chest, feeling the tight muscles beneath his shirt, giving in to her own sensuality. Looking in his eyes, she untucked his shirt and slowly began to pull it up over his torso. Raising his arms, she slipped it over his head and leaned into him, listening as it dropped to the floor. She kissed his chest, then his neck, shivering as his hands moved to the front of her blouse. Giving him room, she leaned back as he slowly worked his way downward, unbuttoning each button carefully.

When her blouse fell open, he slid his arms around her back and pulled her to him, feeling the heat of her skin against his. He kissed her neck and nibbled on her earlobe as his hands traced the outline of her spine. She parted her lips, feeling the tenderness of his touch. His fingers stopped at her bra, and he unfastened it with an expert twist, making her breath catch. Then, continuing to kiss her, he pulled the straps over her shoulders, freeing her breasts. He bent down and kissed them tenderly, one at a time, and she leaned her head back, feeling his heated breath and the moisture from his mouth wherever it touched her.

She was short of breath as she reached for the snap on his jeans. Meeting his eyes again, she unsnapped them, then slowly slid the zipper down. Still watching him, she ran her finger across his waist, skimming her nail softly against his navel before tugging on the waist of his pants. They loosened slightly and he stepped back for a moment, removing them. Then, stepping in to kiss her again, he lifted her in his arms and gently carried her across the room, putting her on the bed.

Lying beside him, she ran her hands over his chest again, now damp with perspiration, and felt his hands gently move on to her jeans. He unsnapped them, and lifting her bottom slightly, she took them off, one leg at a time, while his hands continued to explore her body. She caressed his back and bit softly on his neck, listening as breathing quickened. He began to take off his boxer shorts while she slipped off her own panties, and when they were finally naked, their bodies pressed together.

She was beautiful in the candlelight. He ran his tongue between her breasts, down her belly, and past her navel and up again. Her hair caught the light, making it sparkle, and her skin was soft and inviting as they clung to each other. He felt her hands on his back, pulling him closer.

Instead he continued to kiss her body, not rushing the moment. He put the side of his face to her belly and rubbed gently. The stubble on his chin felt erotic against her skin, and she lay back on the bed, her hands in his hair. He went on until she couldn't take it anymore, then he moved up and did the same thing to her breasts.

She pulled him back to her, arching her back as he slowly moved atop her. He kissed her fingertips one at a time, and as they finally joined as one, she closed her eyes with a sigh. Kissing softly, they made love with a passion kept stifled for the last three years.

Their bodies moved as one, each of them fully aware of the other's needs, each trying to please the other. Garrett kissed her almost continually, the moistness of his mouth lingering wherever it touched, and she felt her body began to tingle with the growing urgency of something wonderful. When it finally happened, she pressed her fingers hard into his back, but the moment it ended another one started to build again and she began to climax in long sequences, one right after the next. When they finished making love, Theresa was exhausted, and she wrapped her arms around him, holding him close. She relaxed by his side, his hands still gently tracing her skin, and she watched as the candles slowly burned toward their base, reliving the moment they had just shared together.

They lay together for most of the night, making love again and again, holding each other tightly afterward. Theresa fell asleep in his arms, feeling wonderful, and Garrett watched as she slept beside him. Just before he fell asleep, he gently brushed her hair from her face, trying hard to remember everything.

Right before daybreak, Theresa opened her eyes, realizing instinctively that he was gone. She turned in the bed, looking for him. Not seeing him, she rose and went to his closet, finding a bathrobe. Wrapping it around her, she left the bedroom and glanced toward the darkness of the kitchen. Not there. She looked in the living room, but he wasn't there, either, and suddenly she knew exactly where he would be.

Stepping outside, she found him sitting in the chair, wearing only his boxers and a gray sweatshirt. Turning around, he saw her and smiled.

"Hey there."

She stepped toward him, and he motioned for her to sit in his lap. He kissed her as he pulled her to him, and she put her arms around his neck. Then, pulling back when she sensed that something was wrong, she touched his cheek.

"You all right?"

It took a moment for him to answer.

"Yeah," he said, quietly, without looking at her.

"You sure?"

He nodded, again without meeting her eyes, and she used her finger to make him face her. She said gently:

"You look sort of . . . sad."

He gave a weak smile without answering.

"Are you sad about what happened?"

"No," he said. "Not at all. I don't regret any of it."

"Then what is it?"

He didn't answer, and again his eyes shifted away.

She spoke softly. "Are you out here because of Catherine?"

He waited for a moment without answering, then took her hand in his. Finally he met her gaze.

"No. I'm not out here because of Catherine," he said, almost whispering the words. "I'm out here because of you."

Then, with a tenderness that reminded her of a small child, he gently pulled her close and held her without saying another word, not letting go until the sky began to lighten and the first person appeared on the beach.

What do you mean, you can't have lunch with me today? We've been doing this for years—how could you forget?"

"I didn't forget, Dad, I just can't do it today. We'll pick it up again next week, okay?"

Jeb Blake paused on the other end of the phone, drumming his fingers on the desktop.

"Why do I get the feeling you're not telling me something?"

"There's nothing to tell."

"You sure?"

"Yeah, I'm sure."

Theresa called to Garrett from the shower, asking him to bring her a towel. Garrett covered the mouthpiece and told her he'd be right there. When he returned his attention to the phone, he heard his father inhale sharply.

"What was that?"

"Nothing."

Then, in a tone of sudden understanding: "That Theresa gal's there, isn't she?"

Knowing he couldn't hide the truth from him now, Garrett replied: "Yeah, she's here."

Jeb whistled, obviously pleased. "It's about damn time."

Garrett tried to downplay it. "Dad, don't make a big deal out of this. . . ."

"I won't—I promise."

"Thanks."

"But can I ask you something?"

"Sure." Garrett sighed.

"Does she make you happy?"

It took a moment for him to answer. "Yeah, she does," he said finally.

"It's about damn time," he said again with a laugh before hanging up. Garrett stared at the phone as he replaced it in its cradle.

"She really does," he whispered to himself with a small smile on his face. "She really does."


Theresa emerged from the bedroom a few minutes later, looking rested and fresh. Smelling coffee brewing, she went to the kitchen for a cup. After putting a piece of bread in the toaster, Garrett walked to her side.

"Good morning, again," he said, kissing the back of her neck.

"Good morning again to you, too."

"Sorry about leaving the bedroom last night."

"Hey, it's okay. . . . I understand."

"You mean that?"

"Of course I do." She turned and faced him with a smile. "I had a wonderful night."

"So did I," he said. Fishing a coffee cup out of the cupboard for Theresa, he asked over his shoulder, "Do you want to do something today? I called the shop and told them I wasn't coming in."

"What did you have in mind?"

"How about showing you around Wilmington?"

"We could do that." She didn't sound convinced.

"Did you have anything else you wanted to do instead?"

"How about we just sort of hang around here today?"

"And do what?"

"Oh, I can think of a couple of things," she said, putting her arms around him. "That is, if you don't have a problem with that."

"No," he said with a grin. "No problem at all."

For the next four days, Theresa and Garrett were inseparable. Garrett ceded control of the shop to Ian, even allowing him to teach the dive classes on Saturday, something he'd never done before. Twice, Garrett and Theresa went sailing; on the second night they stayed out all night on the ocean, lying together in the cabin, rocked by the gentle swells of the Atlantic. Later that evening she asked him to tell her more adventure stories about early sailors, and she stroked his hair as the sound of his voice reverberated against the interior of the hull.

What she didn't know was that after she'd fallen asleep, Garrett left her side as he had their first night together and paced the deck alone. He thought about Theresa sleeping inside and the fact that she would be leaving soon, and with that thought came another memory from years before.

*"I really don't think you should go," Garrett said, looking at Catherine with concern in his eyes.*

*She stood beside the front door, her suitcase beside her, frustrated with his comment. "C'mon, Garrett, we've already talked about this. I'm only going to be gone for a few days."*

*"But you haven't been yourself lately."*

*Catherine felt like throwing up her hands. "How many times do I have to tell you that I'm fine? My sister really needs me—you know how she is. She's worried about the wedding, and Mom isn't much help at all."*

*"But I need you, too."*

*"Garrett—just because you have to be at the shop all day long doesn't mean I have to stay here, too. We're not joined at the hip."*

*Garrett took an involuntary step backward, as if she'd struck him. "I didn't say we were. I'm just not sure whether you should go when you're feeling this way."*

*"You never want me to go anywhere."*

*"Can I help it if I miss you when you're gone?"*

*Her face softened just a little. "I may leave, Garrett, but you know I'll always come back."*

When the memory faded, Garrett walked back inside the cabin and saw Theresa lying under the sheet. Quietly he slipped in beside her and held her tightly against him.

✳      ✳      ✳

The following day was spent at the beach, sitting near the pier where they'd first had lunch. When Theresa got sunburned by the early morning rays, Garrett walked to one of the many shops right off the beach and brought back some lotion. He applied it to her back, rubbing it into her skin, as gently as if she were a child, and even though she didn't want to believe it, deep down she could feel that there were moments when his mind was drifting somewhere else. But then, just as suddenly, the moments would pass and she would wonder whether she'd been mistaken.

They had lunch at Hank's again, holding hands and staring at each other from across the table. They talked quietly, oblivious to the throngs around them, neither one of them noticing when the check was brought to the table and the lunch crowd emptied out.

Theresa watched him carefully, wondering if Garrett had been as intuitive with Catherine as he seemed to be with her. It was as if he could almost read her mind whenever they were together—if she wanted him to hold her hand, he reached for it before she said anything. If she just wanted to talk for a while without interruption, he listened quietly. If she wanted to know how he was feeling about her at any particular moment, the way he looked at her made it all clear. No one—not even David—had ever understood her as well as Garrett seemed to, yet how long had she known him? A few days? How, she wondered, could that be? Late at night, she thought about the answer as he lay sleeping by her side, and the answer always came back to the bottles she had originally found. The more she had come to know Garrett, the more she believed that she was destined to find his messages to Catherine, as if there were some great force that had directed them to her, with the intention of bringing them together.

On Saturday evening Garrett cooked another dinner for her, which they ate on the back deck under the stars. After making love, they lay in his bed, holding each other. Both of them knew that she had to return to Boston the following day. It was a subject they had both avoided talking about until now.

"Will I ever see you again?" she asked.

He was quiet, almost too quiet. "I hope so," he said finally.

"Do you want to?"

"Of course I do." As he said it, he sat up in the bed, pulling slightly away from her. After a moment she sat up and turned on the bedside lamp.

"What is it, Garrett?"

"I just don't want it to end," he said, looking down. "I don't want us to end, I don't want this week to end. I mean, you come into my life and turn it upside-down, and now you're leaving."

She reached for his hand and spoke quietly.

"Oh, Garrett—I don't want it to end, either. This has been one of the best weeks I've ever had. It seems like I've known you forever. We can make it work, if we try. I could come down here or you could come up to Boston. Either way, we can try, can't we?"

"How often would I see you? Once a month? Less than that?"

"I don't know. I think that depends on us and what we're willing to do. I think if we're both willing to give a little, we can make it work."

He paused for a long moment. "Do you really think it's possible if we don't see each other very much? When would I get to hold you? When would I be able to see your face? If we only see each other once in a while, we won't be able to do the things that we need to . . . to continue feeling the way we do. Every time we saw each other, we'd know it's only for a couple of days. There wouldn't be time for anything to grow."

His words stung, partly from the truth and partly because he seemed to want to simply end it here and now. When he finally turned to her, a regretful smile on his face, she didn't know what to say. She released his hand, confused.

"You don't want to try, then? Is that what you're saying? You just want to forget everything that's happened—"

He shook his head. "No—I don't want to forget it. I can't forget it. I don't know. . . . I just want to see you more than it sounds like we'll be able to."

"So do I. But we can't, so let's just make the best of what we can. Okay?"

He shook his head almost dismissively. "I don't know. . . . "

She watched him closely as he spoke, sensing the presence of something else.

"Garrett, what's wrong?"

He didn't answer, and she went on. "Is there a reason you don't want to try?"

Still he remained quiet. In the silence, he turned toward Catherine's picture on the nightstand.

*"How was the trip?" Garrett grabbed Catherine's bag from the backseat as she stepped out of the car. Catherine smiled, though he could tell she was tired.*

*"It was good, but my sister's still a wreck. She wants everything flawless, and we found out that Nancy is pregnant and her bridesmaid's dress isn't going to fit."*

*"So what? She'll just get it adjusted."*

"That's what I said, but you know how she is. She's making a big deal out of everything."

Catherine put her hands on her hips and stretched her back, making a small grimace as she did so.

"You okay?"

"Just stiff, is all. I was tired the whole time I was there, and my back's been kind of achy for a couple of days."

She started toward the front door, Garrett right beside her.

"Catherine, I just wanted to tell you that I'm sorry about the way I acted before you left. I'm glad you went, but I'm even happier that you're back."


"Garrett, talk to me."

She stared at him, concerned. Finally he spoke:

"Theresa . . . it's just so hard right now. The things I've been going through . . ."

He trailed off, and Theresa suddenly knew what he was talking about. She felt her stomach tighten.

"Is this about Catherine? Is that what this is about?"

"No, it's just that . . ." He paused, and she knew with a sudden sinking sureness that she'd been right.

"It is, isn't it? You don't want to even try with us . . . because of Catherine."

"You just don't understand."

Despite herself, she felt a flash of anger. "Oh, I understand. You were able to spend time with me this week, simply because you knew I'd be leaving. And then, once I was gone, you could go back to what you had before. I was just a fling, wasn't I?"

He shook his head. "No, you weren't. You weren't a fling. I really care about you—"

She stared hard at him. "But not enough to even *try* to make this work."

He looked at her, pain evident in his eyes. "Don't be like this. . . ."

"How should I be? Understanding? Do you want me to simply say, 'Oh, okay, Garrett, we'll just end it here because it's difficult and we won't be able to see each other very much. I understand. It was nice meeting you.' Is that what you want me to say?"

"No, that's not what I want you to say."

"Then what do you want? I've already said I'm willing to try. . . . I've already said that I'd like to try—"

He shook his head, unable to meet her eyes. Theresa could feel tears beginning to form.

"Look, Garrett, I know you lost a wife. I know you suffered terribly for it. But you're acting like a martyr now. You've got your whole life ahead of you. Don't throw it all away by living in the past."

"I'm not living in the past," he said defensively.

Theresa fought back her tears with effort. Her voice softened.

"Garrett . . . I may not have lost a wife, but I did lose someone I really cared about, too. I know all about pain and hurt. But to be quite frank, I'm tired of being alone all the time. It's been over three years for me—just like you—and I'm tired of it. I'm ready to go on now and find someone special to be with. And you should, too."

"I know that. Don't you think I know that?"

"Right now, I'm not so sure. Something wonderful has happened between us, and I don't want us to lose sight of that."

He paused for a long moment.

"You're right," he began, struggling with his words. "In my mind, I know you're right. But my heart . . . I just don't know."

"But what about my heart? Doesn't that matter to you at all?"

The way she looked at him made his throat tighten.

"Of course it does. It matters more than you think." When he reached out to take her hand, she flinched and he saw how much he had hurt her. He spoke gently, trying to control his own emotions.

"Theresa, I'm sorry for putting you—putting us—through this on our last night. I didn't mean for it to happen. Believe me, you weren't a fling for me. God—you were anything but that. I told you I really care about you, and I mean that."

He opened his arms, his eyes pleading with her to come to his side. She hesitated for a second, then finally leaned into him, myriad conflicting feelings rushing through her. She lowered her face onto his chest, not wanting to see his expression. He kissed her hair, speaking softly as his lips fluttered over her.

"I do care. I care so much that it scares me. I haven't felt like this in so long, it's almost like I've forgotten how important another person could be to me. I don't think I could just let you go and forget you, and I don't want to. And I definitely don't want us to end right now." For a moment there was only the soft, even sound of his breathing. Finally he whispered, "I promise to do everything I can to see you. And we'll try to make it work."

The tenderness in his voice made her tears begin to fall. He went on, almost too quietly for her to hear.

"Theresa, I think I'm in love with you."

*I think I'm in love with you,* she heard again. *I think . . .*
*I think . . .*

Not wanting to respond, she simply whispered: "Just hold me, okay? Let's not talk anymore."

They made love first thing in the morning and held each other until the sun had risen high enough to let them know it was time for Theresa to get ready. Even though she hadn't spent much time at all at the hotel and had brought her suitcase over to Garrett's house, she hadn't checked out, just in case Kevin or Deanna called.

They showered together, and after dressing, Garrett made Theresa breakfast while she finished packing her things. Zipping her suitcase, Theresa heard the sound of sizzling in the kitchen as the smell of bacon wafted through the house. After drying her hair and putting on some makeup, she walked into the kitchen.

Garrett was sitting at the table, drinking coffee. He winked at her when she entered. On the counter he'd left a cup by the coffeemaker, and she poured herself some. Breakfast was already on the table—scrambled eggs, bacon, and toast. Theresa sat in the chair closest to him.

"I didn't know what you wanted for breakfast," he said, motioning toward the table.

"I'm not hungry, Garrett, if that's all right with you."

He smiled. "That's fine. I'm not that hungry, either."

She got up from her chair and went to him, sitting in his lap. She wrapped her arms around him and buried her face in his neck. He held her tightly in return, running his hands through her hair.

Finally she pulled back. Their time in the sun this week had left her tanned. In her jeans shorts and clean white shirt, she looked like a carefree teenager. For a moment she stared down at the small flower designs stitched into her sandals. Her suitcase and purse stood waiting next to the bedroom door.

"My plane leaves soon, and I've still got to check out of the hotel and return the rental car," she said.

"Are you sure you don't want me to come with you?"

She nodded, her lips pursed. "No, I'll be rushing just to catch my flight as it is, and besides, you'd have to follow me in your truck. We can say good-bye just as easily here."

"I'm going to call you tonight."

She smiled. "I was hoping you would."

Her eyes began to well with tears, and he pulled her close.

"I'm going to miss having you here," he said as she started to cry in earnest. He brushed away the tears with his fingers, his touch light against her skin.

"And I'll miss having you cook for me," she whispered, feeling foolish.

He laughed, breaking the tension. "Don't be so sad. We're going to see each other again in a couple of weeks, aren't we?"

"Unless you're having second thoughts."

He smiled. "I'll be counting the days. And this time you're going to bring Kevin, right?"

She nodded.

"Good, I'd like to meet him. If he's anything at all like you, I'm sure we'll get along great."

"I'm sure you will, too."

"And until then, I'll be thinking about you all the time."

"You will?"

"Absolutely. I'm already thinking about you."

"That's because I'm on your lap."

He laughed again, and she gave him a watery smile. Then she stood and wiped the wetness from her cheeks. Garrett moved to her suitcase and picked it up, and they both left the house. Outside, the sun was already climbing in the sky, and it was warming up quickly. Theresa retrieved the sunglasses she kept in the side pocket of her purse, holding them in her hand as they walked to her rental car.

She unlocked the trunk, and he placed her things inside. Then, taking her in his arms, he kissed her once gently and released her. After opening her car door, he helped her inside and she put the key in the ignition.

With the door open, they stared at each other until she started the car.

"I've got to go, if I'm going to catch my plane."

"I know."

He stepped back from the door and closed it. She rolled down the window and put her hand out. Garrett took it in his for just a moment. Then she shifted the car into reverse.

"You'll call tonight?"

"I promise."

She pulled her hand in, smiling at him, and slowly started forward. Garrett watched her as she waved one last time before driving off, wondering how on earth he'd get through the next two weeks.

Despite the traffic, Theresa made it to the hotel quickly and checked out. There were three messages from Deanna, each seemingly more desperate than the last. "What's going on down there? How did your date go?" read the first one; "Why didn't you call? I'm waiting to hear all about it," read the second; and the third said simply, "You're killing me! Call me with the details—please!" There was also one message from Kevin—she'd called him a couple of times from Garrett's house—and it seemed to be at least a couple of days old.

She returned the rental car and reached the airport with less than a half hour to spare. Luckily the line to check her bags was short, and she made it to the gate just as they were boarding. After handing her ticket to the stewardess, she boarded the plane and took her seat. The flight to Charlotte was only partly full, and the seat next to her was vacant.

Theresa closed her eyes, thinking back on the amazing events of the past week. Not only had she found Garrett, but she had come to know him better than she would ever have imagined possible. He had stirred deep feelings in her, feelings she had long thought were buried.

But did she love him?

She approached the question gingerly, wary of what an admission like that would mean.

Idly she ran through their conversation of last night. His fears of letting go of the past, his feelings about not seeing her as much as he wanted to. These things she understood completely. But . . .

*I think I'm in love with you.*

She frowned. Why did he add the word "think"? Either he was in love or he wasn't . . . wasn't he? Had he said it to appease her? Or had he said it for another reason?

*I think I'm in love with you.*

In her mind, she heard him say it over and over again, his voice edged with . . . what? Ambivalence? Thinking about it now, she almost wished he'd said nothing at all. At least then she wouldn't be trying to figure out exactly what he'd meant.

But what about her? Did she love Garrett?

She shut her eyes tiredly, suddenly unwilling to confront her warring emotions. One thing was for sure, though—she wasn't ever going to tell him that she loved him until she was certain he could put Catherine behind him.

That night, in Garrett's dreams, a violent storm was well under way. Rain pelted hard against the side of the house, and Garrett ran frantically from one room to the next. It was the house he lived in now, and though he knew exactly where he was going, the blinding rain coming in the open windows made it difficult to see. Knowing he had to close them, he rushed to the bedroom and found himself entangled in the curtains as they blew inward. Fighting them off, he reached the window just as the lights went off.

The room went black. Above the storm, he could hear the sound of a distant siren, warning of a hurricane. Lightning illuminated the sky as he struggled with the window. It wouldn't budge. Rain continued to pour inward, wetting his hands and making it impossible to get the grip he needed.

Above him, the roof began to creak with the fury of the storm.

He continued to struggle with the window, but it was jammed and wouldn't move. Finally giving up, he tried the window beside it. Like the first window, it was stuck as well.

He could hear the shingles being torn from the roof, followed by the crash of shattering glass.

He turned and ran to the living room. The window there had

exploded inward, spewing glass over the floor. Rain blew side-ways into the room, and the wind was horrific. The front door was shaking in the frame.

Outside the window, he heard Theresa begin to call for him.

"Garrett, you've got to get out now!"

At that moment, the bedroom windows crashed inward as well. The wind, gusting through the house, began to tear an opening in the ceiling. The house wouldn't be able to stand much longer.

*Catherine.*

He had to get her picture and the other items he kept in the end table.

"Garrett! You're running out of time!" Theresa shouted again.

Despite the rain and blackness, he could see her outside, motioning for him to follow her.

*The picture. The ring. The Valentine's Day cards.*

"C'mon!" she continued to shout. Her arms were waving frantically.

With a roar, the roof separated from the frame of the house and the wind began to tear it away. On instinct, he raised his arms above his head just as part of the ceiling crashed down on him.

In moments everything would be lost.

Not caring about the danger, he started toward the bedroom. He couldn't leave without them.

"You can still make it!"

Something in the sound of Theresa's cry made him stop. He glanced toward Theresa, then toward the bedroom, frozen.

More of the ceiling fell in around him. With a sharp, splintering crack, the roof continued to give way.

He took a step toward the bedroom, and with that, he saw Theresa stop waving her arms. To him it seemed as if she'd suddenly given up.

The wind gusted through the room, an unearthly howl that seemed to blow through him. Furniture toppled over throughout the room, blocking his path.

"Garrett! Please!" Theresa shouted.

Again the sound of her voice made him stop, and with that he realized that if he tried to save the things from his past, he might not make it out at all.

*But was it worth it?*

The answer was obvious.

He gave up his attempt and rushed toward the opening where the window had been. With his fist, he pounded out the shards and stepped out onto the back deck just as the roof was completely torn away. The walls began to buckle then, and as he jumped onto the deck, they crumbled into a pile with a thunderous boom.

He looked for Theresa to make sure she was okay, but strangely, he couldn't see her anymore.

CHAPTER 10

*E*arly the next morning, Theresa was sleeping soundly when the sound of a ringing phone jarred her awake. Fumbling for the phone, she recognized Garrett's voice instantly.

"Did you make it home okay?"

"Yeah, I did," she replied groggily. "What time is it?"

"A little after six. Did I wake you?"

"Yes. I stayed up late last night waiting for your call. I started to wonder if you'd forgotten your promise."

"I didn't forget. I just figured you needed a little time to settle in."

"But you were confident I'd be up at the crack of dawn, right?"

Garrett laughed. "Sorry about that. How was the flight? How are you?"

"Good. Tired, but good."

"So I take it that the pace of the big city has already worn you out again."

She laughed, and Garrett's voice turned serious. "Hey, I want you to know something."

"What?"

"I miss you."

"You do?"

"Yeah—I went in to do work yesterday even though the shop was closed, hoping to get some paperwork done, but I couldn't do much because I kept thinking about you."

"That's good to hear."

"It's the truth. I don't know how I'm going to get any work done over the next couple of weeks."

"Oh, you'll manage."

"I might not be able to sleep, either."

She laughed, knowing he was teasing. "Now, don't go that far. I'm not into those superdependent guys, you know. I like my men to be men."

"I'll try to keep it in check, then."

She paused. "Where are you now?"

"I'm sitting on the back deck, watching the sun come up. Why?"

Theresa thought about the view she was missing. "Is it beautiful?"

"It always is, but this morning, I'm not enjoying it as much as I usually do."

"Why not?"

"Because you're not here with me to enjoy it."

She lay back on the bed, making herself comfortable. "Hey—I miss you, too."

"I hope so. I'd hate to think I was the only one who felt this way."

She smiled, holding the phone to her ear with one hand and absently twirling a strand of her hair with the other, until they finally said a reluctant good-bye twenty minutes later and hung up the phone.

Entering the office later than usual, Theresa felt the effects of her whirlwind adventure finally catching up with her. She hadn't slept much, and when she'd looked in the mirror after talking to Garrett on the phone, she'd felt sure that she looked at least a decade older than she was. As usual, the first place she went once she got to work was the break room for a cup of coffee, and on this morning she added a second packet of sugar to give her an extra jolt.

"Well, hello, Theresa," Deanna said happily, striding in behind her. "I thought you'd never get here. I've been dying to hear everything that happened."

"Good morning," Theresa mumbled, stirring her coffee. "Sorry I'm late."

"I'm just glad you made it at all. I almost ran over to your apartment last night to talk to you, but I didn't know what time you got in."

"I'm sorry for not calling, but I was a little worn out from my week," she said.

Deanna leaned against the counter. "Well, that's not a surprise. I've already put two and two together."

"What do you mean?"

Deanna's eyes were bright. "I take it you haven't seen your desk yet."

"No, I just walked in. Why?"

"Well," she said, raising her eyebrows, "I guess you must have made a good impression."

"What are you talking about, Deanna?"

"Come with me," Deanna said with a conspiratorial grin as she led her back into the newsroom. When Theresa saw her desk, she gasped. Next to the mail that had accumulated while she was gone stood a dozen roses, beautifully arranged in a large clear vase.

"They arrived first thing this morning. I think the delivery man was a little shocked that you weren't there to receive them, but I went ahead and said I was you. Then he *really* looked shocked."

Barely listening to what Deanna had said, Theresa reached for the card leaning against the vase and opened it immediately. Deanna stood behind her, craning over her shoulder. It read:

---

*To the most beautiful woman I know—*
*Now that I'm alone again, nothing is as it once was.*
*The sky is grayer, the ocean is more forbidding.*
*Will you make it right?*
*The only way is to see me again.*

*I miss you,*
*Garrett*

---

Theresa smiled at the note and slipped it back inside the envelope, bending to smell the bouquet.

"You must have had a memorable week," Deanna said.

"Yeah, I did," Theresa answered simply.

"I can't wait to hear about it—every spicy detail."

"I think," Theresa said, glancing around the newsroom at all the people watching her discreetly, "that I'd rather talk to you about it later, when we're alone. I don't need the whole office gossiping about it."

"They already are, Theresa. It's been a long time since flowers have been delivered here. But all right—we'll talk about it later."

"Did you tell them who they were from?"

"Of course not. To be honest, I kind of like leaving them in suspense." She gave a small wink after looking around the newsroom. "Listen, Theresa, I've got some work to do. Do you think we could have lunch today? Then we can talk."

"Sure. Where?"

"How about Mikuni's? I bet you didn't find much sushi down in Wilmington."

"That sounds great. And Deanna . . . thanks for keeping it a secret."

"No problem."

Deanna patted Theresa's shoulder gently and headed back to her office. Theresa leaned over her desk and smelled the roses again before moving the vase to the corner of her desk. She began to sort through her mail for a couple of minutes, pretending not to notice the flowers until the newsroom resumed its chaotic patterns. Making sure that no one was paying attention, she picked up the phone and dialed Garrett at work.

Ian answered the phone. "Hold on, I think he's in his office. Who's calling, please?"

"Tell him it's someone who wants to schedule some dive lessons in a couple of weeks." She tried to sound as distant as she could, not sure if Ian knew about them.

Ian put her on hold, and there was silence for a short moment. Then the line clicked and Garrett came on.

"Can I help you?" he asked, sounding a little frazzled.

She said simply: "You shouldn't have, but I'm glad you did."

He recognized her voice, and his tone brightened. "Hey, it's you. I'm glad they arrived. Do they look okay?"

"They're beautiful. How did you know I loved roses?"

"I didn't, but I've never heard of a woman who didn't, so I took a chance."

She smiled. "So you send lots of women roses?"

"Millions. I have a lot of fans. Dive instructors are almost like movie stars, you know."

"They are, huh?"

"You mean you didn't know? And here I thought you were just another groupie."

She laughed. "Thanks a lot."

"Sure. Did anyone ask who they were from?"

She smiled. "Of course."

"I hope you said good things."

"I did. I told them you were sixty-eight and fat, with a horrible lisp that made it impossible to understand you. But since you were so pitiful, I went ahead and had lunch with you. And now, unfortunately, you're stalking me."

"Hey, that hurts," he said. He paused. "So . . . I hope the roses will remind you that I'm thinking about you."

"They might," she said coyly.

"Well, I am thinking about you and I don't want you to forget it."

She glanced at the roses. "Ditto," she said quietly.

After they had hung up, Theresa sat quietly for a moment, reaching for the card again. She read it once more, and this time, instead of putting it back with the flowers, she placed it in her purse for safekeeping. Knowing this crowd, she was sure someone would read it when she wasn't looking.

"So, what's he like?"

Deanna sat across from Theresa at the table in the restaurant. Theresa handed Deanna the pictures from her vacation.

"I don't know where to start."

Staring at a picture of Garrett and Theresa on the beach, Deanna spoke without looking at her.

"Start at the beginning. I don't want to miss a thing."

Since Theresa had already told her about meeting Garrett at the docks, she picked up her story from the evening they spent sailing. She told Deanna how she had purposely left her jacket on board as an excuse to see him again—to which Deanna replied, "Marvelous!"—moving on to their lunch the next day and finally to their dinner. Recapping the final four days they spent together, she left very little out as Deanna listened with rapt attention.

"It sounds like you had a wonderful time," Deanna said, smiling like a proud mother.

"I did. It was one of the best weeks I've ever spent. It's just that . . ."

"What?"

It took a moment for her to answer. "Well, Garrett said something toward the end that got me wondering where this whole thing was going to go from here."

"What did he say?"

"It wasn't just what he said, but *how* he said it. He sounded as if he weren't sure he wanted us to see each other again."

"I thought you said that you were going down to Wilmington again in a couple of weeks."

"I am."

"Then what's the problem?"

She fidgeted, trying to collect her thoughts. "Well, he's still struggling with Catherine and . . . and I'm not exactly sure whether he'll ever get over it."

Deanna laughed suddenly.

"What's so funny?" Theresa asked, startled.

"*You* are, Theresa. What did you expect? You knew he was still struggling with Catherine before you went down there. Remember, it was his 'undying' love that you found so attractive in the first place. Did you think that he'd completely get over Catherine in a couple of days, just because you two hit it off so well?"

Theresa looked sheepish and Deanna laughed again.

"You *did*, didn't you? That's exactly what you thought."

"Deanna, you weren't there. . . . You don't know how right everything seemed between us, up until the last night."

Deanna's voice softened. "Theresa, I know there's a part of you that believes you can change someone, but the reality is that you can't. You can change yourself, and Garrett can change himself, but you can't do it for him."

"I know that—"

"But you don't," Deanna said, gently cutting her off. "Or if you do, you don't want to see it that way. Your vision, as they say, has become clouded."

Theresa thought for a moment about what she'd said.

"Let's take an objective look at what happened with Garrett, shall we?" Deanna asked.

Theresa nodded.

"Though you knew something about Garrett, he knew absolutely nothing about you. Yet he was the one who asked you to go sailing. So something between you two must have clicked right away. Next, you see him again when you pick up your jacket, and he asks you to lunch. He tells you about Catherine and then asks you to come over for dinner. After that, you spend four wonderful days together getting to know—and care for— each other. Had you told me before you'd left that this is what would have happened, I wouldn't have believed it possible. But it did—that's the thing. And now, you two are planning to see each other again. To me, it sounds like the whole thing was a smashing success."

"Then, you mean I shouldn't worry about whether he'll ever get over Catherine?"

Deanna shook her head. "Not exactly. But look—you've got to take this one step at a time. The fact is, you only spent a few days together so far—that's not enough time to make a decision about something like this. If I were you, I'd see how you both feel over the next couple of weeks, and when you see him the next time, you're bound to know a lot more than you know now."

"Do you think so?" Theresa eyed her friend worriedly.

"I was right about twisting your arm to get you down there in the first place, wasn't I?"

✻        ✻        ✻

While Theresa and Deanna were eating, Garrett was working in his office behind a giant stack of papers when the door opened. Jeb Blake entered, making sure that his son was alone before closing the door behind him. After taking a seat in the chair across from Garrett's desk, Jeb pulled some tobacco and rolling paper from his pocket and began to roll his cigarette.

"Go ahead and sit down. As you can see, I don't have much to do." Garrett gestured toward the pile.

Jeb smiled and continued rolling. "I called the shop a couple of times and they said you hadn't come in all week. What have you been up to?"

Leaning back in his chair, Garrett eyed his father. "I'm sure you already know the answer to your question, and that's probably the reason you're here."

"You were with Theresa the whole time?"

"Yeah, I was."

Continuing to roll his cigarette, Jeb asked nonchalantly, "So, what did you two do with yourselves?"

"We went sailing, walked on the beach, talked. . . . You know, just got to know each other."

Jeb finished with his cigarette and put it in his mouth. He pulled a Zippo lighter from his front shirt pocket, lit up, and inhaled deeply. Exhaling, he gave Garrett a roguish grin.

"Did you cook those steaks like I taught you?"

Garrett smirked. "Of course."

"Was she impressed?"

"She was very impressed."

Jeb nodded and took another drag from his cigarette. Garrett could feel the air in the office beginning to grow stale.

"Well then, she has at least one good quality, doesn't she."

"She's got a lot more than one, Dad."

"You liked her, didn't you?"

"Very much."

"Even though you don't know her very well?"

"I feel like I know everything about her."

Jeb nodded and said nothing for a moment. Finally he asked, "Are you going to see her again?"

"Actually, she's coming down in a couple of weeks with her son."

Jeb watched Garrett's expression carefully. Then, standing, he started toward the door. Before opening it, he turned and faced his son. "Garrett, can I give you some advice?"

Startled at his father's abrupt departure, he answered: "Sure."

"If you like her, if she makes you happy, and if you feel like you know her—then don't let her go."

"Why are you telling me this?"

Jeb looked directly at Garrett and took another drag on his cigarette. "Because if I know you, you're going to be the one who ends it, and I'm here to try to stop you if I can."

"What are you talking about?"

"You know exactly what I'm talking about," he said quietly. Turning around, Jeb opened the door and left Garrett's office without another word.

Later that night, with the remnants of his father's comments rolling through his head, Garrett couldn't sleep. He rose from his bed and went to the kitchen, knowing what needed to be done. In the drawer, he found the stationery he always used when his mind was conflicted, and he sat down with the hopes of putting his thoughts into words.

———

*My darling Catherine,*
*I don't know what's happening to me, and I don't know if I ever will. So much has happened lately that I can't make sense of what I'm going through.*

———

Garrett sat at the table for an hour after writing those first two lines, and no matter how hard he tried, he couldn't think of anything else to say. But when he woke the following morning, unlike most days, his first thought wasn't about Catherine.

Instead it was about Theresa.

Over the next two weeks, Garrett and Theresa spoke on the phone every night, sometimes for hours. Garrett also sent a couple of letters—short notes, really—to let her know that he missed her, and he had another dozen roses delivered the following week, this time with a box of candy.

Theresa didn't want to send him flowers or candy, so instead she sent him a light blue oxford shirt she thought would look good with his jeans, along with a couple of cards.

Kevin arrived home a few days later, and it made the next week pass much more quickly for Theresa than for Garrett. His first night home, Kevin ate dinner with Theresa, telling her about his vacation in fits and starts before collapsing into a deep sleep for almost fifteen hours. When he woke, there was already a long list of things that needed to be done. He needed new clothes for school—he'd already outgrown most of what he'd worn the previous year—and he had to sign up for fall league soccer, which ended up taking almost an entire Saturday. In addition, he'd come home with a suitcase full of dirty laundry that needed to be washed, he wanted to develop the pictures he'd taken on his vacation, and he had a Tuesday afternoon appointment with the orthodontist to see if he needed braces.

In other words, life was back to normal at the Osborne household.

On Kevin's second night back, Theresa told him about her vacation at the Cape, then about her trip to Wilmington. She mentioned Garrett, trying to convey how she felt about him without alarming Kevin. At first, when she explained how they were going to visit him the following weekend, Kevin didn't sound so sure about it. But after she told him what Garrett did for a living, Kevin began to show some signs of interest.

"You mean he might teach me how to scuba dive?" he asked as she was vacuuming the house.

"He said that he would, if you wanted to."

"Cool," he said, returning to whatever he'd been doing before.

A few nights later she took him to the store to get him a few magazines about diving. By the time they were ready to leave, Kevin knew the name of every piece of equipment it was possible to own, obviously dreaming about his upcoming adventure.

Garrett, meanwhile, plunged ahead with work. He worked late, thinking about Theresa while he did so, acting much the same way he had after Catherine's death. When he mentioned to his father how much he missed Theresa, his father only nodded and smiled. Something in his father's assessing gaze made Garrett wonder what exactly was going through the old man's mind.

By prior agreement, both Theresa and Garrett had decided it would be best if she and Kevin didn't stay at Garrett's house, but because it was still summer, nearly every room in town was booked. Luckily Garrett knew the owner of a small motel a mile up the beach from Garrett's house, and he had been able to make arrangements for their stay.

When the day finally came for Theresa and Kevin to visit, Garrett bought some groceries, washed his truck inside and out, and showered before heading to the airport.

Dressed in khaki pants, Top-Siders, and the shirt that Theresa had bought him, he waited nervously at the gate.

In the last two weeks his feelings for Theresa had grown. He knew now that whatever happened between him and Theresa wasn't based simply on physical attraction—his longing hinted at something much deeper, more lasting. As he craned his neck for a glimpse of her among the passengers, he felt a pang of anxiety. It had been so long since he'd felt this way about anyone— and where was it all going?

When Theresa stepped off the plane with Kevin beside her, all his nervousness suddenly faded away. She was beautiful— more so than he remembered. And Kevin—he looked exactly like his picture and a lot like his mother. He was a little over five feet, with Theresa's dark hair and eyes, and gangly—both his arms and his legs seemed to have grown a little faster than the rest of him. He was wearing long Bermuda shorts, Nike shoes, and a shirt from a concert by Hootie and the Blowfish. His choice of apparel was clearly inspired by MTV, and Garrett couldn't help but smile to himself. Boston, Wilmington . . . it really didn't matter, did it? Kids would be kids.

When Theresa saw him she waved, and Garrett moved toward them, reaching for their carry-on bags. Not sure whether he should kiss her in front of Kevin, he hesitated until Theresa leaned over and gaily kissed him on the cheek.

"Garrett, I'd like you to meet my son, Kevin," she said proudly.

"Hi, Kevin."

"Hi, Mr. Blake," he said stiffly, as if Garrett were his teacher.

"Call me Garrett," he said, holding out his hand. Kevin shook it, a little unsure. Until this point, no adult other than Annette had said that he could use their first name.

"How was your flight?" Garrett asked.

"Good," Theresa responded.

"Did you get anything to eat?"

"Not yet."

"Well, how about we grab a bite before I take you to your motel?"

"Sounds good."

"Do you want anything in particular?" Garrett asked Kevin.

"I like McDonald's."

"Oh, honey, no," Theresa said quickly, but Garrett stopped her with a shake of his head.

"McDonald's is fine with me."

"You sure?" Theresa asked.

"Positive. I eat there all the time."

Kevin looked delighted at his answer, and the three of them started walking toward the baggage claim area. As they left the gates, Garrett asked:

"Are you a good swimmer, Kevin?"

"Pretty good."

"Are you up for some scuba lessons this weekend?"

"I think so—I've been reading up on it," he said, trying to sound older than he was.

"Well, good. I was hoping you'd say that. If we're lucky, we may even be able to get you certified before you head back."

"What does that mean?"

"It's a license that allows you to dive whenever you want—kind of like a driver's license."

"You can do that in a few days?"

"Sure. You're required to take a written test and spend a few hours in the water with an instructor. But since you'll be my only student this weekend—unless your mother wants to learn, too—we should have more than enough time."

"Cool," Kevin said. He turned toward Theresa. "Are you gonna learn, too, Mom?"

"I don't know. Maybe."

"I think you should," Kevin said. "It would be fun."

"He's right—you should learn, too," Garrett added with a smirk, knowing she would feel cornered by the two of them and probably give in.

"Fine," she said, rolling her eyes, "I'll go, too. But if I see any sharks, I'm quitting."

"You mean there might be sharks?" Kevin asked quickly.

"Yeah, we'll probably see some sharks. But they're little and they don't bother people."

"How little?" Theresa asked, remembering the story he'd told about the hammerhead he'd encountered.

"Little enough that you won't have anything to worry about."

"Are you sure?"

"Positive."

"Cool," Kevin repeated to himself, and Theresa glanced at Garrett, wondering if he was telling the truth.

After picking up their bags and stopping for a bite to eat, Garrett drove Theresa and Kevin to the motel. Once their things were inside, Garrett went back to his truck, returning with a book and some papers under his arms.

"Kevin—these are for you."

"What are they?"

"It's the book and the tests you need to read for your certification. Don't worry—it looks like there's more to read than there is. But if you want to head out tomorrow, you have to have the first two sections read and complete the first test."

"Is it hard?"

"No—it's pretty easy, but you still have to do it. And you can use the book to find the answers you're not sure about."

"You mean I can look up the answers while I take the test?"

Garrett nodded. "Yeah. When I give these to my classes, they're supposed to do them at home and I'm sure almost everyone uses the book. The important thing is that you try to learn what you need to know. Diving is a lot of fun, but it can be dangerous if you don't know what you're doing."

Garrett handed Kevin the book as he went on.

"If you can finish by tomorrow—it's about twenty pages to read, plus the test—we'll head to the pool for the first part of your certification. You'll learn how to put on your equipment and then we'll practice for a while."

"We're not going in the ocean?"

"Not tomorrow—you have to spend some time getting comfortable with the equipment first. After we spend a few hours doing that, then we'll be ready. We'll probably hit the ocean on Monday and Tuesday for your first open-water dives. And if you get enough hours in the water, you'll have a temporary certification by the time you step on the plane to go home. Then, all you have to do is mail an application, and you'll get the actual certification in the mail in a couple of weeks."

Kevin began to flip through the pages. "Does Mom have to do it, too?"

"If she wants to be certified, she does."

Theresa walked over, peeking over Kevin's shoulder as he glanced through the book. The information didn't look too daunting.

"Kevin," she said, "we can do it together tomorrow morning, if you're too tired to start now."

"I'm not too tired," he said quickly.

"Then would you mind if Garrett and I talked on the patio for a while?"

"No, go ahead," he said absently, already turning to the first page.

Once outside, Garrett and Theresa sat across from each other. Glancing back at her son, Theresa saw that Kevin was already reading.

"You're not cutting any corners to get him certified, are you?"

Garrett shook his head. "No, not at all. To get a PADI certificate—the certificate for recreational divers—you need to pass the tests and spend a certain amount of time in the water with an instructor—that's all. Usually we pace it out over three or four weekends, but that's because most people don't have time to do it during the week. He'll get the same number of hours—it's just more condensed."

"I appreciate your doing this for him."

"Hey—you forget this is what I do for a living." After making sure that Kevin was still reading, he scooted his chair a little closer. "I missed you these last couple of weeks," he said quietly, taking her hand in his.

"I missed you, too."

"You look wonderful," he added. "You were easily the prettiest woman who got off the plane."

Despite herself, Theresa blushed.

"Thanks. . . . You look good yourself—especially wearing that shirt."

"I thought you might like it."

"Are you disappointed that we're not staying at your place?"

"Not really. I understand your reasons—Kevin doesn't know me from Adam, and I'd rather let him get comfortable with me on his own terms than push it on him. Like you said, he's been through enough already."

"You know that it means we won't be able to spend much time alone this weekend, don't you?"

"I'll take you any way I can get you," he said.

Theresa glanced inside again, and when she saw that Kevin was immersed in the book, she leaned over and kissed Garrett. Despite the fact that she wouldn't be with him all night, she found herself surprisingly happy. Sitting beside him and seeing the way he looked at her made her heartbeat surge.

"I wish we didn't live so far apart," she said. "You're kind of addicting."

"I'll take that as a compliment."

*       *       *

Three hours later, long after Kevin was asleep, Theresa quietly led Garrett to the door. After stepping out into the hall and closing the door behind them, they kissed for a long time, both of them finding it hard to let each other go. In his arms Theresa felt like a teenager again, as if she were sneaking a kiss on her parents' porch, and it somehow added to the excitement she was feeling.

"I wish you could stay here tonight," she whispered.

"I do, too."

"Is it as difficult for you to say good night as it is for me?"

"I'd be willing to bet it's a lot more difficult for me. I'm going home to an empty house."

"Don't say that. You'll make me feel guilty."

"Maybe a little guilt is a good thing. Lets me know you care."

"I wouldn't be down here if I didn't." They kissed again, hungrily.

Pulling back, he mumbled, "I should really be going." He didn't sound as if he meant it.

"I know."

"But I don't want to," he said with a boyish smile.

"I know what you mean," she said. "But you have to. You've got to teach us how to dive tomorrow."

"I'd rather teach you a couple of other things I know."

"I think you did that the last time I was here," she said coyly.

"I know. But practice makes perfect."

"Then we'll have to find some time to practice while I'm here."

"You think that might happen?"

"I think," she said honestly, "that when it comes to us, anything is possible."

"I hope you're right."

"I'm right," she said before kissing him one last time. "I usually am." She gently pulled away from him and backed toward the door.

"That's what I like about you, Theresa—your confidence. You always know what's going on."

"Go home, Garrett," she said demurely. "And do me a favor?"

"Anything."

"Dream about me, okay?"

Kevin woke early the next morning and opened the curtains, letting sunlight flood into the room. Theresa squinted and rolled over, trying to get a few more minutes' rest, but Kevin was persistent. "Mom—you've got to take the test before we go," he said excitedly.

Theresa groaned. Turning over, she checked the clock. A little after six A.M. She'd been in bed less than five hours.

"It's too early," she said, closing her eyes again. "Can you give me a few more minutes, honey?"

"We don't have time," he said, sitting on her bed and nudging her shoulder gently. "You haven't even read the first section yet."

"Did you finish it all last night?"

"Yep," he said. "My test is over there, but don't copy, okay? I don't want to get into trouble."

"I don't think you'd get in trouble," she said groggily. "We know the teacher, you know."

"But it wouldn't be fair. And besides, you have to know this stuff, just like Mr. Blake . . . I mean Garrett . . . said, otherwise you could run into trouble."

"Okay, okay," she said, sitting up slowly. She rubbed her eyes. "Do they have any instant coffee in the bathroom?"

"I didn't see any, but if you want, I'll run down the hall and get you a Coke."

"I have some change in my purse. . . ."

Kevin jumped up and began rummaging through her handbag. After finding a few quarters, he ran out the front door, his hair tousled from sleeping. She heard his feet thumping as he raced down the hall. After standing and stretching her arms above her head, she made her way to the small table. She picked up the book and started in on the first chapter just as he returned with two Cokes. "Here you go," he said, putting one on the table beside her. "I'm going to shower and get ready. Where'd you put my swimsuit?"

*Ah, the endless energy of childhood*, she thought. "It's in the top drawer, next to your socks."

"Okay," he said, pulling the drawer open, "got it." He went to the bathroom and Theresa listened as the shower was turned on. Opening her Coke, she returned to the book.

Luckily Garrett had been right when he'd told her that the information wasn't difficult. It was easy reading with pictures describing the equipment, and she was finished by the time Kevin was dressed. After finding her test, she set it in front of her. Kevin walked over and stood behind her as she glanced at the first question. Remembering where she'd read about it, she began to flip back through the book to the appropriate page.

"Mom, that's an easy one. You don't need the book for that."

"At six in the morning, I need all the help I can get," she

grumbled, not feeling the least bit guilty about it. Garrett had said she could use the book, hadn't he?

Kevin continued to look over her shoulder as she answered the first couple of questions, commenting, "No, you're looking in the wrong place," or, "Are you sure you read the chapters?" until she finally told him to go watch television.

"But there's nothing on," he said, sounding dejected.

"Then read something."

"I didn't bring anything."

"Then sit quietly."

"I am."

"No, you're not. You're standing over my shoulder."

"I'm just trying to help."

"Just sit on the bed, okay? And don't say anything."

"I'm not saying anything."

"You're talking right now."

"That's because you're talking to me."

"Can't you let me take the test in peace?"

"Okay. I won't say another word. I'll be as quiet as a mouse."

And he was—for two minutes. Then he started whistling.

She put her pen down and faced him. "Why are you whistling?"

"I'm bored."

"Then turn on the TV."

"There's nothing on. . . ."

And so it went until she finally finished. It had taken almost an hour to do something she could have done in her office in half the time. She took a long, hot shower and dressed, putting on her swimsuit beneath her clothes. Kevin, now famished, wanted to go to McDonald's again, but she drew the line and suggested that they have breakfast at the Waffle House across the street.

"But I don't like their food."

"You haven't ever eaten there before."

"I know."

"Then how do you know you don't like it?"

"I just know."

"Are you omniscient?"

"What does that mean?"

"It means, young man, that we're going to eat where I want to eat for once."

"Really?"

"Yes," she said, looking forward to a cup of coffee more than she had in a long time.

Garrett knocked at the front door of their motel room promptly at nine, and Kevin raced to the door to answer it.

"Are you two ready?" he asked.

"We sure are," Kevin answered quickly. "My test is over there. Let me get it for you."

He skipped over to the table as Theresa rose from the bed and gave Garrett a quick kiss good morning.

"How was your morning?" he asked.

"It already seems like afternoon. Kevin got me up at the crack of dawn to take the test."

Garrett smiled as Kevin returned with his test.

"Here it is, Mr. Blake. Garrett, I mean."

Garrett took it and began to look through his answers.

"My mom had some trouble with a couple, but I helped her

out," Kevin went on, and Theresa rolled her eyes. "Ready to go, Mom?"

"Whenever you are," she said, picking up the room key and her purse.

"Then c'mon," Kevin said, leading the way down the hall, toward Garrett's truck.

Throughout the morning and early afternoon, Garrett taught them the basics of scuba diving. They learned how the equipment worked, how to put it on and test it, and finally how to breathe through the mouthpiece, first on the side of the pool, then underwater. "The most important thing to remember," Garrett explained, "is to breathe normally. Don't hold your breath, don't breathe too quickly or slowly. Just let it come naturally." Of course, nothing seemed natural about it to Theresa, and she ended up having more trouble with it than Kevin. Kevin, always the adventurer, thought that after a few minutes underwater he knew all there was to know.

"This is easy," he said to Garrett. "I think I'll be ready for the ocean this afternoon."

"I'm sure you would, but we still have to do the lessons in the proper order."

"How's Mom doing?"

"Good."

"As good as me?"

"You're both doing great," he said, and Kevin put the mouthpiece back in. He went back underwater just as Theresa came up and took out her mouthpiece.

"It feels funny when I breathe," she said.

"You're doing fine. Just relax and breathe normally."

"That's what you said the last time I came up gagging."

"The rules haven't changed in the last few minutes, Theresa."

"I know that. I just wonder if something isn't wrong with my tank."

"The tank is fine. I double-checked it this morning."

"But you're not the one using it, are you?"

"Would you like me to test it out?"

"No," she muttered, squinting in frustration, "I'll manage." Underwater she went again.

Kevin popped up and took his mouthpiece out again. "Is Mom okay? I saw her come up."

"She's fine. Just getting used to it, like you are."

"Good. I'd feel really bad if I got my certification and she didn't."

"Don't you worry about that. Just keep practicing."

"Okay."

And so it went.

After a few hours in the water, both Kevin and Theresa were tired. They had lunch, and once again Garrett told his diving stories, this time for Kevin's benefit. Kevin asked what seemed like a hundred wide-eyed questions. Garrett answered each one patiently, and Theresa was relieved at how well they seemed to get along.

After stopping at the motel to pick up the book and the lesson for the following day, Garrett brought them both to his house. Though Kevin had planned on starting the next few chapters right away, the fact that Garrett lived on the beach changed everything. Standing in the living room and looking toward the ocean, he asked:

"Can I go down to the water, Mom?"

"I don't think so," she said gently. "We've just spent all day in the pool."

"Ah, Mom . . . please? You don't have to go with me—you can watch me from the deck."

She hesitated, and Kevin knew he had her. "Please," he said again, giving her his most earnest smile.

"All right, you can go. But don't go out too deep, okay?"

"I won't, I promise," he said excitedly. After seizing the towel Garrett handed him, he ran down to the water. Garrett and Theresa sat on the deck and watched him as he began to splash around.

"He's quite a young man," Garrett said quietly.

"Yes, he is," she said. "And I think he likes you. At lunch when you went to the bathroom, he said you were *cool*."

Garrett smiled. "I'm glad. I like him, too. He's one of the better students I've had."

"You're just saying that to please me."

"No, I'm not. He really is. I meet a lot of young kids in my classes, and he's very mature and well-spoken for his age. And he's nice, too. Too many kids are spoiled these days, but I don't get that sense about him."

"Thank you."

"I mean it, Theresa. After hearing about your worries, I wasn't sure what to expect. But he's really a great kid. You've done a good job raising him."

She reached for his hand and kissed it gently. She spoke quietly.

"It means a lot to me to hear you say that. I haven't met many men who want to talk about him, let alone spend time with him."

"Then it's their loss."

She smiled. "How come you always know exactly what to say to make me feel good?"

"Maybe it's because you bring out the best in me."

"Maybe I do."

That evening Garrett took Kevin to the video store to pick up a couple of movies he wanted to watch and ordered pizza for the three of them. They watched the first movie together, eating in the living room. After dinner Kevin slowly began to fade. By nine o'clock he'd fallen asleep in front of the television. Theresa nudged him gently, telling him it was time to leave.

"Can't we just sleep here tonight?" he mumbled, only half-conscious.

"I think we should go," she said quietly.

"If you want, you two can sleep in my bed," Garrett offered. "I'll stay out here and sleep on the couch."

"Let's do that, Mom. I'm really tired."

"Are you sure?" she asked, but by then Kevin had already begun to stagger in the direction of the bedroom. They heard the springs squeak as Kevin plopped down on Garrett's bed. Following him, they peeked in the door. In a moment he was sleeping again.

"I don't think he's giving you much choice," Garrett whispered.

"I'm still not sure it's a good idea."

"I'll be a perfect gentleman—I promise."

"I'm not worried about you—I just don't want to give Kevin the wrong impression."

"You mean you don't want him to know we care about each other? I think he already knows that."

"You know what I mean."

"Yeah, I know." He shrugged. "Look, if you want me to help you get him out to the truck, I'd be glad to do it."

She stared at Kevin for a moment, listening to his deep, even breaths. He looked dead to the world.

"Well, maybe one night wouldn't hurt," she relented, and Garrett winked.

"I was hoping you'd say that."

"Now don't forget your promise to be a perfect gentleman."

"I won't."

"You sound so sure about it."

"Hey . . . a promise is a promise."

She gently closed the door and put her arms around Garrett's neck. She kissed him, biting him teasingly on the lip. "That's good, because if it was just up to me, I don't think I could control myself."

He winced. "You really know how to make it tough on a guy, don't you?"

"Does that mean you think I'm a tease?"

"No," he said quietly. "It means I think you're perfect."

Instead of watching the second movie, Garrett and Theresa sat on the couch, sipping wine and talking. Theresa checked on Kevin a couple of times, making sure he was still asleep. He looked as if he hadn't moved at all.

By midnight Theresa was yawning steadily, and Garrett suggested that she get some sleep.

"But I came down here to see you," she protested drowsily.

"But if you don't get your sleep, I'll look blurry."

"I'm fine, really," she said before yawning again. Garrett rose and went to the closet. He pulled out a sheet, blanket, and pillow and brought them to the couch.

"I insist. Try to get some sleep. We have the next few days to see each other."

"Are you sure?"

"Positive."

She helped Garrett get the couch ready and went to the bedroom. "If you don't want to sleep in your clothes, there are some sweats in the second drawer," he said.

She kissed him again. "I had a wonderful day today," she said.

"So did I."

"I'm sorry for being so tired."

"You've done a lot today. It's completely understandable."

With their arms entwined, she whispered in his ear, "Are you always this easy to get along with?"

"I try."

"Well, you're doing a heck of a job."

A few hours later Garrett woke to the sensation of someone nudging him in the ribs. Opening his eyes, he saw Theresa sitting next to him. She was wearing the sweats he'd mentioned earlier.

"Are you okay?" he asked, sitting up.

"I'm fine," she whispered, stroking his arm.

"What time is it?"

"A little after three."

"Is Kevin still sleeping?"

"Like a rock."

"Can I ask why you got out of bed?"

"I had a dream and I couldn't fall back to sleep."

He rubbed his eyes. "What was the dream about?"

"You," she said in hushed tones.

"Was it a good dream?" he asked.

"Oh, yes . . ." She trailed off. She leaned over to kiss his chest, and Garrett pulled her closer. He glanced toward the bedroom door. She had closed it behind her.

"Aren't you worried about Kevin?" he asked.

"A little, but I'm going to trust you to be as quiet as possible."

She reached under the blanket and ran her fingers across his belly. Her touch was electric.

"Are you sure about this?"

"Uh-huh," she said.

They made love tenderly, quietly, and afterward they lay beside each other. For a long time, neither of them spoke. When the faintest hint of light began to brush the horizon, they kissed good night and she returned to the bedroom. Within a few minutes she was sleeping soundly, and Garrett watched her from the doorway.

For some reason, he found it impossible to fall asleep again.

The following morning, Theresa and Kevin did the workbook together while Garrett ran off to pick up some fresh bagels for breakfast. Again they headed off to the pool. This time the lessons were a little more advanced, covering a number of different skills. Theresa and Kevin practiced "buddy breathing" in the event that either one of them ran out of air when underwater and had to share one tank, and Garrett warned of the dangers of panicking while diving and rushing to the surface too quickly. "If you do that, you'll get what's called 'the bends.' It's not only painful—it can be life-threatening."

They also spent time in the deep end of the pool, swimming underwater for extended periods, getting used to the equipment and practicing how to clear their ears. Toward the end of their lesson, Garrett showed them how to jump off the side of the pool without having their masks come off. Predictably, both of them were tired after a few hours and ready to call it a day.

"Will we go into the ocean tomorrow?" Kevin asked as they were walking back to the truck.

"If you'd like to. I think you're ready, but if you'd rather spend another day in the pool, we could do that instead."

"No, I'm ready."

"Are you sure? I don't want to rush you."

"I'm sure," he said quickly.

"How about you, Theresa? Are you ready for the ocean?"

"If Kevin's ready, then I'm ready."

"Am I still going to get certified by Tuesday?" Kevin asked.

"If the ocean dives go well, you both will."

"Awesome."

"What's up for the rest of the day?" Theresa asked.

Garrett started loading the tanks in the back of the truck. "I thought we'd go sailing. It looks like it's going to be great weather."

"Can I learn how to do that, too?" Kevin asked eagerly.

"Sure. I'll make you my first mate."

"Do I need to be certified for that, too?"

"No—that's up to the captain, and since I'm the captain, I can do it right now."

"Just like that?"

"Just like that."

Kevin looked at Theresa with wide eyes, and she could almost read his thoughts. *First I learn how to dive, then I become a first mate. Wait until I tell my friends.*

Garrett was accurate in predicting ideal weather, and the three of them had a wonderful time on the water. Garrett taught Kevin the basics of sailing—from how and when to tack to anticipating the direction of the wind based on the clouds. As on their first date together, they had sandwiches and salads, but this time they were treated to a family of porpoises that frolicked around the boat as they ate.

It was late by the time they made it back to the docks, and after Garrett showed Kevin how to close up the boat to protect it from unexpected storms, Garrett brought them back to their motel. Since all three of them were exhausted, Theresa and Garrett said good-bye quickly, and both Theresa and Kevin were in bed by the time Garrett arrived back at his house.

The following day, Garrett took them out for their first ocean dive. After the initial nervousness wore off, they began to enjoy themselves and ended up going through two tanks each over the course of the afternoon. Thanks to the calm, coastal weather, the water was clear, with excellent visibility. Garrett took a few photos of them as they explored one of the shallow-water wrecks off the North Carolina coast. He promised to have them developed that week and to send them up as soon as he could.

They spent the evening at Garrett's house again. After Kevin fell asleep, Garrett and Theresa sat close to each other on the deck, caressed by the warm, humid air.

After talking about their earlier dive, Theresa was quiet for a little while. "I can't believe we'll be leaving tomorrow night," she said finally, a trace of sadness in her voice. "These last couple of days have flown by."

"That's because we've been so busy."

She smiled. "Now you have a sense of what my life is like in Boston."

"Always racing around?"

She nodded. "Exactly. Kevin is the best thing that ever happened to me, but he sometimes wears me out. He always has to be doing something."

"You wouldn't change it, though, would you? I mean, you don't want to raise a TV junkie or a kid who sits in his room listening to music all day, do you?"

"No."

"Then count your blessings. He's a great kid—I've really enjoyed spending time with him."

"I'm so glad. I know he feels the same way." She paused. "You know, even though we haven't spent much time alone on this trip, it seems like I know you a lot better now than when I first came down here by myself."

"What do you mean? I'm still the same guy I was before."

She smiled. "You are and you aren't. The last time I was here, you had me all to yourself, and we both know it's easier to get involved with someone when you can spend a lot of exclusive time together. This time, you saw what it would really be like with Kevin around . . . and yet you handled the whole thing better than I could have imagined."

"Well, thanks, but it wasn't that hard. As long as you're around, it doesn't matter what we do. I just like spending time with you."

He put his arm around her, pulling her close. She rested her head on his shoulder. In the silence, they listened as the waves rolled up along the beach.

"Are you going to stay over again tonight?" he asked.

"I was giving it some serious consideration."

"Would you want me to be a perfect gentleman again?"

"Maybe. Maybe not."

He raised his eyebrows. "Are you flirting with me?"

"I'm trying," she confessed, and he laughed. "You know, Garrett, I really feel comfortable around you."

"Comfortable? You make it sound like I'm a couch."

"I don't mean it like that. I mean I just feel good about myself when we're together."

"You should. I feel pretty good about you."

"Pretty good? That's it?"

He shook his head. "No, that's not all." He looked almost bashful for a second. "After you left the last time, my dad came in and lectured me."

"What did he say?"

"He said that if you made me happy, that I shouldn't let you go."

"And how do you intend to do that?"

"I guess I'll have to bowl you over with my charisma."

"You've already done that."

He glanced at her, then looked out over the water. After a moment he spoke quietly. "Then I guess I'll have to tell you that I love you."

*I love you.*

Overhead, the stars were out in full, twinkling in the darkened sky. Distant clouds rode the horizon, reflecting the light of
a crescent moon. Theresa listened as the words rolled through
her head again.

*I love you.*

No ambivalence this time, no doubt about what he'd said.

"Do you really?" she whispered finally.

"Yes," he said, turning to face her, "I do." When he answered,
she saw something in his eyes she hadn't seen before.

"Oh, Garrett . . . ," she began uncertainly, before Garrett interrupted her with a shake of his head.

"Theresa, I don't expect you to feel the same way. I just
wanted you to know how I feel." He thought for a moment and
found himself remembering the dream he'd had. "Over the last
two weeks, a lot of things have happened. . . ." He paused.

She started to say something, but Garrett shook his head. It
took a moment for him to continue.

"And I'm not sure I understand everything, but I do know
how I feel about you."

His finger gently moved across her cheek and lips. "I love
you, Theresa."

"I love you, too," she said softly, trying out the words and
hoping they were true.

They held each other for a long time afterward, then went inside and made love, whispering to each other until the early
morning hours. But this time, after Theresa went to the bedroom, Garrett slept soundly while Theresa stayed awake, thinking about the miracle that had brought them together.

*         *         *

The next day passed wonderfully. Whenever they had a chance, Garrett and Theresa held hands, stealing a few furtive kisses when Kevin wasn't looking.

They spent their day practicing as they had before, and once they had finished their final diving lesson, Garrett gave them their temporary certificates right on the boat. "You can dive whenever and wherever you want now," he said to Kevin, who handled the certificate almost as if it were gold. "Just send this form in and you'll have your PADI certificate in a couple of weeks. But remember—it's never safe to dive alone. Always go with someone else."

Since it was their last day in Wilmington, Theresa checked them out of the motel, and the three of them went to Garrett's house. Kevin wanted to spend their last few hours on the beach, and Theresa and Garrett sat with him near the water's edge. For a while Garrett and Kevin played Frisbee, and realizing it was getting late in the afternoon, Theresa went inside and found something to eat.

They had a quick dinner on the back deck—hot dogs on the grill—before Garrett drove them to the airport. After Theresa and Kevin had safely boarded, Garrett stayed a few minutes, watching until the plane finally began to back out of the gate. When it drew out of sight, he walked back to the truck and returned home, already watching the clock to see how long it would be until he could call her that evening.

In their seats, Theresa and Kevin thumbed through magazines. Halfway through the first leg of their trip home, Kevin suddenly turned to her and asked:

"Mom, do you like Garrett?"

"Yes, I do. But more important, do you like him?"

"I think he's cool. For a grownup, I mean."

Theresa smiled. "You two seemed to have hit it off. Are you glad we came?"

He nodded. "Yeah, I'm glad." He paused, fidgeting with the magazine. "Mom, can I ask you something?"

"Anything."

"Are you gonna marry Garrett?"

"I don't know. Why?"

"Do you want to?"

It took her a few moments to answer. "I'm not sure. I do know that I don't want to marry him right now. We're still getting to know each other."

"But you might want to marry him in the future?"

"Maybe."

Kevin looked relieved. "I'm glad. You seemed like you were really happy when you were with him."

"Could you tell?"

"Mom, I'm twelve. I know more than you think."

She reached over and touched his hand. "Well, what would you have said if I'd told you I did want to marry him now?"

He was quiet for a moment. "I guess I'd wonder where we were gonna live."

For the life of her, Theresa couldn't think of a good response. Where indeed?

CHAPTER 11

_F_our days after Theresa left Wilmington, Garrett had another dream, only this time it was about Catherine. In the dream
they were in a grassy field bordered by a cliff overlooking the
ocean. They were walking together, holding hands and talking,
when Garrett said something that made her laugh. All at once
she broke away from him. Looking over her shoulder and laughing, she called for Garrett to chase her. He did, laughing as well,
feeling much as he had the day they were married.

Watching her run, he couldn't help but notice how beautiful
she was. Her flowing hair reflected the light of the high yellow
sun, her legs were lean and moving rhythmically, effortlessly.
Her smile, despite the fact she was running, looked easy and relaxed, as if she were standing still.

"Chase me, Garrett. Can you catch me?" she called.

The sound of laughter after she said it floated in the air around him, sounding musical.

He was slowly gaining on her when he noticed that she was heading toward the cliff. In her excitement and joy, she didn't seem to realize where she was going.

*But that's ridiculous*, he thought. *She has to know.*

Garrett called for her to stop, but instead she began to run faster.

She was approaching the edge of the cliff.

With a feeling of certain dread, he saw that he was still too far behind her to catch her.

He ran as fast as he could, screaming for her to turn around. She didn't appear to hear him. He felt the adrenaline rush through his body, fed by a paralyzing fear. "Stop, Catherine!" he shouted, his lungs exhausted. "The cliff—you're not watching where you're going!" The more he shouted, the softer his voice became, until it turned into a whisper.

Catherine kept on running, unaware. The cliff was only a few feet away.

He was closing ground.

But he was still too far behind.

"Stop!" he screamed again, though this time he knew she couldn't hear it. His voice had diminished to nothing. The panic he felt then was greater than anything he'd ever known. With everything he had, he willed his legs to move faster, but they began to tire, turning heavier with every step he took.

*I'm not going to make it*, he thought, panicking.

Then, just as suddenly as she had broken away, she stopped. Turning to face him, she seemed oblivious of any danger.

She stood only inches from the edge.

"Don't move," he shouted, but again it came out in a whisper. He stopped a few feet from her and held out his hand, breathing heavily.

"Come toward me," he pleaded. "You're right on the edge."

She smiled and glanced behind her. Noticing how close she was to falling, she turned toward him.

"Did you think you were going to lose me?"

"Yes," he said quietly, "and I promise not to ever let it happen again."


Garrett woke and sat up in bed, staying awake for several hours afterward. When he finally fell back to sleep, it was fitful at best, and it was almost ten o'clock the next morning before he was able to get up. Still exhausted and feeling depressed, he found it impossible to think about anything but the dream. Not knowing what to do, he called his father, who met him for breakfast in their usual place.

"I don't know why I feel this way," he told his father after a few minutes of small talk. "I just don't understand it."

His father didn't answer. Instead he watched his son over his coffee cup, remaining silent as his son went on.

"It's not like she did anything to upset me," he continued. "We just spent a long weekend together, and I really care for her. I met her son, too, and he's great. It's just that . . . I don't know. I don't know if I'm going to be able to keep this up."

Garrett paused. The only sound came from the tables around them.

"Keep what up?" Jeb Blake finally asked.

Garrett stirred his coffee absently. "I don't know whether I can see her again."

His father cocked an eyebrow but didn't reply. Garrett went on.

"Maybe it's just not meant to be. I mean, she doesn't even live here. She's a thousand miles away, she's got her own life, she's got her own interests. And here I am, living down here and leading an entirely separate life. Maybe she'd do better with someone else, someone she could see on a regular basis."

He thought about what he'd said, knowing that he didn't quite believe himself. Still, he didn't want to tell his father about the dream.

"I mean, how can we build a relationship if we don't see each other very often?"

Again his father said nothing. Garrett carried on, as if talking to himself.

"If she lived here and I could see her every day, I think I'd feel differently. But with her being gone . . ."

He trailed off, trying to make sense of his thoughts. After a while he spoke again.

"I just don't see how we can make it work. I've thought about it a lot, and I don't see how it could be possible. I don't want to move to Boston, and I'm sure she doesn't want to move here, so where would that leave us?"

Garrett stopped and waited for his father to say something—anything—in response to what he'd said up to that point. But for a while, he didn't make a sound. Finally he sighed and looked away.

"It sounds to me like you're making excuses," Jeb said quietly.

"You're trying to convince yourself, and you're using me to listen to yourself talk."

"No, Dad, I'm not. I'm just trying to figure out this whole thing."

"Who do you think you're talking to, Garrett?" Jeb Blake shook his head. "Sometimes, I swear you think I just fell off the turnip truck and bumbled through life without learning anything along the way. But I know exactly what you're going through. You've gotten so caught up in being alone that you're afraid of what might happen if you actually find someone else that can take you away from it."

"I'm not afraid," Garrett protested.

His father cut him off sharply. "You can't even admit it to yourself, can you?"

The disappointment in his tone was unmistakable. "You know, Garrett, when your mom died, I made excuses, too. Over the years, I told myself all sorts of things. And you wanna know where it got me?"

He stared at his son. "I'm old and tired, and most of all, I'm alone. If I could go back in time, I'd change a lot about myself, and I'll be damned if I'm going to let you do the same things I did."

Jeb paused before going on, his tone softening. "I was wrong, Garrett. I was wrong not to try to find someone else. I was wrong to feel guilty about your mom. I was wrong to keep living my life the way I did, always suffering inside and wondering what she would have thought. Because you know what? I think your mom would have wanted me to find someone else. Your mom would have wanted me to be happy. And you know why?"

Garrett didn't answer.

"Because she loved me. And if you think that you're showing your love to Catherine by suffering the way you've been doing, then somewhere along the way, I must have messed up in raising you."

"You didn't mess up. . . ."

"I must have. Because when I look at you, I see myself, and to be honest, I'd rather see someone different. I'd like to see someone who learned that it's okay to go on, that it's okay to find someone that can make you happy. But right now, it's like I'm looking in the mirror and seeing myself twenty years ago."

Garrett spent the rest of the afternoon alone, walking on the beach, thinking about what his father had said. Looking back, he knew he'd been dishonest from the start of the conversation and wasn't surprised that his father had figured it out. Why, then, had he wanted to talk to him? Had he wanted his father to confront him as he had?

As the afternoon wore on, his depression gave way to confusion, then to a sort of numbness. By the time he called Theresa later in the evening, the feelings of betrayal he'd felt as a result of the dream had subsided enough to speak with her. They were still there, though not as strong, and when she answered the phone, he felt them diminish even further. The sound of her voice reminded him of the way he felt when they were together.

"I'm glad you called," she said cheerfully, "I thought a lot about you today."

"I thought about you, too," he said. "I wish you were here right now."

"Are you okay? You sound a little down."

"I'm fine. . . . Just lonely, that's all. How was your day?"

"Typical. Too much to do at work, too much to do at home. But it's better now that I've heard from you."

Garrett smiled. "Is Kevin around?"

"He's in his room reading a book about scuba diving. He tells me he wants to be a dive instructor when he grows up."

"Where could he have gotten that idea?"

"I haven't the slightest," she said, amusement in her tone. "How about you? What did you do today?"

"Not much, actually. I didn't go into the shop—I sort of took the day off and wandered the beaches."

"Dreaming about me, I hope?"

The irony of her comment was not lost on him. He didn't answer directly.

"I just really missed you today."

"I've only been gone a few days," she said gently.

"I know. And speaking of that, when will we get to see each other again?"

Theresa sat at the dining room table and glanced at her Day-Timer.

"Umm . . . how about in three weeks? I was thinking that maybe you could come up here this time. Kevin has a week-long soccer camp, and we'd be able to spend some time alone."

"Would you like to come down here instead?"

"It would be better if you came up here, if that's okay. I'm running low on vacation days, and I think we'd be able to work around my schedule. And besides, I think it's about time you got out of North Carolina, just so you can see what the rest of the country has to offer."

As she spoke, he found himself staring at Catherine's picture on the nightstand. It took him a few seconds to respond. "Sure . . . I guess I could do that."

"You don't sound too sure about it."

"I am."

"Is there something else, then?"

"No."

She paused uncertainly. "Are you really okay, Garrett?"

It took him a few days and several phone calls to Theresa to feel somewhat normal again. More than once he found himself calling her late in the evening, just to hear her voice.

"Hey," he'd say, "it's me again."

"Hi, Garrett, what's up?" she'd ask sleepily.

"Not much. I just wanted to say good night before you crawled into bed."

"I'm already in bed."

"What time is it?"

She glanced toward the clock. "Almost midnight."

"Why are you awake? You should be sleeping," he'd tease, and then he'd let her hang up the phone so she could get her rest.

Sometimes, if he couldn't sleep, he'd think about his week with Theresa, remembering how good her skin felt to his touch, overwhelmed by his desire to hold her again.

Then, walking into the bedroom, he'd see Catherine's picture by his bed. And at that moment the dream would rush forward with crystal clarity.

He knew he was still unsettled by the dream. In the past he would have written a letter to Catherine to help him get it into perspective. Then, taking *Happenstance* out on the same route he and Catherine had sailed for the first time after *Happenstance* had been restored, he'd seal it and toss it into the ocean.

Strangely, he wasn't able to do it this time. When he sat down to write, the words simply wouldn't come. Finally growing frustrated, he willed himself to remember, instead.

*"Now there's a surprise,"* Garrett said as he pointed at Catherine's plate. On it, she was piling spinach salad from the buffet in front of them.

*Catherine shrugged dismissively. "What's wrong with wanting a salad?"*

*"Nothing's wrong with it," he said quickly. "It's just that this is the third time you've eaten it this week."*

*"I know. I've just been craving it. I don't know why."*

*"If you keep eating it like you do, you're going to turn into a rabbit."*

*She laughed and poured on the salad dressing. "If that were the case," she said, looking at his plate, "if you keep eating that seafood, you'll turn into a shark."*

*"I am a shark," he said, raising his eyebrows.*

*"You may be a shark, but if you keep teasing me, you'll never get the chance to prove it with me."*

*He smiled. "Why don't I prove it this weekend?"*

*"When? You'll be working this weekend."*

*"Not this weekend. Believe it or not, I've cleared my schedule so that we can spend some time together. We haven't spent a whole weekend alone since I don't know when."*

*"What did you have in mind?"*

*"I don't know. Maybe sailing, maybe something else. Whatever you want to do."*

*She laughed. "Well, I did have big plans—my trip to Paris for a little shopping, a quick safari or two . . . but I guess I can rearrange things."*

*"Then it's a date."*

*       *       *

As the days passed, the image of the dream began to fade. Each time Garrett talked to Theresa, he found himself feeling a little more renewed. He also spoke to Kevin a couple of times, and his enthusiasm for Garrett's presence in their lives helped him regain his footing as well. Even though the heat and humidity of August seemed to make time pass more slowly than usual, he kept himself as busy as he could, doing his best not to think about the complexities of his new situation.

Two weeks later—a few days before he was leaving for Boston—Garrett was cooking in the kitchen when the phone rang.

"Hiya, stranger," she said. "Got a few minutes?"

"I always have a few minutes to talk when it comes to you."

"I was just calling to find out what time your flight is coming in. You weren't sure the last time we talked."

"Hold on," he said, rummaging through the kitchen drawer for his itinerary. "Here it is—I'll be getting into Boston a few minutes after one."

"That works out perfectly. I've got to drop Kevin off a few hours earlier, and it'll give me time to get the apartment in shape."

"Cleaning up for me?"

"You get the full treatment. I'm even going to dust."

"I feel honored."

"You should. Only you and my parents get that kind of attention."

"Should I pack a pair of white gloves to make sure you've done a good job?"

"If you do, you won't live to see the evening."

He laughed and changed the subject. "I'm looking forward to seeing you again," he said earnestly. "These last three weeks were a lot harder than the first two."

"I know. I could hear it in your voice. You were really down for a few days, and . . . well, I was beginning to get worried about you."

He wondered whether she suspected the reason for his melancholy. Clearing his mind, he went on. "I was, but I'm over it now. I've already packed my bags."

"I hope you didn't take up any space with unnecessary items."

"Like what?"

"Like . . . I don't know . . . pajamas."

He laughed. "I don't own any pajamas."

"That's good. Because even if you did, you wouldn't need them."

Three days later, Garrett Blake arrived in Boston.

After picking him up from the airport, Theresa showed him around the city. They had lunch at Faneuil Hall, watched the skullers gliding on the Charles River, and took a quick tour of the Harvard campus. As usual, they held hands most of the day, reveling in each other's company.

More than once, Garrett found himself wondering why the last three weeks had been so difficult for him. He knew that part of his anxiety stemmed from the dream, but spending time with Theresa made the dream's troubling feelings seem distant and insubstantial. Every time Theresa laughed or squeezed his hand, she reaffirmed the feelings he'd had when she was last in Wilmington, banishing the dark thoughts that plagued him in her absence.

When the day began to cool and the sun dipped below the trees, Theresa and Garrett stopped for some Mexican food to bring back to her apartment. Sitting on her living room floor in the glow of candlelight, Garrett looked around the room.

"You have a nice place," he said, forking up some beans with a tortilla chip. "For some reason, I thought it would be smaller than it is. It's bigger than my house."

"Only by a little, but thanks. It works for us. It's real convenient to everything."

"Like restaurants?"

"Exactly. I wasn't kidding when I told you I didn't like to cook. I'm not exactly Martha Stewart."

"Who?"

"Never mind," she said.

Outside her apartment, the sound of traffic was clearly audible. A car screeched on the street below, a horn blared, and all at once the air was filled with noise as other cars joined in the chorus.

"Is it always this quiet?" he asked.

She nodded toward the windows. "Friday and Saturday nights are the worst—usually it's not so bad. But you get used to it if you live here long enough."

The sounds of city living continued. A siren blared in the distance, growing steadily louder as it approached.

"Would you like to put on some music?" Garrett asked.

"Sure. What kind do you like?"

"I like *both* kinds," he said, pausing dramatically. "Country *and* western."

She laughed. "I don't have anything like that here."

He shook his head, enjoying his own joke. "I was kidding,

anyway. It's an old line. Not too funny, but I've been waiting for my chance to say it for years."

"You must have watched a lot of *Hee-Haw* as a kid."

Now it was his turn to laugh.

"Back to my original question—what kind of music do you like?" she persisted.

"Anything you have is fine."

"How about some jazz?"

"Sounds good."

Theresa got up and chose something she thought he might like and slipped it into the CD player. In a few moments the music started, just as the traffic congestion outside seemed to clear.

"So what do you think of Boston so far?" she asked, reclaiming her seat.

"I like it. For a big city, it's not too bad. It doesn't seem as impersonal as I thought it would be, and it's cleaner, too. I guess I pictured it differently. You know—crowds, asphalt, tall buildings, not a tree in sight, and muggers on every corner. But it's not like that at all."

She smiled. "It is nice, isn't it? I mean, it's not beachfront, but it has its own appeal. Especially if you consider what the city has to offer. You could go to the symphony, or to museums, or just stroll around in the Commons. There's something for everyone here—they even have a sailing club."

"I can see why you like it here," he said, wondering why it sounded as if she were selling the place.

"I do. And Kevin likes it, too."

He changed the subject: "You said he's at soccer camp?"

She nodded. "Yeah. He's trying out for an all-star team for

twelve and under. I don't know if he'll make it, but he thinks he has a pretty good shot. Last year, he made the final cut as an eleven-year-old."

"It sounds like he's good."

"He is," she said with a nod. She pushed their now empty plates to the side and moved closer. "But enough about Kevin," she said softly. "We don't always have to talk about him. We can talk about other things, you know."

"Like what?"

She kissed his neck. "Like what I want to do with you now that I have you all to myself."

"Are you sure you just want to talk about it?"

"You're right," she whispered. "Who wants to talk at a time like this?"

The next day, Theresa again took Garrett on a tour of Boston, spending most of the morning in the Italian neighborhoods of the North End, wandering the narrow, twisting streets and stopping for the occasional cannoli and coffee. Though Garrett knew she wrote columns for the paper, he didn't know exactly what else her job entailed. He asked her about it as they made their way leisurely through the city.

"Can't you write a column from your home?"

"In time, I suppose I can. But right now, it's not possible."

"Why not?"

"Well, it's not in my contract, for starters. Besides, I have to do a lot more than sit at my computer and write. Often, I have to interview people, so there's time involved in that—sometimes even a little travel. Plus, there's all the research I have to do, especially when I write about medical or psychological issues, and when I'm in the office, I have access to a lot more sources. And then there's the fact that I need a place where I can be reached. A lot of the stuff I do is human interest, and I get calls from people all day long. If I worked out of my home, I know a lot of people would call in the evenings when I'm spending time with Kevin, and I'm not willing to give up my time with him."

"Do you get calls at home now?"

"Occasionally. But my number isn't listed, so not all that often."

"Do you get a lot of crazy calls?"

She nodded. "I think all columnists do. A lot of people call the paper with stories they want printed. I get calls about people who are locked up in prison who shouldn't be, I get calls about city services and how the garbage isn't being picked up on time. I get calls about street crime. It seems like I've gotten calls about everything."

"I thought you said you write about parenting."

"I do."

"Then why would they call you? Why don't they call someone else?"

She shrugged. "I'm sure they do, but it still doesn't stop them from calling me. A lot of people begin their calls with, 'No one else will listen to me and you're my last hope.'" She glanced at him before going on. "I guess they think I'll be able to do something about their problems."

"Why?"

"Well, columnists are different from other newspaper writers. Most things printed in the newspaper are impersonal—straightforward reporting, facts and figures, and the like. But if people read my column every day, I guess they think they know me.

They begin to see me as a friend of sorts. And people look to their friends to help them out when they need it."

"It must put you in an awkward position sometimes."

She shrugged. "It does, but I try not to think about it. Besides, there are good parts about my job, too—giving information that people can use, keeping up with the latest medical data and spelling it out in laymen's terms, even sharing lighthearted stories just to make the day a little easier."

Garrett stopped at a sidewalk store selling fresh fruit. He picked out a couple of apples from the bin, then handed one to Theresa.

"What's the most popular thing you've ever written about in your column?" he asked.

Theresa felt her breath catch. *The most popular? Easy—I found a message in a bottle once, and I got a couple of hundred letters.*

She forced herself to think of something else. "Oh . . . I get a lot of letters when I write about teaching disabled children," she said finally.

"That must be rewarding," he said, paying the shopkeeper.

"It is."

Before taking a bite of his apple, Garrett asked: "Could you still write your column even if you changed papers?"

She considered the question. "It would be hard to do, especially if I want to continue to syndicate. Since I'm so new and still establishing my name, having the *Boston Times* behind me really helps. Why?"

"Just curious," he said quietly.

The next morning Theresa went into work for a few hours but was home for the day a little after lunchtime. They spent the afternoon at the Boston Commons, where they ate a picnic lunch. Their lunch was interrupted twice by people who recognized her from her picture in the paper, and Garrett realized that Theresa was actually more well-known than he had thought.

"I didn't know you were such a celebrity," he said wryly after the second person walked away.

"I'm not really a celebrity. It's just that my picture appears above my column, so people know what I look like."

"Does this sort of thing happen a lot?"

"Not really. Maybe a few times a week."

"That's a lot," he said, surprised.

She shook her head. "Not when you consider real celebrities. They can't even go to the store without someone taking their picture. I pretty much lead a normal life."

"But it still must be odd to have total strangers coming up to you."

"Actually, it's kind of flattering. Most people are very nice about it."

"Either way, I'm glad I didn't know you were so famous right off the bat."

"Why?"

"I might have been too intimidated to ask you to go sailing."

She reached over and took his hand. "I can't imagine you being intimidated about anything."

"Then you don't know me very well."

She was quiet for a moment. "Would you really have been intimidated?" she asked sheepishly.

"Probably."

"Why?"

"I guess I'd wonder what someone like you could possibly see in me."

She leaned over to kiss him. "I'll tell you what I see. I see the man that I love, the man who makes me happy . . . someone I want to continue to see for a long time."

"How come you always know just what to say?"

"Because," she said quietly, "I know more about you than you would ever suspect."

"Such as?"

A lazy smile played over her lips. "For instance, I know you want me to kiss you again."

"I do?"

"Absolutely."

And she was right.

Later that evening Garrett said, "You know, Theresa, I can't find a single thing wrong with you."

They were in the tub together, surrounded by mountains of bubbles, Theresa leaning against his chest. He used a sponge to wash her skin as he spoke.

"What's that supposed to mean?" she asked curiously, turning her head to look at him.

"Just what I said. I can't find a single thing wrong with you. I mean, you're perfect."

"I'm not perfect, Garrett," she said, pleased nonetheless.

"But you are. You're beautiful, you're kind, you make me laugh, you're intelligent, and you're a great mother as well. Toss in the fact that you're famous, and I don't think there's anyone who can measure up to you."

She caressed his arm, relaxing against him. "I think you see me through rose-colored glasses. But I like it. . . ."

"Are you saying I'm biased?"

"No—but you've only seen my good side so far."

"I didn't know you had another side to you," he said, squeezing both of her arms simultaneously. "Both sides feel pretty good right now."

She laughed. "You know what I mean. You haven't seen my dark side yet."

"You don't have a dark side."

"Sure I do. Everyone does. It's just that when you're around, it likes to keep itself hidden."

"So, how would you describe your dark side?"

She thought for a moment. "Well, for starters, I'm stubborn, and I can get mean when I'm angry. I tend to lash out and say the first thing that pops in my head, and believe me, it's not pretty. I also have a tendency to tell others exactly what I'm thinking, even when I know it would be best just to walk away."

"That doesn't sound so bad."

"You haven't been on the receiving end yet."

"It still doesn't sound so bad."

"Well . . . let me put it this way. When I first confronted David about the affair, I called him some of the worst names in the English language."

"He deserved it."

"But I'm not sure he deserved to have a vase thrown at him."

"Did you do that?"

She nodded. "You should have seen the look on his face. He'd never seen me like that before."

"What did he do?"

"Nothing—I think he was too shocked to do anything. Especially when I started in with the plates. I cleaned out most of the cupboard that night."

He grinned in admiration. "I didn't know you were so feisty."

"It's my midwest upbringing. Don't mess with me, buster."

"I won't."

"That's good. I'm much more accurate these days."

"I'll remember that."

They sank deeper into the warm water. Garrett continued to move the sponge over her body.

"I still think you're perfect," he said softly.

She closed her eyes. "Even with my dark side?" she asked.

"Especially with your dark side. It adds an element of excitement."

"I'm glad, because I think you're pretty perfect yourself."


The rest of their vacation flew by. In the mornings Theresa would go into work for a few hours, then come home and spend the afternoons and evenings with Garrett. In the evenings they would either order something in or head to one of the many small restaurants near her apartment. Sometimes they rented a movie to watch afterward, but usually they preferred to spend their time without other distractions.

On Friday night Kevin called from the soccer camp. Excitedly he explained that he'd made the all-star team. Though it meant more games would be played outside of Boston and they'd have to travel most weekends, Theresa was happy for him. Then, surprising her, Kevin asked to speak to Garrett. Garrett listened as he described what had happened that week and congratulated him. After hanging up, Theresa opened a bottle of wine and the two of them celebrated Kevin's good fortune until the early morning hours.

On Sunday morning—the day he was leaving—they had brunch with Deanna and Brian. Garrett saw immediately what Theresa loved about Deanna. She was both charming and amusing, and Garrett found himself laughing throughout his meal. Deanna asked him about diving and sailing, while Brian speculated that if he owned his own business, he'd never get anything done because golf would simply take over his life.

Theresa was pleased that they seemed to get along so well. Excusing themselves after they'd eaten, Deanna and Theresa headed together into the bathroom to chat.

"So, what do you think?" Theresa asked expectantly.

"He's great," Deanna admitted. "He's even better looking than he was in the pictures you brought back."

"I know. My heart skips a beat whenever I look at him."

Deanna primped her hair, doing her best to add a little body to it. "Did your week turn out as well as you hoped?"

"Even better."

Deanna beamed. "I could tell by the way he was looking at you that he really cares about you, too. The way you two act together reminds me of Brian and me. You seem like a good match."

"Do you really think so?"

"I wouldn't say it if I didn't mean it."

Deanna took some lipstick out of her purse and began to apply it. "So, how did he like Boston?" she asked offhandedly.

Theresa took out her own lipstick as well. "It's not what he's used to, but he seemed to have enjoyed himself. We went to a lot of fun places."

"Did he say anything in particular?"

"No . . . why?" She looked at Deanna curiously.

"Because," Deanna answered evenly, "I was just wondering if he'd said anything that might make you think he'd move here if you asked him to."

Her comment made Theresa think about something she'd been avoiding.

"We haven't talked about it yet," she said finally.

"Were you planning to?"

*The distance between us is a problem, but there's still something else, isn't there?* she heard a voice inside her whisper.

Not wanting to think about it, she shook her head. "I don't think it's the right time—at least not yet." She paused, gathering her thoughts. "I mean—I know we have to talk about it sometime, but I don't think we've known each other long enough to start making decisions about the future. We're still getting to know each other."

Deanna eyed her with motherly suspicion. "But you've known him long enough to fall in love with him, haven't you?"

"Yes," Theresa conceded.

"Then you know that this decision is coming, whether you want to face it or not."

It took a moment for her to answer. "I know."

Deanna put her hand on Theresa's shoulder. "What if it comes down to losing him or leaving Boston?"

Theresa pondered the question and its implications. "I'm not sure," she said quietly, and looked at Deanna uncertainly.

"Can I give you some advice?" Deanna asked.

Theresa nodded. Deanna led her out of the bathroom by the

arm, leaning toward Theresa's ear so that no one could overhear them.

"Whatever you decide to do, remember that you have to be able to go forward in life without looking back. If you're sure that Garrett can give you the kind of love you need and that you'll be happy, then you have to do whatever it takes to keep him. True love is rare, and it's the only thing that gives life real meaning."

"But doesn't the same thing apply to him? Shouldn't he be willing to sacrifice as well?"

"Of course."

"Then where does that leave me?"

"It leaves you with the same problem you had before, Theresa—one that you're definitely going to have to think about."

Over the next two months, their long-distance relationship began to evolve in a way that neither Theresa nor Garrett expected though both should have foreseen.

Working around each other's schedules, they were able to get together three more times, each time for a weekend. Once, Theresa flew down to Wilmington so they could be alone, and they spent their time holed up in Garrett's house, except for an evening they spent sailing. Garrett traveled to Boston twice, spending much of his time on the road for Kevin's soccer tournaments, though he hadn't minded. They were the first soccer games he'd ever attended, and he found himself caught up in the action more than he thought he would.

"How come you're not as excited as I am?" he'd asked Theresa during one particularly frenzied moment on the field.

"Why don't you wait until you've seen a few hundred games, and then I'm sure you could answer your own question," she'd replied playfully.

When they were together during those weekends, it was as if nothing else mattered in the world. Usually Kevin would spend one of the nights at a friend's house so they could be alone, at least for a little while. They spent hours talking and laughing, holding each other close, and making love, trying to make up for weeks spent apart. Yet neither of them broached the subject of what was going to happen to their relationship in the future. They lived moment to moment, neither of them exactly sure of what to expect from the other. Not that they weren't in love. Of that, at least, they were certain.

But because they didn't see each other very often, their relationship had more ups and downs than either of them had experienced before. Since everything felt right when they were together, everything felt wrong when they weren't. Garrett, especially, found himself struggling with the distance between them. Usually the good feelings he'd had when they saw each other lasted for a few days afterward, but then he'd find himself growing depressed as he anticipated the weeks before he saw her again.

Of course, he wanted them to spend more time together than was possible. Now that summer had passed, it was easier for him to get away than it was for her. Even with most of the employees gone, there wasn't much to do around the shop. But Theresa's schedule was completely different, if only because of Kevin. He was in school again, he had tournaments on the weekends, and it was difficult for her to break away, even for a few days. Although Garrett was willing to visit Boston to see her more often, Theresa simply didn't have the time. More than once he'd suggested another trip up to see her, but for one reason or another, it hadn't worked out.

True, he knew there were couples who faced living situations more difficult than theirs. His father told him stories of how he and his mother hadn't spoken for months at a time. He'd gone to Korea and spent two years with the marines, and when times were tough in the shrimping business, he used to find work with passing freighters on their way to South America. Sometimes those trips lasted months. The only thing his parents had during those times were letters, which were infrequent at best. Garrett and Theresa had something less difficult, but that still didn't make it easy.

He knew the distance between them was a problem, but it didn't seem as if it were going to change anytime in the near future. As he saw it, there were only two solutions—he could move, or she could move. No matter how he looked at it—and no matter how much they cared for each other—it always came down to one of those two choices.

Deep down, he suspected that Theresa was having the same thoughts he was, which was why neither of them wanted to talk about it. It seemed easier not to bring it up, since it would mean starting down a path that neither was sure they wanted to follow.

One of them was going to have to change his or her life dramatically.

But which one?

He had his own business in Wilmington, the kind of life he wanted to live, the only life he knew how to live. Boston was nice to visit, but it wasn't home. He'd never even contemplated living somewhere else. And then there was his father—he was getting up in years, and despite the strong exterior, his age was catching up with him and Garrett was all he had.

On the other hand, Theresa had strong ties to Boston. Though her parents lived elsewhere, Kevin was in a school he liked, she had a blossoming career with a major newspaper, and she had a network of friends she'd have to leave. She'd worked hard to get where she was, and if she left Boston, she'd probably have to give it up. Would she be able to do that without resenting him for what he'd made her do?

Garrett didn't want to think about it. Instead he focused on the fact that he loved Theresa, clinging to the belief that if they were meant to be together, they would find a way to do it.

Deep down, however, he knew it wasn't going to be that easy, and not just because of the distance between them. After he'd returned from his second trip to Boston, he had a picture of Theresa enlarged and framed. He set it on the bedstand opposite Catherine's picture, but despite his feelings for Theresa, it seemed out of place in his bedroom. A few days later he moved the picture across the room, but it still didn't help. Wherever he put it, it seemed to him as if Catherine's eyes would follow it. *This is ridiculous*, he told himself after moving it yet again. Nonetheless he found himself finally slipping Theresa's picture into the drawer and reaching for Catherine's instead. Sighing, he sat on the bed and held it in front of him.

"We didn't have these problems," he whispered as he ran his finger over her image. "With us, everything always seemed so easy, didn't it?"

When he realized the picture wouldn't answer, he cursed his foolishness and retrieved Theresa's picture.

Staring at them both, even he understood why he was having so much trouble with it all. He loved Theresa more than he ever thought he could . . . but he still loved Catherine. . . .

Was it possible to love them both at once?

"I can't wait to see you again," Garrett said.

It was the middle of November, a couple of weeks before Thanksgiving. Theresa and Kevin were flying home to see her parents for the holidays, and Theresa had made arrangements to come down the weekend before to spend some time with Garrett. It had been a month since they'd seen each other.

"I'm looking forward to it, too," she said. "And you promised that I'd finally get to meet your father, right?"

"He's planning on cooking an early Thanksgiving dinner for us at his place. He keeps asking me what you like to eat. I think he wants to make a good impression."

"Tell him he doesn't have to worry. Anything he makes will be fine."

"That's what I keep telling him. But I can tell he's nervous about it."

"Why?"

"Because you'll be the first guest we've ever had over. For years, it's just been the two of us."

"Am I interrupting a family tradition?"

"No—I like to think that we're starting a new one. Besides, he was the one who volunteered, remember?"

"Do you think he'll like me?"

"I know he will."

*       *       *

When he found out Theresa was coming, Jeb Blake did some things he hadn't ever done before. First, he hired someone to come in and clean the small house where he lived, a job that ended up taking almost two days because he was so adamant that the house be spotless. He also bought a new shirt and tie. Emerging from his bedroom in his new clothes, he couldn't help but notice the surprise in Garrett's eyes.

"How do I look?" he asked.

"You look fine, but why are you wearing a tie?"

"It's not for you—it's for dinner this weekend."

Garrett continued to stare at his father, a wry smile on his face. "I don't think I've ever seen you in a tie before."

"I've worn them before. You just haven't noticed."

"You don't have to wear a tie just because Theresa is coming."

"I know that," he replied tersely, "I just felt like wearing one to dinner this year."

"You're nervous about meeting her, aren't you?"

"No."

"Dad—you don't have to be someone you're not. I'm sure Theresa would like you no matter how you were dressed."

"That doesn't mean I can't look nice for your lady friend, does it?"

"No."

"Then I guess it's settled, isn't it? I didn't come out here to get your advice about it, I came out here to see if I looked okay."

"You look fine."

"Good."

He turned and started back to the bedroom, already untucking his shirt and loosening the tie. Garrett watched him vanish from sight, and a moment later he heard his father call his name.

"What now?" Garrett asked.

His father peeked his head around the corner. "You're wearing a tie, too, aren't you?"

"I wasn't planning on it."

"Well, change your plans. I don't want Theresa to find out that I raised someone who didn't know how to dress for company."

The day before her arrival, Garrett helped his father finish his preparations. Garrett mowed the lawn while Jeb unpacked the wedding china he seldom, if ever, used anymore and washed the dishes by hand. After searching for matching silverware—easier said than done—Jeb found a tablecloth in the closet, deciding it would be a nice touch. He tossed it into the washing machine just as Garrett came inside after finishing the yard. Garrett walked to the cupboard and pulled a glass from the shelf.

"What time is she coming in tomorrow?" Jeb asked from around the corner.

Garrett filled the glass with water and answered over his shoulder. "Her plane gets in about ten o'clock. We should be here around eleven or so."

"What time do you think she'll want to eat?"

"I don't know."

Jeb walked into the kitchen. "You didn't ask her?"

"No."

"Then how will I know when to put the turkey in the oven?"

Garrett took a drink of water. "Just plan on us eating sometime in the middle of the afternoon. Anytime is fine, I'm sure."

"Do you think you should call and ask her?"

"I really don't think it's necessary. It's not that big of a deal."

"Maybe not to you. But it's the first time I'll be meeting her, and if you two end up getting married, I don't want to be the subject of any humorous stories later on."

Garrett raised his eyebrows. "Who said we're getting married?"

"No one."

"Then why did you bring it up?"

"Because," he said quickly, "I figured one of us had to, and I wasn't sure you were ever going to get around to it."

Garrett stared at his father. "So, you think I should marry her?"

Jeb winked as he answered. "It doesn't matter what I think, it's what you think that's important, isn't it?"

Later that evening, Garrett opened his front door just as the phone began to ring. After rushing to the phone, he picked it up and heard the voice he expected.

"Garrett?" Theresa asked. "You sound out of breath."

He smiled. "Oh, hey, Theresa. I just walked in. My father had me over at his house all day getting the place ready—he's really looking forward to meeting you."

There was an uncomfortable pause. "About tomorrow . . . ," she said finally.

He felt his throat tighten. "What about tomorrow?"

It took a moment for her to answer. "I'm really sorry, Garrett . . . I don't know how to tell you this, but I'm not going to be able to make it down to Wilmington after all."

"Is something wrong?"

"No, everything's fine. It's just that something came up at the last minute—a big conference that I've got to go to."

"What kind of conference?"

"It's for my job." She paused again. "I know it sounds terrible, but I wouldn't go unless it was really important."

He closed his eyes. "What's it for?"

"It's for bigwig editors and media types—they're meeting in Dallas this weekend. Deanna thinks it would be a good idea if I met some of them."

"Did you just find out about it?"

"No . . . I mean, yes. Well—I knew there was going to be a meeting, but I wasn't supposed to go. Usually, columnists aren't invited, but Deanna pulled some strings and arranged for me to go with her." She hesitated. "I'm really sorry, Garrett, but like I said, it would be wonderful exposure, and it's an opportunity of a lifetime."

He was silent for a moment. Then he said simply, "I understand."

"You're angry with me, aren't you."

"No."

"Are you sure?"

"I'm sure."

She knew by his tone that he wasn't telling the truth, but she didn't think there was anything she could say that would make him feel any better.

"Will you tell your father that I'm sorry?"

"Yeah, I'll tell him."

"Can I call you this weekend?"

"If you want to."

The next day he ate dinner with his father, who did his best to play down the whole affair.

"If it's like she said," his father explained, "she had a good reason. It's not like she can put her job on the back burner. She has a son to support, and she's got to do her best to provide for him. Besides, it's just one weekend—not much in the grand scheme of things."

Garrett nodded, listening to his father but still upset about the whole thing. Jeb went on.

"I'm sure you two will be able to work it out. In fact, she's probably going to do something real special the next time you two are together."

Garrett said nothing. Jeb took a couple of bites before speaking again.

"You've got to understand, Garrett—she's got responsibilities, just like you do, and sometimes those responsibilities take priority. I'm sure that if something happened in the shop that you had to take care of, you would have done the same thing."

Garrett leaned back, pushing his half-eaten plate to the side. "I understand all that, Dad. It's just that I haven't seen her for a month now, and I was really looking forward to her visit."

"Don't you think she wanted to see you, too?"

"She said she did."

Jeb leaned across the table and pushed Garrett's plate in front of him again. "Eat your dinner," he said. "I spent all day cooking, and you're not going to waste it."

Garrett looked at his plate. Though he wasn't hungry anymore, he picked up his fork and took a small bite.

"You know," his father said as he picked at his own food, "this isn't the last time this is going to happen, so you shouldn't get so down about it now."

"What do you mean?"

"I mean that as long as you two continue to live a thousand miles apart, things like this are going to come up and you won't see each other as much as either one of you wants."

"Don't you think I know that?"

"I'm sure you do. But I don't know if either one of you has the guts to do something about it."

Garrett looked at his father, thinking, Gee, Dad, tell me how you really feel. Don't hold back.

"When I was young," Jeb continued, oblivious of his son's sour expression, "things were a lot simpler. If a man loved a woman, he asked her to marry him, and then they lived together. It was as simple as that. But you two—it's like you don't know what to do."

"I've told you before—it's not that easy. . . ."

"Sure it is—if you love her, then find a way to be with her. It's as simple as that. That way, if something comes up and you don't see each other one weekend, you don't end up acting like your life is over."

Jeb paused before continuing. "It just isn't natural what you two are trying to do, and in the long run, it isn't going to work. You know that, don't you?"

"I know," Garrett said simply, wishing his father would stop talking about it.

His father cocked his eyebrow, waiting. When Garrett didn't add anything else, Jeb spoke again.

" 'I know'? That's all you have to say?"

He shrugged. "What else can I say?"

"You can say that the next time you see her, you two are going to figure this out. That's what you can say."

"Fine—we'll try to figure it out."

Jeb put his fork down and glared at his son. "I didn't say try, Garrett, I said that you two *are going* to figure this out."

"Why are you so adamant about it?"

"Because," he said, "if you two don't figure it out, you and me are going to keep eating alone for the next twenty years."

The following day, Garrett took *Happenstance* out first thing in the morning and stayed on the water until after the sun went down. Though Theresa had left a message for him with her hotel information in Dallas, he hadn't called last night, telling himself that it was too late and that she was already asleep. It was a lie and he knew it, but he simply didn't feel like talking to her yet.

The fact was, he didn't feel like talking to anyone. He was still angry at what she'd done, and the best place for him to think about it was out on the ocean, where no one could bother him. Most of the morning he found himself wondering if she realized how much this whole thing bothered him. More than likely she didn't—he convinced himself—otherwise she wouldn't have done it.

That is, if she cared about him.

By the time the sun rose higher in the sky, however, his anger began to fade. As he thought more clearly about the situation, he decided that his father had been right—as usual. Her reason for not coming didn't reflect on him as much as it reflected on the differences in their lives. She *did* have responsibilities she couldn't ignore, and as long as they continued to live separate lives, things like this were going to keep coming up.

Though he wasn't happy about it, he wondered if all relationships had moments like these. If truth be told, he didn't know. The only other real relationship he'd ever had was with

Catherine, and it wasn't easy to compare the two. He and Catherine were married and living under the same roof, for one thing. Even more, they'd known each other most of their lives, and because they were younger, they didn't have the same responsibilities that either Garrett or Theresa had now. They were fresh out of college, they didn't own a home, and there certainly weren't any children to care for. No—what they had was completely different from what he and Theresa had now, and it wasn't fair to try to link them.

Still, there was one thing he couldn't ignore, one thing that nagged at him throughout the afternoon. Yes, he knew there were differences—yes, he knew it wasn't fair to compare them—but in the end, what stood out for him was the fact that he had never questioned whether he and Catherine were a *team*. Never once did he question the future with her, never once did it enter his mind that either one of them wouldn't sacrifice everything for the other. Even when they'd had their fights—about where to live, whether to start the shop, or even what to do on Saturday nights—it wasn't as if either one of them doubted their relationship. There was something long-term in the way they interacted with each other, something that reminded him that they would always be together.

Theresa and he, on the other hand, didn't have that yet.

By the time the sun went down, he realized it wasn't fair to think this way. He and Theresa had known each other only for a short period of time—it wasn't realistic to expect it so soon. Given enough time—and the right circumstances—they would become a team as well.

Wouldn't they?

Shaking his head, he realized he wasn't exactly sure.

He wasn't sure about a lot of things.

But one thing he did know—he hadn't ever analyzed his relationship with Catherine the way he was doing with Theresa, and this wasn't fair, either. Besides, analysis wasn't going to help him in this situation. All the analysis in the world didn't change the fact that they didn't see each other as much as they wanted—or needed—to.

No—what they needed now was action.

Garrett called Theresa as soon as he got home that evening.

"Hello," she answered sleepily.

He spoke softly into the phone. "Hey, it's me."

"Garrett?"

"I'm sorry for waking you up, but you'd left a couple of messages on my answering machine."

"I'm glad you called. I wasn't sure you were going to."

"For a while, I didn't want to."

"Are you still mad at me?"

"No," he said quietly. "Sad, maybe, but not mad."

"Because I'm not there this weekend?"

"No. Because you're not here most weekends."

That night he dreamed again.

In his dream Theresa and he were in Boston, walking along one of the busy city streets, crowded with the usual collection of individuals—men and women, old and young, some dressed in suits, others in the baggy clothing typical of today's youth. For a while, they window-shopped just as they had on one of his previous visits. The day was clear and bright, without a cloud in the sky, and Garrett was enjoying spending the day with her.

Theresa stopped at the window of a small craft store and asked if Garrett wanted to go inside. Shaking his head, he said, "You go ahead. I'll wait for you here." Theresa made sure he was certain, then stepped inside. Garrett stood outside the door, relaxing in the shade of the tall buildings, when he saw something familiar out of the corner of his eye.

It was a woman, walking along the sidewalk a little distance away, her blond hair just brushing her shoulders.

He blinked, glanced away for a moment, and turned back quickly. Something in the way she moved struck him, and he watched her as she slowly moved away. Finally the woman stopped and turned her head, as if remembering something. Garrett felt his breath catch.

*Catherine.*

It couldn't be.

He shook his head. At this distance he couldn't tell if he was mistaken or not.

She started to walk away again just as Garrett called to her.

"Catherine—is it you?"

She didn't seem to hear him above the noise of the street. Garrett glanced over his shoulder and spotted Theresa in the shop, browsing. When he looked back up the street, Catherine—or whoever she was—was turning the corner.

He started toward her, walking quickly, then he began to jog. The sidewalks were becoming more crowded by the second, as if a subway had suddenly opened its doors, and he had to dodge around throngs of people before he reached the corner.

He turned where she had.

Once around the corner, the street grew steadily—menacingly—darker. He picked up his pace again. Though it hadn't been raining, he felt his feet splashing through puddles. He stopped for a moment to catch his breath, his heart pounding in his chest. As he did so, fog began to roll in, almost like a wave, and soon he couldn't see anything more than a few feet away.

"Catherine—are you here?" he shouted. "Where are you?"

He heard laughter in the distance, though he couldn't make out exactly where it was coming from.

He started walking again, slowly. Again he heard the laughter—childlike, happy. He stopped in his tracks.

"Where are you?"

Silence.

He looked from side to side.

Nothing.

The fog grew steadily thicker as a light rain began to fall. He started moving again, unsure where he was going.

Something darted into the fog, and he moved quickly toward it.

She was walking away, only a few feet in front of him.

The rain began to fall harder now, and suddenly everything seemed to be moving in slow motion. He began to jog . . . slowly . . . slowly . . . he could see her just ahead . . . the fog growing thicker by the second . . . rain coming down in showers . . . a glimpse of her hair . . .

And then she was gone. He stopped again. The rain and fog made it impossible to see anymore.

"Where are you?" he shouted again.

Nothing.

"Where are you?" he shouted, even louder this time.

"I'm here," a voice said from the rain and mist.

He wiped the rain from his face. "Catherine? . . . Is it really you?"

"It's me, Garrett."

But it wasn't her voice.

Theresa stepped out of the fog. "I'm here."

Garrett woke and sat up in bed, sweating profusely. Wiping his face with the sheet, he sat up for a long time afterward.

Later that day, Garrett met with his father.

"I think I want to marry her, Dad."

They were fishing together at the end of the pier with a dozen other people, most of whom seemed lost in thought. Jeb looked up in surprise.

"Two days ago, it didn't seem like you wanted to see her again."

"I've done a lot of thinking since then."

"You must have," Jeb said quietly. He reeled in his line, checked the bait, then cast again. Even though he doubted he'd catch anything he wanted to keep, fishing was, in his estimation, one of life's greatest pleasures.

"Do you love her?" Jeb asked.

Garrett looked at him, surprised. "Of course I do. I've told you that a few times."

Jeb Blake shook his head. "No . . . you haven't," he said sincerely. "We've talked about her a lot—you've told me that she makes you happy, that you feel like you know her, and that you don't want to lose her—but you've never told me that you love her."

"It's the same thing."

"Is it?"

                    ✻      ✻      ✻

After he'd gone home, the conversation he'd had with his father kept repeating itself in his mind.

"*Is it?*"

"Of course it is," he'd said right away. "And even if it isn't, I do love her."

Jeb stared at his son for a moment before finally turning away. "You want to marry her?"

"I do."

"Why?"

"Because I love her, that's why. Isn't that enough?"

"Maybe."

Garrett reeled in his line, frustrated. "Weren't you the one who thought we should get married in the first place?"

"Yeah."

"So why are you questioning it now?"

"Because I want to make sure you're doing it for the right reasons. Two days ago, you weren't even sure if you wanted to see her again. Now, you're ready for marriage. It just seems like a mighty big turnaround to me, and I want to make sure it's because of the way you feel about Theresa—and that it doesn't have anything to do with Catherine."

Bringing up her name stung a little.

"Catherine doesn't have anything to do with this," Garrett said quickly. He shook his head and sighed deeply. "You know, Dad, I don't understand you sometimes. You've been pushing me into this the whole time. You kept telling me I had to put the past behind me, that I had to find someone new. And now that I have, it seems like you're trying to talk me out of it."

Jeb put his free hand on Garrett's shoulder. "I'm not talking you out of anything, Garrett. I'm glad you found Theresa, I'm glad that you love her, and yes, I do hope that you end up marrying her. I just said that if you're going to get married, then you'd better be doing it for the right reasons. Marriage is between two people, not three. And it's not fair to her if you go into it otherwise."

It took a moment for him to respond.

"Dad, I want to get married because I love her. I want to spend my life with her."

His father stood silently for a long time, watching. Then he said something that made Garrett look away.

"So, in other words, you're telling me that you're completely over Catherine?"

Though he felt the expectant weight of his father's gaze, Garrett didn't know the answer.

"Are you tired?" Garrett asked.

He was lying on his bed as he spoke with Theresa, with only the bedside lamp turned on.

"Yeah, I got in just a little while ago. It was a long weekend."

"Did it turn out as well as you hoped it would?"

"I hope so. There's no way to tell just yet, but I did meet a lot of people who could eventually help me out with my column."

"It's a good thing you went, then."

"Good and bad. Most of the time, I wished I'd gone to visit you instead."

He smiled. "When do you leave for your parents'?"

"Wednesday morning. I'll be gone until Sunday."

"Are they looking forward to seeing you?"

"Yeah, they are. They haven't seen Kevin for almost a year,

and I know they're looking forward to having him around for a few days."

"That's good."

There was a short pause.

"Garrett?"

"Yeah."

She spoke softly. "I just want you to know that I'm still really sorry about this weekend."

"I know."

"Can I make it up to you?"

"What did you have in mind?"

"Well . . . can you come up here to visit the weekend after Thanksgiving?"

"I suppose so."

"Good, because I'm going to plan a special weekend just for the two of us."

It was a weekend that neither of them would ever forget.

Theresa had called him more than usual in the preceding two weeks. Usually it had been Garrett who called, but it seemed that every time he'd wanted to talk to her, she had anticipated it. Twice, while he was walking to the phone to dial her number, it started ringing before he got there, and the second time it happened, he simply answered the phone with, "Hi, Theresa." It had surprised her, and they joked for a while about his psychic abilities before settling into an easy conversation.

When he arrived in Boston two weeks later, Theresa met him at the airport. She had told him to wear something dressy, and he walked off the plane wearing a blazer, something she'd never seen him in before.

"Wow," she'd said simply.

He adjusted the blazer self-consciously. "Do I look okay?"

"You look great."

They went straight from the airport to dinner. She'd made reservations at the most elegant restaurant in town. They had a leisurely, wonderful meal, and afterward Theresa took Garrett to *Les Misérables*, which was currently showing in Boston. The play was sold out, but because Theresa knew the manager, they found themselves seated in the best section of the house.

It was late by the time they got back, and to Garrett, the following day seemed just as rushed. Theresa took him to her office and showed him around—introducing him to a couple of people—and afterward they visited the Museum of Fine Arts for the rest of the afternoon. That evening they met Deanna and Brian for dinner at Anthony's—a restaurant on the top floor of the Prudential Building that offered wonderful views of the entire city.

Garrett had never seen anything like it.

Their table was near the window. Deanna and Brian both rose from their seats to greet them. "You remember Garrett from brunch, don't you?" Theresa asked, trying not to sound too ridiculous.

"Of course I do. It's good to see you again, Garrett," Deanna said, leaning in for a quick hug and kiss on the cheek. "I'm sorry I forced Theresa to come with me a couple of weeks ago. I hope you haven't been too hard on her."

"It's okay," he said, nodding stiffly.

"I'm glad. Because looking back, I think it was worth it."

Garrett looked at her curiously. Theresa leaned in and asked, "What do you mean, Deanna?"

Deanna's eyes sparkled. "I got some good news yesterday, after you left."

"What is it?" Theresa asked.

"Well," she said nonchalantly, "I talked to Dan Mandel, the head of Media Information Inc., for about twenty minutes or so, and it turns out he was very impressed with you. He liked the way you handled yourself and thought you were quite a pro. And best of all . . ."

Deanna paused dramatically, doing her best to stifle a smile.

"Yes?"

"He's going to pick up your column in all his papers, starting in January."

Theresa put her hand to her mouth to stifle her scream, but it was still loud enough that the people at the nearby tables turned their heads. She huddled toward Deanna, talking quickly. Garrett took a small step backward.

"You're kidding," Theresa cried, disbelieving.

Deanna shook her head, smiling broadly. "No. I'm telling you what he told me. He wants to talk to you again on Tuesday. I've got a conference call set up for ten o'clock."

"You're sure about this? He wants my column?"

"Positive. I faxed him your media kit along with a number of your columns, and he called me. He wants you—no doubt about it. It's something he's already decided."

"I can't believe it."

"Believe it. And I heard through the grapevine that a couple of others are interested as well."

"Oh . . . Deanna . . ."

Theresa leaned in and impulsively hugged Deanna, excitement animating her face. Brian nudged Garrett with his elbow.

"Great news, huh?"

It took a moment for Garrett to answer.

"Yeah . . . great."

After settling in for dinner, Deanna ordered a bottle of champagne and made a toast, congratulating Theresa on her bright future. The two of them chatted nonstop throughout the rest of the evening. Garrett was quiet, not knowing quite what to add. As if sensing his discomfort, Brian leaned over to Garrett.

"They're like schoolgirls, aren't they? Deanna was parading around the house all day, just waiting to tell her."

"I just wish I understood it all a little better. I don't really know what to say."

Brian took a drink, shaking his head. His words came out slightly slurred.

"Don't worry about that—even if you did understand, you probably wouldn't get a word in edgewise. They talk like this all the time. If I didn't know better, I'd swear they were twins in another life."

Garrett glanced across the table at Theresa and Deanna. "You might be right."

"Besides," Brian added, "you'll understand it better when you live with it full-time. After a while, you'll understand it almost as well as they do. I know I do."

The comment was not lost on him. *When you live with it full-time?*

When Garrett didn't respond, Brian changed the subject. "So how long are you staying?"

"Until tomorrow night."

Brian nodded. "It's tough not seeing each other much, isn't it?"

"Sometimes."

"I can imagine. I know Theresa gets down about it now and then."

Across the table, Theresa smiled at Garrett. "What are you two talking about over there?" she asked cheerfully.

"This and that," Brian said, "your good fortune, mainly."

Garrett nodded briefly without answering, and Theresa watched as he adjusted himself in his seat. It was obvious he felt uncomfortable—though she wasn't sure why—and she found herself puzzling over it.

"You were kind of quiet tonight," Theresa said.

They were back in her apartment, sitting on the couch with the radio playing softly in the background.

"I guess I didn't have much to say."

She took his hand and spoke quietly. "I'm glad you were with me when Deanna told me the news."

"I'm happy for you, Theresa. I know it means a lot to you."

She smiled uncertainly. Changing the subject, she asked: "Did you have a good time talking to Brian?"

"Yeah . . . he's easy to get along with." He paused. "But I'm not very good in groups, especially when I'm sort of outside the loop. I just . . ." He stopped, considering whether he should say anything else, and decided not to.

"What?"

He shook his head. "Nothing."

"No—what were you going to say?"

After a moment he answered, choosing his words carefully. "I was just going to say that this whole weekend has been strange for me. The show, expensive dinners, going out with your friends . . ." He shrugged. "It isn't what I expected."

"Aren't you having a good time?"

He ran his hands through his hair, looking uncomfortable again. "It's not that I haven't had fun. It's just . . ." He shrugged. "It's not me. None of this is anything I'd normally do."

"That's why I planned the weekend like I did. I wanted to introduce you to new things."

"Why?"

"For the same reason you wanted me to learn how to dive—because it's something exciting, something different."

"I didn't come up here to do something different. I came up here to spend some quiet time with you. I haven't seen you for a long time, and ever since we've been up here, it seems like we've been rushing from place to place. We haven't even had a chance to talk yet and I'm leaving tomorrow."

"That's not true. We were alone at dinner last night, and again at the museum today. We've had plenty of time to talk."

"You know what I mean."

"No, I don't. What did you want to do—sit around in the apartment?"

He didn't answer. Instead he sat quietly for a moment. Then he rose from the couch, walked across the room, and turned off the radio.

"There's something important I've wanted to say since I came up here," he said without turning around.

"What is it?"

He lowered his head. *It's now or never,* he whispered to himself.

Finally turning around and gathering his courage, he took a deep breath.

"I guess it's just been really hard this past month not seeing you, and right now, I'm not sure if I want to keep going on like this."

Her breath caught for a second.

Seeing her expression, he moved toward her, feeling a strange tightness in his chest at what he was about to say. "It's not what you're thinking," he said quickly. "You've got it completely wrong. It's not that I don't want to see you anymore, I want to see you all the time." When he reached the couch, he kneeled in front of her. Theresa looked at him, surprised. He took her hand in his.

"I want you to move to Wilmington."

Though she'd known this was coming sometime, she hadn't expected it to come up now, and certainly not like this. Garrett went on.

"I know it's a big step, but if you move down, we won't have these long periods apart anymore. We could see each other every day." He reached up, caressing her cheek. "I want to walk the beach with you, I want to go sailing with you. I want you to be there when I get home from the shop. I want it to feel like we've known each other all our lives . . ."

The words were coming quickly, and Theresa tried to make sense of them. Garrett kept talking.

"I just miss you so much when we're not together. I realize your job is here, but I'm sure the local paper would take you on. . . ."

The more he talked, the more her head began to spin. To her, it almost sounded as if he were trying to re-create his relationship with Catherine. "Wait a minute," she finally said, cutting him off. "I can't just pick up and leave. I mean . . . Kevin's in school . . ."

"You don't have to come right away," he countered. "You can wait until school is out if that would be better. We've made it this long—another few months won't make much difference."

"But he's happy here—this is his home. He's got his friends, his soccer . . ."

"He can have all that in Wilmington."

"You don't know that. It's easy for you to say that he will, but you don't know that for sure."

"Didn't you see how well we got along?"

She let go of his hand, growing frustrated. "That has nothing to do with it, don't you see? I know you two got along, but you weren't asking him to change his life. *I* wasn't asking him to change his life." She paused. "And besides, this isn't all about him. What about me, Garrett? You were there tonight—you know what happened. I just got some wonderful news about my column and now you want me to give that up, too?"

"I don't want to give *us* up. There's a big difference."

"Then why can't you move to Boston?"

"And do what?"

"The same thing you do in Wilmington. Teach diving, go sailing, whatever. It's a lot easier for you to leave than it would be for me."

"I can't do that. Like I said, this"—he motioned around the room and toward the windows—"isn't me. I'd be lost up here."

Theresa stood up and walked across the room, agitated. She ran her hand through her hair. "That isn't fair."

"What isn't fair?"

She faced him. "This whole thing. Asking me to move, asking me to change my whole life. It's like you've put a condition on it—'We can be together, but it's got to be my way.' Well, what about my feelings? Aren't they important, too?"

"Of course they're important. You're important—we're important."

"Well—you don't make it sound that way. It's like you're only thinking about yourself. You want me to give up everything I've worked for, but you're not willing to give up anything." Her eyes never left his.

Garrett rose from the couch and moved toward her. When he got close, she pulled back, raising her arms like a barrier.

"Look, Garrett—I don't want you to touch me right now, okay?"

He dropped his hands to his sides. For a long moment neither of them said anything. Theresa crossed her arms and glanced away.

"Then I guess your answer is that you're not coming," he finally said, sounding angry.

She spoke carefully. "No. My answer is that we're going to have to talk this out."

"So you can try to convince me that I'm wrong?"

His comment didn't deserve a response. Shaking her head, she walked to the dining room table, picked up her purse, and started toward the front door.

"Where are you going?"

"I'm going to get some wine. I need a drink."

"But it's late."

"There's a store at the end of the block. I'll be back in a couple of minutes."

"Why can't we talk about it now?"

"Because," she said quickly, "I need a few minutes alone so I can think."

"You're running out?" It sounded like an accusation.

She opened the door, holding it as she spoke. "No, Garrett, I'm not running out. I'll be back in a few minutes. And I don't appreciate you talking to me like that. It's not fair of you to make me feel guilty about this. You've just asked me to change my entire life, and I'm taking a few minutes to think about it."

She left the apartment. Garrett stared at the door for a couple of seconds, waiting to see if she would come back. When she didn't, he cursed himself silently. Nothing had turned out as he thought it would. One minute he asked her to move to Wilmington, the next she's out the door, needing to be alone. How had it gotten away from him?

Not knowing what else to do, he paced around the apartment. He glanced in the kitchen, then Kevin's room, and kept moving. When he reached her bedroom, he paused for a moment before entering. After walking over to her bed, he sat down, putting his head into his hands.

Was it fair of him to ask her to leave? Granted, she had a life here—a good life—but he felt sure that she could have that in Wilmington. No matter how he looked at it, it would probably be much better than their life together up here. Looking around, he knew there was no way he could live in an apartment. But even if they moved to a house—would it have a view? Or would they live in a suburb, surrounded by a dozen houses that looked exactly the same?

It was complicated. And somehow, everything he'd said had come out wrong. He hadn't wanted her to feel as if he were giving her an ultimatum, but thinking back, he realized that was exactly what he had done.

Sighing, he wondered what to do next. Somehow he didn't think there was anything he could say when she got back that wouldn't lead to another argument. Above all, he didn't want that. Arguments rarely led to solutions, and that's what they needed now.

But if he couldn't say anything, what else was there? He thought for a moment before finally deciding to write her a letter, outlining his thoughts. Writing always made him think more clearly—especially over the last few years—and maybe she would be able to understand where he was coming from.

He glanced toward her bedside table. Her phone was there—she probably took messages now and then—but he didn't see either a pen or pad. He opened the drawer, rifled through it, and found a ballpoint near the front.

Looking for some paper, he continued shuffling—through magazines, a couple of paperback books, some empty jewelry boxes—when something familiar caught his eye.

A sailing ship.

It was on a piece of paper, wedged between a slim Day-Timer and an old copy of *Ladies' Home Journal*. He reached for it, assuming it was one of the letters he'd written to her over the last couple of months, then suddenly froze.

*How could that be?*

The stationery had been a gift from Catherine, and he used it only when he wrote to her. His letters to Theresa had been written on different paper, something he'd picked up at the store.

He found himself holding his breath. He quickly made room

in the drawer, removing the magazine and gently lifted out, not one, but five—five!—pieces of the stationery. Still confused, he blinked hard before glancing at the first page, and there, in his scrawl, were the words:

*My Dearest Catherine...*

*Oh, my God.* He turned to the second page, a photocopy.

*My Darling Catherine...*

The next letter.

*Dear Catherine...*

"What is this," he muttered, unable to believe what he was seeing. "It can't be—" He looked over the pages again just to make sure.

But it was true. One was real, two were copies, but they were his letters, the letters he had written to Catherine. The letters he had written after his dreams, the letters he dropped from *Happenstance* and never expected to see again.

On impulse he began to read them, and with each word, each phrase, he felt his emotions rushing to the surface, coming at him all at once. The dreams, his memories, his loss, the anguish. He stopped.

His mouth went dry as he pressed his lips together. Instead of reading any more, he simply stared at them in shock. He barely heard the front door open and then close. Theresa called out, "Garrett, I'm back." She paused, and he could hear her walking through the apartment. Then, "Where are you?"

He didn't answer. He couldn't do anything but try to grasp how this had happened. How could she have them? They were his letters . . . his *personal* letters.

The letters to his *wife*.

Letters that were *no one else's* business.

Theresa stepped into the room and looked at him. Though he didn't know it, his face was pale, his knuckles white as they gripped the pages he held.

"Are you okay?" she asked, not realizing what was in his hands.

For a moment, it was as if he hadn't heard her. Then, looking up slowly, he glared at her.

Startled, she almost spoke again. But she didn't. Like a wave, everything hit her at the same time—the open drawer, the papers in his hand, the expression on his face—and she knew immediately what had happened.

"Garrett . . . I can explain," she said quickly, quietly. He didn't seem to hear her.

"My letters . . . ," he whispered. He looked at her, a mixture of confusion and rage.

"I . . ."

"How did you get my letters?" he demanded, the sound of his voice making her flinch.

"I found one washed up at the beach and—"

He cut her off. "You found it?"

She nodded, trying to explain. "When I was at the Cape. I was jogging and I came across the bottle. . . ."

He glanced at the first page, the only original letter. It was the one he had written earlier that year. But the others . . .

"What about these?" he asked, holding up the copies. "Where did they come from?"

Theresa answered softly. "They were sent to me."

"By whom?" Confused, he rose from the bed.

She took a step toward him, holding out her hand. "By other people who'd found them. One of the people read my column. . . ."

"You published my letter?" He sounded as if he'd just been hit in the stomach.

She didn't answer for a moment. "I didn't know . . . ," she began.

"You didn't know what?" he said loudly, the hurt evident in his tone. "That it was wrong to do that? That this wasn't something that I wanted the world to see?"

"It was washed up on the beach—you had to know someone would find it," she said quickly. "I didn't use your names."

"But you put it in the paper. . . ." He trailed off in disbelief.

"Garrett . . . I—"

"Don't," he said angrily. Again he glanced at the letters, then looked back at her, as if he were seeing her for the first time. "You *lied* to me," he said, almost as if it were a revelation.

"I didn't lie. . . ."

He wasn't listening. "You lied to me," he repeated, as if to himself. "And you came to find me. Why? So you could write another column. Is that what this is about?"

"No . . . it isn't like that at all. . . ."

"Then what was it?"

"After reading your letters, I . . . I wanted to meet you."

He didn't understand what she was saying. He kept looking from the letters to her and back again. His expression was pained.

"You lied to me," he said for the third time. "You *used* me."

"I didn't. . . ."

"Yes, you did!" he shouted, his voice echoing in the room. Remembering Catherine, he held the letters out in front of him, as if Theresa had never seen them before. "These were mine— my feelings, my thoughts, my way of dealing with the loss of my wife. Mine—not yours."

"I didn't mean to hurt you."

He stared hard at her without saying anything. His jaw muscles tensed.

"This whole thing is a sham, isn't it," he said finally, not waiting for her to answer. "You took my feelings for Catherine and tried to manipulate them into something *you* wanted. You thought that because I loved Catherine, I would love you, too, didn't you?"

Despite herself, she paled. She felt suddenly incapable of speech.

"You planned all this from the beginning, didn't you?" He paused again, running his free hand through his hair. When he spoke, his voice began to crack. "The whole thing was set up—"

He seemed dazed for a moment, and she reached out to him.

"Garrett—yes, I admit I wanted to meet you. The letters were so beautiful—I wanted to see what kind of person writes like that. But I didn't know where it would lead, I didn't plan on anything after that." She took his hand. "I love you, Garrett. You've got to believe me."

When she finished speaking, he pulled his hand free and moved away.

"What kind of person are you?"

The comment stung, and she responded defensively, "It's not what you think. . . ."

Garrett pressed on, oblivious of her response. "You got caught up in some weird fantasy. . . ."

That was too much. "Stop it, Garrett!" she cried angrily, hurt by his words. "You didn't listen to anything I said!" As she shouted, she felt tears welling up in her eyes.

"Why should I listen? You've been lying to me ever since I've known you."

"I didn't lie! I just never told you about the letters!"

"Because you knew it was wrong!"

"No—because I knew you wouldn't understand," she said, trying to regain her composure.

"I understand all right. I understand what kind of person you are!"

Her eyes narrowed. "Don't be like this."

"Be like what? Mad? Hurt? I just found out this whole thing was a charade, and now you want me to stop?"

"Shut up!" she shouted back, her anger suddenly rising to the surface.

He seemed stunned by her words, and he stared at her without speaking. Finally, with breaking voice, he held out the letters again.

"You think you understand what Catherine and I had together, but you don't. No matter how many letters you read—no matter how well you know me—you'll never understand. What she and I had was *real*. It was real, and she was real. . . . "

He paused, collecting his thoughts, regarding her as if she were a stranger. Then, stiffening, he said something that hurt her worse than anything he'd said so far.

"We've never even come close to what Catherine and I had."

He didn't wait for a response. Instead he walked past her, toward his suitcase. After throwing everything inside, he zipped it quickly. For a moment she thought to stop him, but his comment had left her reeling.

He stood, lifting his bag. "These," he said, holding the letters, "are mine, and I'm taking them with me."

Suddenly realizing what he intended to do, she asked, "Why are you leaving?"

He stared at her. "I don't even know who you are."

Without another word, he turned around and strode through the living room and out the door.

CHAPTER 12

Not knowing where else to go, Garrett caught a cab to the airport after leaving Theresa's apartment. Unfortunately no flights were available, and he ended up staying in the terminal the rest of the night, still angry and unable to sleep. Pacing the terminal for hours, he wandered past shops that had long since closed up for the evening, stopping only occasionally to look through the barricades that kept nighttime travelers at bay.

The following morning he caught the first flight he could and made it home a little after eleven and then went straight to his room. As he lay in bed, however, the events of the evening before kept running through his head, keeping him awake. Trying and failing to fall asleep, he eventually gave up. He showered and dressed, then sat on his bed again. Staring at the photograph of Catherine, he eventually picked it up and carried it with him into the living room. On the coffee table he found the letters where he'd left them. In Theresa's apartment he'd been too shocked to make sense of them, but now, with her picture in front of him, he read the letters slowly, almost reverently, sensing Catherine's presence filling the room.

*"Hey, I thought you'd forgotten about our date," he said as he watched Catherine walking down the dock with a grocery bag.*

*Smiling, Catherine took his hand as she stepped on board. "I didn't forget, I just had a little detour on the way."*

*"Where?"*

*"Actually, I went to see the doctor."*

*He took the bag from her and set it off to one side. "Are you okay? I know you haven't been feeling well—"*

*"I'm okay," she said, cutting him off gently. "But I don't think I'm up for a sail tonight."*

*"Something is wrong, isn't it?"*

*Catherine smiled again as she leaned over and pulled a small package out of one of the bags. Garrett watched as she began to open it.*

*"Close your eyes," she said, "and I'll tell you all about it."*

*Still a little unsure, Garrett nonetheless did as she asked and heard as tissue paper was unwrapped. "Okay, you can open them now."*

*Catherine was holding up baby clothes in front of her.*

*"What's this?" he asked, not understanding.*

*Her face was buoyant. "I'm pregnant," she said excitedly.*

*"Pregnant?"*

*"Uh-huh. I'm officially eight weeks along."*

*"Eight weeks?"*

*She nodded. "I think I must have gotten pregnant the last time we went sailing."*

*Hesitating from the shock, Garrett took the baby clothes and held them delicately in his hand, then finally leaned forward and gave Catherine a hug. "I can't believe it. . . ."*

*"It's true."*

*A broad smile crossed his lips as the realization finally began to sink in. "You're pregnant."*

*Catherine closed her eyes and whispered in his ear, "And you're going to be a father."*

Garrett's thoughts were interrupted by the squeaking of the door. His father peeked his head into the room.

"I saw your truck out front. I wanted to make sure everything was okay," he said in explanation. "I didn't expect you back here until this evening." When Garrett didn't respond, his father walked in and immediately spotted Catherine's picture on the table. "You okay, son?" he asked cautiously.

They sat in the living room while Garrett explained the situation from the beginning—the dreams he'd been having over the years, the messages he'd been sending by bottle, finally moving on to the argument they'd had the night before. He left nothing out. When he finished, his father took the letters from Garrett's hand.

"It must have been quite a shock," he said, glancing at the pages, surprised that Garrett had never mentioned the letters to him. He paused. "But don't you think you were a little rough on her?"

Garrett shook his head tiredly. "She knew everything about me, Dad, and she never told me. She set the whole thing up."

"No, she didn't," he said gently. "She may have come down to meet you, but she didn't make you fall in love with her. You did that on your own."

Garrett looked away before finally returning his gaze to the picture on the table. "But don't you think it was wrong of her to hide it from me?"

Jeb sighed, not wanting to answer the question, knowing it would lead Garrett to retread old ground. Instead he tried to think of another way to get through to his son. "A couple of weeks ago, when we were talking on the pier, you told me you wanted to marry Theresa because you loved her. Do you remember that?"

Garrett nodded absently.

"Why has that changed?"

Garrett looked at his father, confused. "I've already told you that—"

Jeb gently cut him off before he could finish.

"Yeah, you've explained your reasons, but you haven't been honest about it. Not with me, not with Theresa, not even with yourself. She may not have told you about the letters, and granted, maybe she should have. But that's not why you're still angry now. You're angry because she made you realize something that you didn't want to admit."

Garrett looked at his father without responding. Then, rising from the couch, he went to the kitchen, suddenly feeling the urge to escape the conversation. In the refrigerator, he found a pitcher of sweet tea and poured himself a glass. Holding the freezer open, he pulled out the metal tray to crack out a couple of cubes. In a sudden spurt of frustration, he pulled the lever too hard and ice cubes flew over the counter and onto the floor.

As Garrett muttered and cursed in the kitchen, Jeb stared at the picture of Catherine, remembering his own wife from long ago. He put the letters beside it and walked to the sliding glass door. Opening it, he watched as cold December winds from the Atlantic made the waves crash violently, the sounds echoing through the house. Jeb contemplated the ocean, watching it churn and roll until he heard a knock at the door.

He turned, wondering who it could be. Strangely, he realized that in all of his visits here, no one had ever come to the door.

In the kitchen, Garrett apparently hadn't heard the knock. Jeb went to answer it. Behind him, the wind chimes hanging over the back deck were ringing loudly.

"Coming," he called out.

When the front door swung open, wind gusted through the living room, scattering the letters to the floor. Jeb, however, didn't notice. All his attention was focused on the visitor on the porch. He couldn't help but stare.

Standing before him was a dark-haired young woman he'd never seen before. He paused in the doorway, knowing exactly who she was but finding himself at a loss for words. He moved aside to make room for her.

"C'mon in," he said quietly.

As she entered, closing the door behind her, the wind abruptly died. She glanced at Jeb, uncomfortable. For a moment, neither spoke.

"You must be Theresa," Jeb finally said. In the background, Jeb could hear Garrett mumbling to himself as he cleaned up the ice in the kitchen. "I've heard a lot about you."

She crossed her arms, hesitating. "I know I'm not expected. . . ."

"It's okay," Jeb encouraged.

"Is he here?"

Jeb nodded his head in the direction of the kitchen. "Yeah, he's here. He's getting something to drink."

"How is he?"

Jeb shrugged and gave her a slow, wry smile. "You'll have to talk to him. . . ."

Theresa nodded, suddenly wondering whether coming down was a good idea. She glanced around the room and immediately spied the letters spread around the floor. She also noticed Garrett's bag sitting by his bedroom door, still packed from his visit. Other than that, the house looked exactly the same as it always did.

Except, of course, for the photograph.

She spotted it over Jeb's shoulder. Normally it was in his room, and for some reason, now that it was in plain view, she couldn't take her eyes off it. She was still staring at the picture when Garrett reentered the living room.

"Dad, what happened in here—"

He froze. Theresa faced him uncertainly. For a long moment, neither of them said anything. Then Theresa took a deep breath.

"Hello, Garrett," she said.

Garrett said nothing. Jeb picked up his keys from the table, knowing it was time to leave.

"You two have a lot to talk about, so I'll get out of here."

He went to the front door, glancing sidelong at Theresa. "It was nice meeting you," he murmured. But as he spoke, he raised his eyebrows and shrugged slightly, as if to wish her luck. In a moment he was outside, making his way down the walk.

"Why are you here?" Garrett asked evenly once they were alone.

"I wanted to come," she said quietly. "I wanted to see you again."

"Why?"

She didn't answer. Instead, after a moment's hesitation, she walked toward him, her eyes never leaving his. Once she was close, she put her finger to his lips and shook her head to stop him from speaking. "Shh," she whispered, "no questions . . . just for now. Please . . ." She tried to smile, but now that he could see her better, he knew she'd been crying.

There was nothing she could say. There were no words to describe what she'd been going through.

Instead she wrapped her arms around him. Reluctantly he drew his arms around her as she rested her head against him. She kissed his neck and pulled him closer. Running her hand through his hair, she moved her mouth tentatively to his cheek, then to his lips. She kissed them lightly at first, her lips barely brushing against them, then she kissed him again, more passionate now. Without conscious thought, he began to respond to her advances. His hands slowly traveled up her back, molding her against him.

In the living room, with the roar of the ocean echoing through the house, they held each other tightly, giving in to their growing desires. Finally Theresa pulled back, reaching for his hand as she did so. Taking it in hers, she led him to the bedroom.

Letting go, she crossed the room as he waited just inside the door. Light from the living room spilled in, casting shadows across the room. Hesitating only slightly before facing him again, she began to undress. Garrett made a small movement to close the bedroom door, but she shook her head. She wanted to see him this time, and she wanted him to see her. She wanted Garrett to know he was with her and no one else.

Slowly, ever so slowly, she shed her garments. Her blouse . . . her jeans . . . her bra . . . her panties. She removed her clothing deliberately, her lips slightly parted, her eyes never leaving his. When she was naked, she stood before him, letting his gaze travel over all of her.

Finally she approached him. Standing close, she ran her hands over him—his chest, his shoulders, his arms, touching him gently, as if she wanted to remember the way he felt forever. Stepping back to allow him to undress, she watched him, her eyes taking everything in as his clothes fell to the floor. Moving to his side, she kissed his shoulders, then slowly worked around him, her mouth against his skin, the wetness of her lips lingering everywhere she touched. Then, leading him to the bed, she lay down, pulling him with her.

They made love fiercely, clinging desperately to each other. Their passion was unlike any time they'd made love before— each painfully conscious of the other's pleasure, every touch more electric than the last. As if fearful of what the future would bring, they worshiped each other's bodies with a single-minded intensity that would sear their memories forever. When they finally climaxed together, Theresa threw back her head and cried aloud, not attempting to stifle the sound.

Afterward she sat up in the bed, cradling Garrett's head in her lap. She ran her hands through his hair, rhythmically, steadily, listening as the sound of his breathing gradually deepened.

Later that afternoon, Garrett woke up alone. Noticing that

Theresa's clothes were gone as well, he grabbed his jeans and shirt. Still buttoning his shirt as he left his bedroom, he quickly searched the house for her.

The house was cold.

He found her in the kitchen. She was seated at the table, wearing her jacket. On the table in front of her, he saw a cup of coffee, nearly empty, as if she'd been sitting there for some time. The coffeepot was already in the sink. Checking the clock, he realized he'd been asleep for almost two hours.

"Hey there," he said uncertainly.

Theresa glanced over her shoulder at him. Her voice was subdued.

"Oh, hey . . . I didn't hear you get up."

"You okay?"

She didn't answer directly. "Come sit with me," she said instead. "There's a lot I've got to tell you."

Garrett sat down at the table. He smiled tentatively at her. Theresa fidgeted with the coffee cup for a moment, her eyes downcast. He reached over, brushing a loose strand of hair away from the side of her face. When she didn't respond, he pulled back.

Finally, without looking at him, she reached into her lap and removed the letters, laying them on the table. Apparently she'd gathered them up while he slept.

"I found the bottle when I was jogging last summer," she began, her voice steady but distant, as if recalling something painful. "I didn't have any idea what the letter inside would say, but after reading it, I started to cry. It was just so beautiful—I knew it had come straight from your heart, and the way it was written . . . I guess I related to the things you wrote because I felt so alone, too."

She looked at him. "That morning, I showed it to Deanna. Publishing it was her idea. I didn't want to at first . . . I thought it was too personal, but she didn't see the harm in it. She thought it would be a nice thing for people to read. So I relented, and assumed that would be the end of it. But it wasn't."

She sighed. "After I got back to Boston, I got a call from someone who'd read the column. She sent me the second letter, one that she'd found a few years ago. After I read it, I was intrigued, but again, I didn't think it would go any further."

She paused. "Have you ever heard of *Yankee* magazine?"

"No."

"It's a regional magazine. It's not well-known outside of New England, but it publishes some good stories. That's where I found the third letter."

Garrett looked at her in surprise. "It was published there?"

"Yes, it was. I tracked down the author of the article and he sent me the third letter, and . . . well, curiosity got the best of me. I had three letters, Garrett—not just one but three—and every one of them touched me the same way the first one had. So, with Deanna's help, I found out who you were and I came down to meet you."

She smiled sadly. "I know it sounds like you said—that it was some sort of fantasy—but it wasn't. I didn't come down here to fall in love with you. I didn't come down here to write a column. I came down to see who you were, that was all. I wanted to meet the person who wrote those beautiful letters. So I went to the docks and there you were. We talked, and then, if you remem-

ber, you asked me to go sailing. If you hadn't, I probably would
have gone home that day."

He didn't know what to say. Theresa reached over and placed
her hand carefully over his.

"But you know what? We had a good time that night, and I
realized I wanted to see you again. Not because of the letters,
but because of how you treated me. And everything just seemed
to grow naturally from there. After that first meeting, nothing
that happened between us was part of a plan. It just happened."

He sat quietly for a moment, looking at the letters. "Why
didn't you tell me about them?" he asked.

She took her time answering. "There were times when I
wanted to, but . . . I don't know . . . I guess I convinced myself
that it didn't matter how we met. The only thing that mattered
was how well we got along." She paused, knowing there was
more. "Besides, I didn't think you'd understand. I didn't want to
lose you."

"If you'd told me earlier, I would have understood."

She watched him carefully as he answered. "Would you, Garrett? Would you *really* have understood?"

Garrett knew it to be a moment of truth. When he didn't respond, Theresa shook her head and glanced away.

"Last night, when you asked me to move, I didn't say yes right
away because I was afraid of *why* you'd asked." She hesitated. "I
needed to be sure you wanted *me*, Garrett. I needed to be sure
you asked me because of *us*, and not because you were running
from something. I guess I wanted you to convince me when I got
back from the store. But you found these instead. . . ."

She shrugged, speaking more softly now. "Deep down, I

guess I knew it all along, but I wanted to believe that everything would work itself out."

"What are you talking about?"

She didn't answer directly. "Garrett—it isn't that I don't think you love me, because I know you do. That's what makes this whole thing so hard. I *know* you love me, and I love you, too—and if the circumstances were different, perhaps we could get through all this. But right now, I don't think we can. I don't think you're ready yet."

Garrett felt as if he'd been punched in the stomach. She looked directly at him, meeting his eyes.

"I'm not blind, Garrett. I knew why you would get so quiet sometimes when we weren't together. I knew why you wanted me to move down here."

"It was because I missed you," he interjected.

"That was part of it . . . but not all of it," Theresa said, pausing to blink back tears. Her voice began to crack. "It's also because of Catherine."

She dabbed at the corner of her eye, clearly fighting tears, determined not to break down.

"When you first told me about her, I saw the way you looked . . . it was obvious that you still loved her. And last night—despite your anger—I saw the same look again. Even after all the time we've spent together, you're still not over her. And then . . . the things you said . . ." She took a deep, uneven breath. "You weren't angry simply because I found the letters, you were angry because you felt I threatened what you and Catherine shared—and still do."

Garrett looked away, hearing the echo of his father's accusation. Again she reached over and touched his hand.

"You are who you are, Garrett. You're a man who loves deeply, but you're also a man who loves forever. No matter how much you love me, I don't think it's in you to ever forget her, and I can't live my life wondering whether I measure up to her."

"We can work on it," he began hoarsely. "I mean . . . I can work on it. I know it can be different—"

Theresa cut him off with a brief squeeze of his hand.

"I know you believe that, and part of me wants to believe it, too. If you put your arms around me now and begged me to stay, I'm sure I would, because you added something to my life that was lacking for a long time. And we'd go on again like we had been, both believing everything was okay. . . . But it wouldn't be, don't you see? Because the next time we had an argument . . ." She stopped. "I can't compete with her. And as much as I want it to go on, I can't let it, because *you* won't let it."

"But I love you."

She smiled gently. Letting go of his hand, she reached up and softly caressed his cheek. "I love you, too, Garrett. But sometimes love isn't enough."

Garrett was quiet when she finished, his face pale. In the long silence between them, Theresa began to cry.

Leaning toward her, he put his arm around her and held her, his arms weak. He rested his cheek against her hair as she buried her face in his chest, her body shaking as she cried into him. It was a long time before Theresa wiped her cheeks and pulled away. They looked at each other, Garrett's eyes issuing a mute plea. She shook her head.

"I can't stay, Garrett. As much as we both want me to, I can't."

The words hit hard. Garrett's head suddenly felt woozy.

"No . . . ," he said brokenly.

Theresa stood, knowing she had to leave before she lost her nerve. Outside, thunder boomed loudly. Seconds later a light, misty rain began to fall.

"I have to go."

She slipped her purse over her shoulder and started for the front door. For a moment, Garrett was too stunned to move.

Finally, in a daze, he rose from his seat and followed her out the door, the rain beginning to fall steadily now. Her rental car was parked in the driveway. Garrett watched as she opened the car door, unable to think of anything to say.

In the driver's seat she fumbled with the key for a moment, then put it in the ignition. She forced a weak smile as she shut the door. Despite the rain, she rolled down the window to see him more clearly. Turning the key, she felt the engine crank to life. They stared at each other as the car idled in his driveway.

His expression as he looked at her cut through all her defenses, her fragile resolve. For just a moment she wanted to take everything back. She wanted to tell him that she didn't mean what she had said, that she still loved him, that it shouldn't end this way. It would be easy to do that, it would feel so right—

But no matter how much she wanted to, she couldn't force herself to say the words.

He took a step toward the car. Theresa shook her head to stop him. This was already painful enough.

"I'll miss you, Garrett," she said beneath her breath, uncertain whether he could even hear her. She slid the transmission into reverse.

The rain began to fall harder: the thicker, colder drops of a winter storm.

Garrett stood, frozen. "Please," he said raggedly, "don't leave." His voice was low, almost obscured by the sound of the rain.

She didn't answer.

Knowing she would start to cry again if she stayed any longer, she rolled up the window. Looking over her shoulder, she began to back out of the drive. Garrett put his hand on the hood as the car started to move, his fingers gliding along the wet surface as it slowly backed away. In a moment the car was on the street, ready to roll, the windshield wipers flapping back and forth.

With sudden urgency, Garrett felt his last chance slipping away. "Theresa," he shouted, "wait!"

With the rain coming down steadily, she didn't hear him. The car was already past the house. Garrett jogged to the end of the drive, waving his arms to get her attention. She didn't seem to notice.

"Theresa!" he shouted again. He was in the middle of the road now, running behind the car, his feet splashing through the puddles that had already begun to form. The brake lights blinked for a second, then steadied as the car came to a halt. Rain and mist swirled around it, making it look like a mirage. Garrett knew she was watching him in the rearview mirror, watching him close the distance. *There's still a chance. . . .*

The brake lights suddenly flicked off and the car started forward again, picking up speed, accelerating more quickly this time. Garrett kept running behind the car, chasing it as it made its way down the street. He watched as the car moved farther into the distance, becoming smaller with each passing moment. His lungs burned, but he kept on going, racing a sense of futility. The rain began to come down in sheets, storm drops, soaking through his shirt and making it difficult for him to see.

Finally he slowed to a jog, then stopped. The air was dense with rain, and he was breathing heavily. His shirt clung to his skin, his hair hanging in his eyes. While the rain came down around him, he stood in the middle of the road, watching as her car turned the corner and vanished from sight.

Still, he didn't move. He stayed in the middle of the road for a long time, trying to catch his breath, hoping she would turn around and come back to him, wishing he hadn't let her go. Wishing for one more chance.

*She was gone.*

A few moments later a car honked its horn behind him and he felt his heart surge. He turned quickly and wiped the rain from his eyes, almost expecting to see her face behind the wind- shield, but immediately saw he was mistaken. Garrett moved to the side of the road to let the car pass, and as he felt the man's curious stare upon him, he suddenly realized he'd never felt so alone.

On the airplane, Theresa sat with her purse resting in her lap. She'd been one of the last to board, making her way onto the plane with only a few minutes to spare.

Looking out the window, she watched the rain coming down in blowing sheets. Below her, on the tarmac, the last of the lug- gage was being loaded, the handlers working quickly to keep the bags from getting soaked. They finished just as the main cabin door closed, and moments later the boarding ramp pulled back to the terminal.

It was dusk, and there were only a few minutes left of wan- ing gray light. The stewardesses made their final run through the cabin, making sure everything was stored properly, then headed for their seats. The cabin lights blinked and the plane began its slow reverse drift, away from the terminal, turning in the direction of the runway.

The plane stopped, waiting for clearance, parallel to the terminal.

Absently she glanced out at the terminal. From the corner of her eye, she saw a solitary figure standing near the terminal window, his hands pressed against the glass.

She looked closer. *Could it be?*

She couldn't tell. The tinted windows of the terminal coupled with the pouring rain obscured her view. Had he not been standing so close to the glass, she wouldn't have known he was there at all.

Theresa continued to stare at the figure, her breath catching in her throat.

Whoever it was didn't move.

The engines roared, then quieted as the plane began its slow roll forward. She knew there were only a few moments left. The gate fell farther behind them as the plane gradually picked up speed.

*Forward . . . toward the runway . . . away from Wilmington . . .*

She turned her head, straining for one last glimpse, but it was impossible to tell whether the person was still there.

While the plane taxied into final position, she continued to stare out the window, wondering whether her sighting had been real or if she'd imagined it. The plane turned sharply, rotating into position, and Theresa felt the thrust of the engines as the plane made its way down the runway, the tires rumbling loudly until they lifted from the ground. Squinting through her tears as the plane rose higher, Theresa watched as Wilmington came into view. She could make out the empty beaches as they passed over them . . . the piers . . . the marina. . . .

The plane started to make its turn, banking slightly, turning north and heading for home. From her window all she could see was the ocean now, the same ocean that had brought them together.

Behind the heavy clouds, the sun was going down, drifting toward the horizon.

Just before they soared into the clouds that would obliterate everything below, she put her hand against the glass and touched it gently, imagining the feel of his hand once more.

"Good-bye," she whispered.

Silently she began to cry.

# CHAPTER  13

Winter arrived early the following year. Sitting on the beach near the spot where she'd first discovered the bottle, Theresa noted that the cold ocean breezes had grown stronger since she'd arrived this morning. Ominous gray clouds rolled overhead, and the waves were starting to rise and crash with greater frequency. She knew the storm was finally getting close.

She'd been out here for most of the day, reliving their relationship up until the day they'd said good-bye, sifting through memories as if searching for a grain of understanding she might have missed before. For the past year she'd been haunted by his expression as he stood in the driveway, the reflection of him in her rearview mirror chasing her car as she drove away. Leaving him then had been the hardest thing she'd ever done. Often she dreamed of turning back the clock and living that day over.

Finally she stood. In silence she started walking along the shore, wishing he were with her. He would enjoy a quiet, misty day like this, and she imagined him walking beside her as she looked toward the horizon. She paused, mesmerized by the churning and rolling of the water, and when she finally turned her head, she realized his image had left her as well. She stood there for a long time, trying to bring him back, but when his image didn't return, she knew it was time to go. She started walking again, though this time more slowly, wondering if he could have guessed at her reason for coming here.

Despite herself, she felt her thoughts returning to the days immediately following their last good-bye. We spend so much time making up for things we failed to say, she mused. *If only*, she began for the thousandth time, the images of those days beginning to flash behind her eyes like a slide show she was powerless to stop.

*If only . . .*


After arriving back in Boston, Theresa had picked up Kevin on the way home from the airport. Kevin, who'd spent the day at a friend's house, excitedly recounted the movie he'd seen, oblivious of the fact that his mother was barely listening. When they got home she ordered a pizza, and they ate in the living room with the television on. When they finished, she surprised Kevin by asking him to sit with her for a while instead of doing his homework. As he rested against her quietly on the couch, he occasionally sent her an anxious glance, but she merely stroked his hair and smiled at him abstractedly, as if she were somewhere far away.

Later, after Kevin had gone to bed and she knew he'd fallen asleep, she slipped on some soft pajamas and poured herself a glass of wine. On her way back to the bedroom, she turned off the answering machine by the phone.

On Monday she had a long lunch with Deanna and told her everything that had happened. She tried to sound strong. Nonetheless Deanna held her hand throughout, listening thoughtfully and barely speaking.

"It's for the best," Theresa said resolutely when she finished. "I'm okay with this." Deanna gazed at her searchingly, her eyes full of compassion. But she said nothing, only nodding at Theresa's brave claims.

For the next few days Theresa did her best to avoid thinking about him. Working on her column was comforting. Concentrating on research and distilling it into words took all the mental energy she had. The hectic atmosphere in the newsroom helped as well, and because the conference call with Dan Mandel had turned out to be everything Deanna promised it would, Theresa approached her work with renewed enthusiasm, preparing two or three columns a day, faster than she'd ever written them before.

In the evenings, however, after Kevin went to bed and she was alone, she found it difficult to keep his image at bay. Borrowing her habits from work, Theresa tried to focus on other tasks instead. She cleaned the house from top to bottom during the next few evenings—scrubbing the floor, cleaning the refrigerator, vacuuming and dusting the apartment, rearranging the closets. Nothing was left untouched. She even sorted through her drawers for clothes that she didn't wear anymore, with the plan of donating them to charity. After boxing them up, she carried the clothes to the car and loaded them in the back. That night she paced through the apartment, looking for something—anything—else that needed to be done. Finally, realizing she'd finished but still unable to sleep, she turned on the television. Flipping through the channels, she stopped when she saw Linda Ronstadt being interviewed on the *Tonight* show. Theresa had always loved her music, but when Linda later walked to the microphone to perform a dreamy ballad, Theresa nonetheless began to cry. She didn't stop for almost an hour.

That weekend she and Kevin went to see the New England Patriots play the Chicago Bears. Kevin had been pressing her to go as soon as soccer season ended, and she finally agreed to take him, though she didn't really understand the game. They sat in the stands, their breaths coming out in little puffs, drinking syrupy hot chocolate and rooting for the home team.

Afterward, when they went to dinner, Theresa reluctantly told Kevin that she and Garrett wouldn't be seeing each other anymore.

"Mom, did something happen when you went to see Garrett last time? Did he do something that made you mad?"

"No," she answered softly, "he didn't." She hesitated before glancing away. "It just wasn't meant to be."

Although Kevin clearly seemed baffled by this answer, it was the closest she could bring herself to explaining it right then.

The following week she was working at her computer when the phone rang.

"Is this Theresa?"

"Yes, it is," she answered, not recognizing the voice.

"This is Jeb Blake . . . Garrett's father. I know this is going to sound strange, but I'd like to talk to you."

"Oh, hi," she stammered. "Um . . . I've got a few minutes now."

He paused. "I'd like to talk to you in person, if it's possible. It's not something I'd be comfortable with over the phone."

"Can I ask what it's about?"

"It's about Garrett," he said quietly. "I know it's asking a lot, but do you think you could fly down here? I wouldn't ask if it weren't important."

Finally agreeing to go, Theresa left work and went to Kevin's school. After picking him up early, she dropped him off with a friend she could trust, explaining that she was probably going to be gone a few days. Kevin tried to ask her about her sudden trip, but her odd, distracted behavior made it clear that her reasons would have to be explained later.

"Say hi for me," he said, kissing her good-bye.

Theresa only nodded, then went to the airport and caught the first flight she could. Once in Wilmington, she went directly to Garrett's house, where Jeb was waiting for her.

"I'm glad you could come," Jeb said as soon as she'd arrived.

"What's going on?" she asked, scanning the house curiously for signs of Garrett's presence.

Jeb looked older than she remembered. Leading her to the kitchen table, he pulled out the chair so she could sit with him. Speaking softly, he began with what he knew.

"From what I could gather from talking to different people," he said quietly, "Garrett took *Happenstance* out later than usual. . . ."

*     *     *

It was simply something he had to do. Garrett knew the dark, heavy clouds on the horizon presaged a coming storm. They seemed far enough away, however, to give him the time he needed. Besides, he was only going out a few miles. Even if the storm did hit, he would be close enough to make it back to port. After pulling on his gloves, he steered *Happenstance* through the rising swells, the sails already in position.

For three years he'd taken the same route whenever he went out, driven by instinct and memories of Catherine. It had been her idea to sail directly east that night, the first night *Happenstance* was ready. In her imagination they were sailing to Europe, a place she'd always wanted to go. Sometimes she would return from the store with travel magazines and look through the pictures as he sat beside her. She wanted to see it all—the famous châteaux of the Loire Valley, the Parthenon, the Scottish highlands, the Basilica—all the places she'd read about. Her ideal vacation ran from the ordinary to the exotic, changing every time she picked up a different magazine.

But, of course, they never made it to Europe.

It was one of his biggest regrets. When he looked back on his life with her, he knew it was the one thing he should have done. He could have given her that much, at least, and thinking back, he knew it would have been possible. After a couple of years of saving, they'd had the money to go and had toyed with travel plans, but in the end they'd used the money to buy the shop. When she realized the responsibility of the business would never leave them with enough time to go, her dream eventually began to fade. She began to bring home the magazines less frequently. After a while she seldom mentioned Europe at all.

The night they first took *Happenstance* out, however, he knew her dream was still alive. She stood on the bow, looking far into the distance, holding Garrett's hand. "Will we ever go?" she asked him gently, and it was that vision of her he always remembered: her hair billowing in the wind, her expression radiant and hopeful, like that of an angel.

"Yes," he promised her, "as soon as we have the time."

Less than a year later, while pregnant with their child, Catherine died in the hospital with Garrett at her side.

Later, when the dreams began, he didn't know what to do. For a while he tried to push his tormented feelings away. Then in a fit of desperation one morning, he tried to find relief by putting his feelings into words. He wrote quickly, without pausing, and the first letter was almost five pages long. He carried the finished letter with him when he went sailing later that day, and reading it again suddenly gave him an idea. Because the Gulf Stream, which flowed northward up the coast of the United States, eventually turned east once it reached the cooler waters of the Atlantic, with a little luck a bottle could drift to Europe and wash up on the foreign soil she had always wanted to visit. His decision made, he sealed the letter in a bottle and threw it overboard with the hopes of somehow keeping the promise he'd made. It became a pattern he would never break.

Since then he'd written sixteen more letters—seventeen, if you counted the one he had with him now. As he stood at the wheel, gliding the boat directly eastward, he absently touched the bottle nestled in his coat pocket. He had written it this morning, as soon as he had risen.

The sky was beginning to turn leaden, but Garrett steered onward, toward the horizon. Beside him, the radio crackled with warnings of the coming storm. After a moment's hesitation, he turned it off and evaluated the sky. He still had time, he decided. The winds were strong and steady, but they weren't yet unpredictable.

After writing this letter to Catherine, he had written a second one as well. That one, he'd already taken care of. Because of the second letter, though, he knew he had to send Catherine's letter today. Storms were lined up across the Atlantic, moving slowly westward in a march toward the eastern seaboard. From the reports he'd seen on television, it didn't look as if he'd be able to get out again for at least a week, and that was too long to wait. He'd already be gone by then.

The choppy seas continued to rise: the swells breaking higher, the troughs bottoming out a little lower. The sails were beginning to strain in the steady, heavy winds. Garrett evaluated his position. The water was deep here, though not quite deep enough. The Gulf Stream—a summer phenomenon—was gone, and the only way the bottle stood a chance of making it across the ocean was if it was far enough out to sea when it was dropped. The storm might otherwise wash it ashore within a few days—and of all the letters he'd written to her, he wanted this one to make it to Europe most of all. He had decided that it would be the last one he'd ever send.

On the horizon, the clouds looked ominous.

He pulled on his rain slicker and buttoned it up. When the rains came, he hoped it would protect him for at least a little while.

*Happenstance* began to bob as she moved farther out to sea. He held the wheel with both hands, keeping her as steady as he could. When the winds shifted and picked up—signaling the front of the storm—he began to tack, moving diagonally across the swells despite the hazards. Tacking was difficult in these conditions, slowing his progress, but he preferred to go against the wind now rather than attempt to tack on the way back if the storm caught up to him.

The effort was exhausting. Every time he shifted the sails, it took all the strength he had just to keep from losing control. Despite his gloves, his hands burned when the lines slid through his hands. Twice, when the wind gusted unexpectedly, he almost lost his balance, saved only because the gust died as quickly as it came.

For almost an hour he continued tacking, all the while watching the storm up ahead. It seemed to have stalled, but he knew it was an illusion. It would hit land in a few hours. As soon as it hit shallower water, the storm would accelerate and the ocean would become unnavigable. Now, it was simply gathering steam like a slowly burning fuse, getting ready to explode.

Garrett had been caught in major storms before and knew better than to underestimate the power of this one. With one careless move, the ocean would take him, and he was determined not to let that happen. He was stubborn, but not foolish. The moment he sensed real danger, he'd turn the boat around and race back to port.

Overhead, the clouds continued to thicken, rolling and twisting into new shapes. Light rain began to fall. Garrett looked upward, knowing it was just beginning. "Just a few more minutes," he muttered under his breath. He needed just a few more minutes—

Lightning flashed across the sky, and Garrett counted off the seconds before he heard the thunder. Two and a half minutes later it finally sounded, booming over the open expanse of the ocean. The center of the storm was roughly twenty-five miles away. With the current wind speed, he calculated, he had over an hour before it hit in full force. He planned to be long gone by then.

The rain continued to fall.

Darkness began to settle in as he forged ahead. As the sun dropped lower, impenetrable clouds above blotted out the remaining sunlight, quickly lowering the air temperature. Ten minutes later the rain began to fall harder and colder.

*Damn!* He was running out of time, but he still wasn't there.

The swells seemed to rise, the ocean churning, as *Happenstance* cut forward. To keep his balance, he spread his legs farther apart. The wheel was steady, but the swells were beginning to come diagonally now, rocking the boat like an unsteady cradle. Resolutely he pressed on.

Minutes later lightning flickered again . . . pause . . . thunder. Twenty miles now. He checked his watch. If the storm progressed at this rate, he'd be cutting it close. He could still make it back to port in time, as long as the winds continued blowing in the same direction.

But if the winds shifted . . .

His mind clicked through the scenario. He was two and a half hours out to sea—going with the wind, he would need an hour and a half to get back at the most, if everything went as planned. The storm would hit land about the same time he did.

"Damn," he said, this time out loud. He had to drop the bottle now, even though he wasn't as far out as he wanted to be. But he couldn't risk going out any farther.

He grasped the now shuddering wheel with one hand as he reached into his jacket and removed the bottle. He pressed on the cork to make sure it was wedged in tightly, then held up the bottle in the waning light. He could see the letter inside, rolled tightly.

Staring at it, he felt a sense of completion, as if a long journey had finally come to an end.

"Thank you," he whispered, his voice barely audible above the crashing of the waves.

He threw the bottle as far as he could and watched it fly, losing it only when it hit the water. It was done.

Now, to turn the boat around.

At that moment, two bolts of lightning split the sky simultaneously. Fifteen miles away now. He hesitated, concerned.

It couldn't be coming that fast, he suddenly thought. But the storm seemed to be gaining speed and strength, expanding like a balloon, coming directly toward him.

He used the loops to steady the wheel while he returned to the stern. Losing precious minutes, he fought furiously to maintain control of the boom. The lines burned in his hands, ripping through his gloves. He finally succeeded in shifting the sails, and the boat leaned hard as it caught the wind. As he made his way back, another gust blew a cold blast from a different direction.

*Warm air rushes to cold.*

He switched on the radio just in time to hear a small-craft advisory being issued. Quickly he turned up the volume, listening closely as the broadcast described the rapidly changing weather patterns. "Repeat . . . small-craft advisory . . . dangerous winds forming . . . heavy rain expected."

The storm was gathering steam.

With the temperature dropping quickly, the winds had picked up dangerously. In the last three minutes they had increased to a steady gale of twenty-five knots.

He leaned into the wheel with a growing sense of urgency.
Nothing happened.

He realized suddenly that the rising swells were lifting the
stern out of the water, not allowing the rudder to respond. The
boat seemed frozen in the wrong direction, teetering precariously.
He rode another swell and the hull slapped hard against the
water, the bow of the boat nearly going under.

"Come on . . . catch," he whispered, the first tendrils of panic
unfurling in his gut. This was taking too long. The sky was growing blacker by the minute, and the rain began to blow sideways in
dense, impenetrable sheets.

A minute later the rudder finally caught and the boat began to
turn. . . .

Slowly . . . slowly . . . the boat still leaning too far to its side . . .

With growing horror he watched the ocean rise around him to
form a roaring, giant swell that was headed straight for him.

He wasn't going to make it.

He braced himself as water crashed over the exposed hull,
sending up white plumes. *Happenstance* leaned even farther and
Garrett's legs buckled, but his grip on the wheel was solid. He
scrambled to his feet again just as another swell hit the boat.

Water flooded onto the deck.

The boat struggled to stay upright in the blasting winds, ac-
tively taking on water now. For almost a minute it poured onto
the deck with the force of a raging river. Then the winds suddenly abated for a moment, and miraculously *Happenstance* began
to right itself, the mast rising slightly into the ebony sky. The
rudder caught again and Garrett turned the wheel hard, knowing
he had to rotate the boat quickly.

Lightning again. Seven miles away now.

The radio crackled. "Repeat . . . small-craft advisory . . . winds expected to reach forty knots . . . repeat . . . winds at forty knots, gusting to fifty . . ."

Garrett knew he was in danger. There was no way he could control *Happenstance* in winds that strong.

The boat continued to make its turn, battling the extra weight and the savage ocean swells. The water at his feet was almost six inches deep now. Almost there . . .

A gale-force wind suddenly began to blow from the opposite direction, stopping his progress cold and rocking *Happenstance* like a toy. Just when the boat was most vulnerable, a large swell crashed against the hull. The mast sank lower, pointing toward the ocean.

This time the gust never stopped.

Freezing rain blew sideways, blinding him. *Happenstance*, instead of correcting, began to tilt even more, the sails heavy with rain-water. Garrett lost his balance again, the angle of the boat defying his efforts to get up. If another swell hit again . . .

Garrett never saw it coming.

Like an executioner's swing, the wave smashed against the boat with terrible finality, forcing *Happenstance* onto her side, the mast and sails crashing into the water. She was lost. Garrett clung to the wheel, knowing if he let go, he'd be swept out to sea.

*Happenstance* began taking on water rapidly, heaving like a great drowning beast.

He had to get to the emergency kit, which included a raft—it was his only chance. Garrett inched his way toward the cabin door, holding on to anything he could, fighting the blinding rain, fighting for his life.

Lightning and thunder again, almost simultaneously.

He finally reached the hatch and gripped the handle. It

wouldn't budge. Desperate, he placed his feet into position for greater leverage and pulled again. When it cracked open, water began to flood inside, and he suddenly realized he'd made a terrible mistake.

The ocean rushed in, quickly obscuring the interior of the cabin. Garrett immediately saw that the kit, normally secured in a bin on the wall, was already underwater. There was nothing, he realized finally, to prevent the boat from being swallowed up by the ocean.

Panicked, he fought to shut the cabin door, but the rush of water and his lack of leverage made it impossible. *Happenstance* began to sink quickly. In seconds half the hull was submerged. His mind suddenly clicked again.

*Life jackets . . .*

They were located under the seats near the stern.

He looked. They were still above water.

Struggling furiously, he reached for the side railings, the only handholds still above water. By the time he grabbed hold, the water was up to his chest and his legs were kicking in the ocean. He cursed himself, knowing he should have put on the life jacket before.

Three-fourths of the boat was underwater now, and it was still going down.

Fighting toward the seats, he placed hand over hand, straining against the weight of the waves and his own leaden muscles. Halfway there, the ocean reached his neck and the futility of the situation finally hit him.

He wasn't going to make it.

The water was up to his chin when he finally stopped trying.

Looking upward, his body exhausted, he still refused to believe that it would end this way.

He let go of the side rail and began to swim away from the boat. His coat and shoes dragged heavily in the water. He treaded water, rising with the swells as he watched *Happenstance* finally slip beneath the ocean. Then, with cold and exhaustion beginning to numb his senses, he turned and began the slow, impossible swim to shore.

Theresa sat with Jeb at the table. Talking in fits and starts, he had taken a long time to tell her what he knew.

Later, Theresa would recall that as she listened to his story, it was not with a sense of fear as much as it was one of curiosity. She knew that Garrett had survived. He was an expert sailor, an even better swimmer. He was too careful, too vital, to be bested by something like this. If anyone could make it, it would be he.

She reached across the table to Jeb, confused. "I don't understand. . . . Why did he take the boat out if he knew there was a storm coming?"

"I don't know," he said quietly. He couldn't meet her eyes.

Theresa furrowed her brow, bewilderment making her surroundings surreal. "Did he say anything to you before he went out?"

Jeb shook his head. He was ashen, his eyes downcast as if hiding something. Absently Theresa looked around the kitchen. Everything was tidy, as if it had been cleaned moments before she arrived. Through the open bedroom door she saw Garrett's comforter spread neatly across the bed. Oddly, two large floral arrangements had been placed atop it.

"I don't understand—he's all right, isn't he?"

"Theresa," Jeb finally said with tears forming in his eyes, "they found him yesterday morning."

"Is he in the hospital?"

"No," he said quietly.

"Then where is he?" she asked, refusing to acknowledge what she somehow knew.

Jeb didn't answer.

It was then that her breathing suddenly became difficult. Beginning with her hands, her body started to tremble. Garrett! she thought. What happened? Why aren't you here? Jeb bowed his head so she wouldn't see his tears, but she could hear his choking gasps.

"Theresa . . . ," he said, trailing off.

"*Where is he?*" she demanded, leaping to her feet in a surge of frantic adrenaline. She heard the chair clatter to the floor behind her as if from a very great distance.

Jeb stared up at her silently. Then, with a single deliberate motion, he wiped the tears with the back of his hand. "They found his body yesterday morning."

She felt her chest constrict as if she were suffocating.

"He's gone, Theresa."

On the beach where it had all begun, Theresa allowed herself to remember the events from one year earlier.

They had buried him next to Catherine, in a small cemetery near his home. Jeb and Theresa stood together at the graveside service, surrounded by the people whose lives Garrett had touched—friends from high school, former diving students, employees from the shop. It was a simple ceremony, and though it began to rain just as the minister finished speaking, the crowd lingered long after it was over.

The wake was held at Garrett's house. One by one, people came through, all offering their condolences and sharing memories. When the last few filed out, leaving Jeb and Theresa alone, Jeb pulled a box from the closet and asked her to sit with him while they looked through it together.

In the box were hundreds of photographs. Over the next few hours she watched Garrett's childhood and adolescence unfold— all the missing pieces of his life that she had only imagined. Then there were the pictures of the later years—high school and college graduations; the restored *Happenstance*; Garrett in front of the remodeled shop prior to its opening. In every one of them, she noticed, his smile never changed. Smiling with him, she saw that for the most part his wardrobe hadn't, either. Unless the photo had been taken for a special occasion, from early childhood on, it seemed he'd always dressed the same—either jeans or shorts, a casual shirt, and Top-Siders without socks.

There were dozens of photographs of Catherine. At first Jeb seemed uncomfortable when she saw them, but strangely, they didn't really affect her. She felt neither sadness nor anger because of them. They were simply a part of another time in his life.

Later that evening, as they sorted through the last few pictures, she saw the Garrett she'd fallen in love with. One shot in particular caught her eye, and she held it in front of her for a long time. Noticing her expression, Jeb explained that it had been taken on Memorial Day, a few weeks before the bottle had washed up at the Cape. In it Garrett stood on his back deck, looking much the same as he had the first time she'd come to his house.

When she was finally able to put it down, Jeb gently took it from her.

The following morning he handed her an envelope. Opening

it, she saw that he'd given it back to her, along with a number of
others. With the pictures were the three letters that had first en-
abled Theresa and Garrett to come together.

"I think he would want you to have these."

Too choked up to respond, she nodded a silent thank-you.


Theresa couldn't remember much about her first few days
back in Boston, and in retrospect she knew she didn't really want
to. She did recall that Deanna was waiting for her at Logan Airport when her plane touched down. After taking one look at her,
Deanna immediately called her husband, instructing him to bring
some clothes to Theresa's because she planned to stay with her
for a few days. Theresa spent most of the time in bed, not even
bothering to get up when Kevin came home from school.

"Is my mom ever going to be okay?" Kevin asked.

"She just needs a little time, Kevin," Deanna answered. "I
know it's hard for you, too, but it's going to be okay."

Theresa's dreams, when she could remember them, were frag-
mented and disorienting. Surprisingly, Garrett never appeared in
them at all. She didn't know if that was an omen of sorts or even
if she should attach any meaning to it. In her daze, she found it
difficult to think about anything clearly, and she went to bed
early and remained there, cocooned in the soothing darkness for
as long as she could.

Sometimes upon awakening, she experienced a split second of
confused unreality when the whole thing seemed like a terrible
mistake, too absurd to have actually occurred. In that split second, everything would be as it should. She would find herself
straining for the sounds of Garrett in the apartment, sure that
the empty bed meant only that he was already in the kitchen,

drinking coffee and reading the paper. She would join him in a moment at the table and shake her head: *I had the most terrible dream. . . .*

Her only other recollection about that week was her relentless need to understand how this could have happened. Before she left Wilmington, she made Jeb promise to call her if he learned anything else about the day Garrett had gone out on *Happenstance.* In a curious twist of reason, she believed that knowing the details— the *why*—would somehow lessen her grief. What she refused to believe was that Garrett had sailed into the storm without planning to return. Whenever the phone rang, her hopes rose in the expectation of hearing Jeb's voice. "I see," she imagined herself saying. "Yes . . . I understand. That makes sense. . . ."

Of course, deep down, she knew that would never happen. Jeb didn't call with an explanation that week, nor did the answer come to her in a moment of contemplation. No, the answer eventually came from a place she would never have predicted.

On the beach at Cape Cod, one year later, she reflected without bitterness on the turn of events that had led her to this place. Ready at last, Theresa reached in her bag. After removing the object she had brought with her, she stared at it, reliving the hour in which her answer had finally come. Unlike her recollection of the days immediately following her return to Boston, this memory was still unshakably clear.

After Deanna had left, Theresa had tried to reestablish a routine of sorts. In her confusion over the last week, she'd ignored the aspects of life that nonetheless had gone on. While Deanna had helped with Kevin and kept the house up, she'd simply piled the mail that accumulated in the corner of the dining room.

After dinner one night while Kevin was at the movies, Theresa absently began to sort through the pile.

There were a few dozen letters, three magazines, and two packages. One package she recognized as an item she'd ordered from a catalog for Kevin's birthday. The second, though, was wrapped in plain brown paper without a return address.

This second package was long and rectangular, sealed with extra tape. There were two "Fragile" stickers—one near the address and the other on the opposite side of the box—and another sticker that said "Handle with Care." Curious, she decided to open it first.

It was then that she saw the postmark from Wilmington, North Carolina, dated from two weeks before. Quickly she scanned the address scrawled on the front.

It was Garrett's handwriting.

"No . . ." She set the package down, her stomach suddenly tight.

She found a pair of scissors in the drawer and shakily began to cut the tape, pulling at the paper carefully as she did so. She already knew what she'd find inside.

After lifting out the object and checking the rest of the package to make sure nothing was still inside, she carefully loosened the surrounding bubble wrap. It was taped tightly at the top and bottom, and she was forced to use the scissors again. Finally, after prying off the remaining pieces, she set the object on her desk and stared at it for a long moment, unable to move. When she lifted it into better light, she saw her own reflection.

The bottle was corked, and the rolled-up letter inside stood on its end. After removing the cork—he'd corked it only loosely—she tipped it upside-down, and the letter spilled out easily. Like the letter she'd found only a few months before, it was wrapped in yarn. She unrolled it carefully, making sure not to rip it.

It was written with a fountain pen. In the top right corner was a picture of an old ship, sails billowing in the wind.

〜

*Dear Theresa,*
*Can you forgive me?*

〜

She laid the letter on the desk. Her throat ached, making it difficult to breathe. The overhead light was making a strange prism of her unbidden tears. She reached for some tissue and rubbed her eyes. Composing herself, she started again.

〜

*Can you forgive me?*
*In a world that I seldom understand, there are winds of destiny that blow when we least expect them. Sometimes they gust with the fury of a hurricane, sometimes they barely fan one's cheek. But the winds cannot be denied, bringing as they often do a future that is impossible to ignore. You, my darling, are the wind that I did not anticipate, the wind that has gusted more strongly than I ever imagined possible. You are my destiny.*

*I was wrong, so wrong, to ignore what was obvious, and I beg your forgiveness. Like a cautious traveler, I tried to protect myself from the wind and lost my soul instead. I was a fool to* ignore my destiny, but even fools have feelings, and I've come to realize that you are the most important thing that I have in this world.

I know I am not perfect. I've made more mistakes in the past few months than some make in a lifetime. I was wrong to have acted as I did when I found the letters, just as I was wrong to hide the truth about what I was going through with respect to my past. When I chased you as you drove down the street and again as I watched you leave from the airport, I knew I should have tried harder to stop you. But most of all, I was wrong to deny what was obvious in my heart: that I can't go on without you.

You were right about everything. When we sat in my kitchen, I tried to deny the things you were saying, even though I knew they were true. Like a man who gazes only backward on a trip across the country, I ignored what lay ahead. I missed the beauty of a coming sunrise, the wonder of anticipation that makes life worthwhile. It was wrong of me to do that, a product of my confusion, and I wish I had come to understand that sooner.

Now, though, with my gaze fixed toward the future, I see your face and hear your voice, certain that this is the path I must follow. It is my deepest wish that you give me one more chance. As you might have guessed, I'm hoping that this bottle will work its magic, as it did once before, and somehow bring us back together.

For the first few days after you left, I wanted to believe that I could go on as I always had. But I couldn't. Every time I watched the sun go down, I thought of you. Every time I walked by the phone, I yearned to call. Even when I went *sailing, I could only think of you and the wonderful times we had. I knew in my heart that my life would never be the same again. I wanted you back, more than I imagined possible, yet whenever I conjured you up, I kept hearing your words in our last conversation. No matter how much I loved you, I knew it wasn't going to be possible unless we—both of us—were sure I would devote myself fully to the path that lay ahead. I continued to be troubled by these thoughts until late last night when the answer finally came to me. Hopefully, after I tell you about it, it will mean as much to you as it did to me:*

*In my dream, I saw myself on the beach with Catherine, in the same spot I took you after our lunch at Hank's. It was bright in the sun, the rays reflecting brilliantly off the sand. As we walked alongside each other, she listened intently as I told her about you, about us, about the wonderful times we shared. Finally, after some hesitation, I admitted that I loved you, but that I felt guilty about it. She said nothing right away but simply kept walking until she finally turned to me and asked, "Why?"*

*"Because of you."*

*Upon hearing my answer, she smiled at me with patient amusement, the way she used to before she died. "Oh, Garrett," she finally said as she gently touched my face, "who do you think it was that brought the bottle to her?"*

Theresa stopped reading. The faint hum of the refrigerator seemed to echo the letter's words:

*Who do you think it was that brought the bottle to her?*

Nicholas Sparks

Leaning back in her chair, she closed her eyes, trying to hold back the tears.

"Garrett," she murmured, "Garrett . . ." Outside her window, she could hear the sounds of cars passing by. Slowly she began reading again.

*When I woke, I felt empty and alone. The dream did not comfort me. Rather, it made me ache inside because of what I had done to us, and I began to cry. When I finally pulled myself together, I knew what I had to do. With shaking hand, I wrote two letters: the one you're holding in your hand right now, and one to Catherine, in which I finally said my good-bye. Today, I'm taking Happenstance out to send it to her, as I have with all the others. It will be my last letter—Catherine, in her own way, has told me to go on, and I have chosen to listen. Not only to her words, but also to the leanings of my heart that led me back to you.*

*Oh, Theresa, I am sorry, so very sorry, that I ever hurt you. I am coming to Boston next week with the hope that you find a way to forgive me. Maybe I'm too late now. I don't know.*

*Theresa, I love you and always will. I am tired of being alone. I see children crying and laughing as they play in the sand, and I realize I want to have children with you. I want to watch Kevin as he grows into a man. I want to hold your hand and see you cry when he finally takes a bride, I want to kiss you when his dreams come true. I will move to Boston if you ask because I cannot go on this way. I am sick and sad*

*without you. As I sit here in the kitchen, I am praying that*
*you will let me come back to you, this time forever.*

*Garrett*

————

It was dusk now, and the gray sky was turning dark quickly. Though she'd read the letter a thousand times, it still aroused the same feelings she'd had when she'd first read it. For the past year, those feelings had stalked her every waking moment.

Sitting on the beach, she tried once again to imagine him as he wrote the letter. She ran her finger across the words, tracing the page lightly, knowing his hand had been there before. Fighting back tears, she studied the letter, as she always did after reading it. In spots she saw smudges, as if the pen were leaking slightly while he wrote; it gave the letter a distinctive, almost rushed appearance. Six words had been crossed out, and she looked at those especially closely, wondering what he'd intended to say. As always, she couldn't tell. Like many things about his last day, it was a secret he'd taken with him. Toward the bottom of the page, she noticed, his handwriting was hard to read, as if he'd been gripping the pen tightly.

When she was finished, she rolled up the letter again and carefully wrapped the yarn around it, preserving it so it would always look the same. She put it back into the bottle and set it off to one side, next to the bag. She knew that when she got home, she would place it back on her bureau, where she always kept it. At night, when the glow of streetlights slanted through her room, the bottle gleamed in the darkness and was usually the last thing she saw before going to sleep.

Next, she reached for the pictures Jeb had given her. She remembered that after she returned from Boston, she'd sifted through them one by one. When her hands began to tremble, she had put them in her drawer and never looked at them again.

But now she thumbed through them, finding the one that had been taken on the back porch. Holding it in front of her, she remembered everything about him—the way he looked and moved, his easy smile, the wrinkles at the corners of his eyes. Perhaps tomorrow, she told herself, she would take in the negative and have another one made, an eight-by-ten that she could set on her nightstand, the same way he had with Catherine's picture. Then she smiled sadly, realizing even now that she wouldn't go through with it. The photos would go back into her drawer where they had been before, beneath her socks and next to the pearl earrings her grandmother had given her. It would hurt too much to see his face every day, and she wasn't ready for that yet.

Since the funeral, she'd kept in sporadic contact with Jeb, calling every now and then to see how he was doing. The first time she called, she had explained to him what she had discovered about why Garrett had taken *Happenstance* out that day, and they both ended up weeping on the phone. As the months rolled on, however, they were eventually able to mention his name without tears, and Jeb would fall to describing his memories of Garrett as a child or relating to Theresa over and over the things he'd said about her in their long absences apart.

In July Theresa and Kevin flew to Florida and went scuba diving in the Keys. The water there, as in North Carolina, was warm, though much clearer. They spent eight days there, diving every morning and relaxing on the beach in the afternoon. On their way back to Boston, they both decided they would do it again the following year. For his birthday, Kevin asked for a subscription to a diving magazine. Ironically, the first issue included a story about the shipwrecks off the North Carolina coast, including the one in shallow water they had visited with Garrett.

Though she'd been asked, she hadn't dated anyone since Garrett's death. People at work, with the exception of Deanna, tried repeatedly to set her up with various men. All were described as handsome and eligible, but she politely declined every invitation. Now and then she overheard her colleagues' whispers: "I don't understand why she's giving up," or, "She's still young and attractive." Others, who were more understanding, simply observed that she'd eventually recover, in her own time.

It was a phone call from Jeb three weeks ago that had led her back to Cape Cod. When she listened to his gentle voice, quietly suggesting that it was time to move on, the walls she'd built finally began to collapse. She cried for most of the night, but the following morning she knew what she had to do. She made the arrangements to return here—easy enough, since it was off-season. And it was then that her healing finally began.

As she stood on the beach, she wondered if anyone could see her. She glanced from side to side, but it was deserted. Only the ocean appeared to be moving, and she was drawn to its fury. The water looked angry and dangerous: it was not the romantic place she remembered it to be. She watched it for a long time, thinking of Garrett, until she heard the growl of thunder echo through the winter sky.

The wind picked up, and she felt her mind drift with it. Why, she wondered, had it ended the way it had? She didn't know. Another gust and she felt him beside her, brushing the hair from her face. He had done that when they said good-bye, and she felt his touch once more. There were so many things she wished she could change about that day, so many regrets. . . .

Now, alone with her thoughts, she loved him. She would always love him. She'd known it from the moment she saw him on the docks, and she knew it now. Neither the passage of time nor his death could change the way she felt. She closed her eyes, whispering to him as she did so.

"I miss you, Garrett Blake," she said softly. And for a moment, she imagined he'd somehow heard her, because the wind suddenly died and the air became still.

The first few raindrops were beginning to fall by the time she uncorked the simple clear bottle she was holding so tightly and removed the letter she had written to him yesterday, the letter she had come to send. After unrolling it, she held it before her, the same way she held the first letter she'd ever found. The little light that remained was barely enough for her to see the words, but she knew them all by heart, anyway. Her hands shook slightly as she began reading.

~

*My Darling,*

*One year has passed since I sat with your father in the kitchen. It is late at night and though the words are coming hard to me, I can't escape the feeling that it's time that I finally answer your question.*

*Of course I forgive you. I forgive you now, and I forgave you the moment I read your letter. In my heart, I had no other choice. Leaving you once was hard enough; to have done it a* second time would have been impossible. I loved you too much to have let you go again. Though I'm still grieving over what might have been, I find myself thankful that you came into my life for even a short period of time. In the beginning, I'd assumed that we were somehow brought together to help you through your time of grief. Yet now, one year later, I've come to believe that it was the other way around.

Ironically, I am in the same position you were, the first time we met. As I write, I am struggling with the ghost of someone I loved and lost. I now understand more fully the difficulties you were going through, and I realize how painful it must have been for you to move on. Sometimes my grief is overwhelming, and even though I understand that we will never see each other again, there is a part of me that wants to hold on to you forever. It would be easy for me to do that because loving someone else might diminish my memories of you. Yet, this is the paradox: Even though I miss you greatly, it's because of you that I don't dread the future. Because you were able to fall in love with me, you have given me hope, my darling. You taught me that it's possible to move forward in life, no matter how terrible your grief. And in your own way, you've made me believe that true love cannot be denied.

Right now, I don't think I'm ready, but this is my choice. Do not blame yourself. Because of you, I am hopeful that there will come a day when my sadness is replaced by something beautiful. Because of you, I have the strength to go on.

I don't know if spirits do indeed roam the world, but even if they do, I will sense your presence everywhere. When I listen to the ocean, it will be your whispers; when I see a dazzling sunset, it will be your image in the sky. You are not gone *forever, no matter who comes into my life. You are standing with God, alongside my soul, helping to guide me toward a future that I cannot predict.*

*This is not a good-bye, my darling, this is a thank-you. Thank you for coming into my life and giving me joy, thank you for loving me and receiving my love in return. Thank you for the memories I will cherish forever. But most of all, thank you for showing me that there will come a time when I can eventually let you go.*

*I love you,*

*T*

After reading the letter for the last time, Theresa rolled it up and sealed it in the bottle. She turned it over a few times, knowing that her journey had come full circle. Finally, when she knew she could wait no longer, she threw it out as far as she could.

It was then that a strong wind picked up and the fog began to part. Theresa stood in silence and stared at the bottle as it began to float out to sea. And even though she knew it was impossible, she imagined that the bottle would never drift ashore. It would travel the world forever, drifting by faraway places she herself would never see.

When the bottle vanished from sight a few minutes later, she started back to the car. Walking in silence in the rain, Theresa smiled softly. She didn't know when or where or if it would ever turn up, but it didn't really matter. Somehow she knew that Garrett would get the message.